C000261599

David!

COD PIECES

Up Yours!

Sid Kipper.

COD PIECES
(Short Stories and Tall Tales)

from
Chris Sugden
and
SIDKIPPER

COD PIECES

Copyright © Chris Sugden 2001

All rights reserved. No part of this publication may be reproduced, stored in a retrieval system, or transmitted, in any form or by any means, electronic, mechanical, photocopying, recording, or otherwise, without the prior consent of the publisher.

First published in 2001 by
Mousehold Press
Victoria Cottage
Constitution Opening
Norwich, NR3 4BD

Cover design by Terence Loan

ISBN 1 874739 19 6

Printed by Watkiss Studios
Biggleswade
Bedfordshire

COD PIECES is an amazing collection of stories from one tiny village. The book's lynch-pin is Sid Kipper, who performs many of the pieces, and from whom the majority of them have been collected.

One person. One village. But a breadth of style, period and character that will delight and amuse you in equal, and sizeable amounts.

Acknowledgements:
The following have all made contributions (large or small, willingly or unwillingly, intended or not) to various stories in this book. My thanks (or, where appropriate, apologies) to them:
Dick Nudds, Adrian Bell, Elaine Cooper, Roger Richardson, Charles Dickens and Adrian Hodges, Mike and Dominique Ward, Ruth Frazer, Tim Laycock, Dylan Thomas, Doris Day, Whitby Folk Week, Bert Vincent, Nick Patrick, Dave Burland, Rudyard Kipling, Martin Ellis, a bloke in a folk club, Stan Hugill, Danny Kaye, Val Simpkin, Cambridge, Ephraim Hicks, Ken Wood, Leonardo DiCaprio and Kate Winslet, Hindringham Cricket Club, any number of bigots, Keith Marsden and Pete Bellamy, Barry Dransfield, Lancaster Maritime Festival, The Bible, Kurt Vonnegut, Tykes News, Henry Kipper, Anon, Trad, and The Folk.

(Sid Kipper is a wholly-owned subsidiary of Chris Sugden who, nevertheless, accepts only limited liability.)

To Val, with all my love

AN INTRODUCTION
by Reverend Derek Bream

We can all learn a lot from stories, can't we? Indeed, did not Our Lord Himself use parables to teach His lessons? I feel fairly sure that He did.

Of course, for many of us stories are just things that grown-ups tell to children at bedtime. But Sidney Kipper continues the tradition of stories that grown-ups tell to each other, after the children have gone. Not that they are, necessarily, vulgar or coarse. They simply deal with matters which would pass over a child's head. Things such as gender, decimalisation, and goats.

This book contains the very best of Sidney's vast repertoire. A few of his offerings do, I'm afraid, contain scenes of a rather dubious nature. But, then, we mustn't be judgemental, must we? (Although, if some people do wish to be judgemental, then that's a valid point of view as well, I suppose.) But this book also contains a lot more than Sidney's stories. It is, in fact, a celebration of the simply super literary culture of my own adopted village of St Just-near-Trunch, in Norfolk. Here you will find not only a veritable shoal of Kippers, but also other published authors, such as Augustus Swineherd, Mrs E. Sopp, and last, and most assuredly least, my good self.

When I was asked to write this little introduction I thought to myself 'Derek, exactly what is a story?' So I took a closer look at the word itself, and I realised that there are clues there, for those who will only see them. A story is, for instance, a store – of wisdom and ideas. It may be old-fashioned, and out of touch. That is the 'tory' part. Or it may stand out as something permanent, formed from the rock of truth. That is, a 'tor'.

It may, conversely, be all about choices, as represented by the 'or'. If told backwards it will probably contain a lot of 'rot'. And, just like a pig, it is enclosed in a 'sty'. I think that all tells us a lot, and I hope it helps you. It certainly does me.

But I expect you'll want me to get off, so that you can get on and read the contents for yourself. So it only remains for me to declare this book open, wish it well, and thank the ladies who made the tea.

Derek, 2001

BIG DICK of WHITTINGTON
as told by Sid Kipper

You may be wondering why Big Dick was called Big Dick. Well, I'll tell you anyhow. It was to extinguish him from his cousin, Big Sarah. And Whittington is a small village two leagues from Downham Market, who are in the Premier Division. It stands on the A134 Lynn to Thetford road. Well, no, it stands either side of the road actually; otherwise it wouldn't be so much a village as a road block, and people would get run over going to make a cup of tea.

Now Big Dick had decided it was time to leave home and go in search of his fortune. Which was daft, of course, because he didn't actually have a fortune. And if he did why would he need to go and search for it? He could just keep it in the Post Office like anyone else. But for some reason he thought he did have a fortune, and what's more he thought that fortune was in Norwich – although how he thought it got there I don't know. He was obsessed, if you-ask me.

And another thing – you had to wonder about Dick. I mean he wasn't exactly a man's man, if you know what I mean. For instance, he never seemed to need to shave. Well, not his face, he didn't, although there were rumours that he had a go at his legs and armpits from time to time. And some other things – he carefully looked after his nails and he always drank sweet sherry. In fact, if you hadn't known better, you might have begun to wonder if he was a real man at all. But don't let that put you off the story, which is just about to start, so brace yourself.

One day Big Dick got out a clean spotted handkerchief, tied it to a stick, slapped his thigh, and set off. And along with him went his faithful cat, Pussy. 'Come along, Pussy,' said Dick, in his soft, rather high-pitched voice; 'You and me are going to Norwich to find my fortune.' But the cat didn't say nothing.

So straightaway they set off. But after a while, as they walked along the road, and just as they reached a milestone, they heard a strange voice. It said, 'Turn again, Dick, three times vice-president of Whittington Pig and Produce Show.' But Dick simply ignored it. He wasn't about to take any advice from a talking milestone! He just straightened the seam of his tights, carried on walking, and said, 'Not on your Nellie – we're going to Norwich to find my fortune, aren't we Pussy?' But the cat didn't say nothing.

And so, after lots of interesting adventures in strange and exotic places like Watton (where Dick fought off some footpads with his hat pin), Wicklewood (where he had to defend his honour from a short-sighted, lusty goatherd), and Barford (where he had to defend the cat's honour from a short-sighted lusty goat), they finally arrived in Norwich. They made their way through the busy streets to an Inn, which they entered. 'Ho, Inn keeper,' called Dick, striking a suitable pose which I'll leave you to imagine for yourselves – suffice it say that it involved thrusting one hip out and slapping his thigh again. 'Tell me, Inn keeper, have you a room for Big Dick and his Pussy?' But apparently this wasn't the way to behave in the big city. Now, it may have been that what he got in his ear was a flea, but if it was it was a hell of a big one, with very sharp corners. As a consequence Dick and Pussy were forced to leave the Inn in a hurry. But Dick wasn't discouraged – just a little concussed.

'Very well, Pussy,' he said, his ample chest straining the buttons of his tunic. 'If we're not welcome there we will press on and go in search of my fortune straight away.' But the cat, of course, didn't say nothing.

The first person they came upon in the streets was a Pedlar. 'Excuse me', said Big Dick, 'I have come to Norwich to find my fortune – do you happen to know where it is?' But the Pedlar ignored him. He just carried on peddling and said, 'Why don't you push off, bumpkin?' Well, Big Dick was speechless. And the cat didn't say nothing.

And the next person they ran into was a Haberdasher. 'Excuse me,' said Big Dick, 'I have come to Norwich to find my fortune – do you happen to know where it is?' But the Haberdasher ignored him too. She just carried on dashing her haber, and said, 'Why don't you push off, bumpkin?' Well, Big Dick was speechless. And the cat didn't say nothing.

Now the third person they met was a Family Butcher. 'Excuse me,' said Big Dick – but you know the rest of that. And the Butcher also ignored him. He just carried on with butchering his family and said – well, you know that as well. And you can probably guess that Big Dick was speechless, and the cat didn't say nothing.

And you'd be right, as a matter of fact. Because the cat didn't say nothing. No – the cat said something. It said, 'Mind your lip, sonny, or I'll shin up your leg and grab your attention.'

3

Well, now it was the turn of the Butcher to be speechless. 'What's the matter?' asked Big Dick, varnishing his fingernails. 'Cat got your tongue?' But the butcher took no notice, because he was staring at the cat. He swallowed a couple of times, and then he said, 'Are you a talking cat?' But the cat just stretched itself out, washed it's whiskers for a while, and then it said, 'No, as a matter of fact, I'm not.' And while the Butcher was trying to work that one out, Big Dick and Pussy walked on.

But they hadn't walked but ten rods, polls or perches when this bloke came up from behind them, doffed his hat, and said, 'Excuse me, Sir; by the cut of your tights I take it you are Big Dick, the man with the talking cat who is seeking his fortune.'

'Well, yes,' said Big Dick, 'though it's all padding, you know. But wait, do you happen to know where my fortune is?'

'Alas, no', said the man. 'But if you'll excuse me I'd like to have a word with your feline friend.' Well, this bloke took the cat off and they had a long conversation while Dick gazed in wonder at the bustling city – and tried to work out what feline meant. But when he looked round again, the bloke and the cat had disappeared.

Well, Dick walked the streets of Norwich for a whole week in his little short tunic and long leather boots, asking after his fortune. And he got some very interesting replies, most of which he didn't understand, which was probably just as well. He looked hi and lo, but no matter how hard he searched he couldn't find his fortune. Which doesn't surprise us, of course, because we know that he never had one in the first place.

But one day, as Dick was passing a theatre, a huge poster caught his eye. It was a giant picture of Dick's cat, wearing a top hat and eating caviar, surrounded by female cats dressed only in fur. And underneath that it said, 'Come and hear the talking pussy – the Turn of the Century'.

So Big Dick bought a ticket, and he went in and he watched the show, which was full of acts that did clever things. There were dancing girls, performing fleas, waltzing donkeys, and things like that. And top of the bill was the talking cat, who gave a short address on the catching of mice. Dick was enthralled. He'd never known there was so much in it.

After the show Dick rushed round to the cat's undressing room, and told it that it was wonderful, darling. And the cat showed Dick its contract, which was for bags and bags and bags of gold.

4

Well, Dick immediately went into a short dance routine, paused for a round of applause that didn't come, and then threw himself at the cat. 'Oh, Pussy,' he cried; 'I knew I would find my fortune here in Norwich, and it is you, faithful feline…' (because he'd worked out what it meant by now, what with being in Norwich and getting sophisticated). '…It is you, faithful feline, who has found it.'

But the cat just threw him back. And as Dick picked himself up from the floor, patting his hair back into shape and adjusting his rather prominent cuffs, the cat leant back in its chair, lit a cigar, looked at Dick, with his stick and his handkie and his ridiculous buckled shoes, and said, 'What do you mean, your fortune? I don't see your paw print on the contract. I tell you what – why don't you push off, bumpkin?'

'But you're my Pussy,' protested Big Dick. 'You're my faithful friend. At least, I always thought you were.'

The cat looked a bit sheepish, but made no comment.

'And another thing,' said Dick: 'all the time you were with me, all the adventures we shared, why did you never let me know that you could speak?'

'Well,' said the cat, 'you were never interested in anything worth speaking about. You just went on and on and on about going to Norwich and finding your fortune, and did your bum look big in this, and, bugger, you'd laddered your tights. Now, if you'd wanted to discuss something interesting like catching birds, or sniffing bottoms, I might have been up for it. But you were too busy doing your make-up and worrying about which neckerchief to wear. I tell you, getting rid of you was the best thing I ever did. Now, why don't you do like I said, bumpkin, and push off?'

And with that the cat turned its back on Dick, and started fishing in a bowl of live goldfish which had been provided for it.

Well, once again it was Big Dick's turn to be speechless. Reluctantly he left the theatre, and if he'd had a tail it would definitely have been between his legs. In the end there was nothing else for it – he could only tuck his long blond hair into his feathered hat and go all the way back home, where the prediction came true, and he was three times Vice-President of Whittington Pig and Produce Show. And, in due course, with his charming ways and girlish good looks, he wooed and wed a rich merchant's daughter, who had a very big disappointment.

And, as for the cat – well, the cat found fame and fortune, and lived nine times happily ever after, until it was finally drowned in cream in a freak dairy accident.

And the moral of the story? Well, that's quite beyond me, as a matter of fact.

So – let that be a lesson to you!

EXPLANATION
by Chris Sugden

In its earliest form the previous tale was one of that large family of stories where good triumphs over evil, persistence overcomes tribulation, faith is rewarded with fortune, and innocence protects its owner from the perils of the big city. And if you've ever come across any of that family you'll know that most of them are extremely difficult to live with.

Luckily for us, however, this particular member of the family left home, loosened up, and stopped moralising all the time. As a result it is now a perfectly healthy story, leading a constructive life in the community – although it has been counselled not to see too much of the rest of its family if it wants to stay that way.

But perhaps I should have told you that before the story began. So from now on I'll get my retaliation in first.

Chris Sugden

DAVID KIPPERFIELD

by Augustus Swineherd

Augustus Swineherd was a writer with style – or, strictly speaking, styles. Unfortunately none of them was his own. He tended to write in the style of whatever author he had been reading most recently – in this case, surely, Charles Dickens. Thus he produced David Kipperfield, *a huge, rambling novel which I believe nobody has ever actually finished. Which is probably just as well. If they had they would discover that Swineherd never finished it either.*

It was published in episodes by The Strand *magazine, a popular periodical with shore-hawkers and beach-combers. This episode finds various of the protagonists spending Christmas together in Mr Rickety's residence on Yarmouth Beach.*

CHAPTER MCXXVI
I Spend Christmas in Great Yarmouth, and Get Change

It was the best of chimes, it was the worst of chimes, but as soon as Mr Rickety heard those chimes he answered the door to the postman.

'Merry Christmas, Smethurst,' he cried, giving the postman his box.

'You wouldn't be so bloomin' merry at this time if you was a bloomin' postman,' came the reply, as Smethurst handed over a brace of seasonal missives. 'And what I'm supposed to put in all these boxes I'm sure I don't know.'

Mr Rickety closed the door on his grumbling, whereupon Mr Macabre, who was in his element in the making of punch, turned to me.

'My dear Kipperfield,' effluxed Macabre, 'I am sure that I speak for Mrs Macabre and myself when I confide how tickled I am to be spending Christmas in company with yourself and these fine people.'

Here he waved his ladle to encompass all those sitting in the stranded boat that was Mr Rickety's house. I had somehow never resolved the conundrum of whether it was a boat-house or a house-boat.

'And I am touched, Sir, quite touched,' continued Mr Macabre, 'to be in such company aboard what, given that it is made from a maritime vessel of some sort, yet nevertheless stands high and dry upon the sand, I can only describe as a veritable ship of the desert.'

'Is that not a camel, my love?' asked Mrs Macabre.

'A camel, you say? No, my dear, you are mistaken, surely. A camel – I am certain that I am correct in this – has a hump, or, in the case of the noble bactrian, a pair of such protuberances and – again I am quite positive of my accuracy – it has a quartet of legs, a brace of ears, a single snout and a solitary tail, although these features, I hasten to append, are not necessarily arranged in the order in which I have named them, but are, nonetheless, present without exception in any animal which wishes to bear the noble name "camel".'

There was a profound silence, broken only by the gentle snoring of the assembled company. We roused soon enough, however, when Macabre loudly announced that the punch had reached a peak – perhaps he said a hump – and must perforce be taken at once. And so, with steaming bowls in hand, we toasted each other quite brown.

Nothing would then do but that we recharge our vessels and drink a drop to Absent Friends.

'Abs and French,' declared Willis the carter. Eggerty, that dearest of creatures, once my nurse, but now Mrs Willis – smiled indulgently. 'Willis is barkin',' she said fondly.

At that point the door was thrown open by a rough fisherman acting in a desperate manner. 'A clipper from Spain have foundered!' he cried. 'She's a-breaking up!'

'From Spain, you say,' said Mr Rickety, thoughtfully. 'Well, now, we aren't about to take ourselves out on a bitter night and get ourselves cold and wet on account of no bunch of foreigners.' And with that he called upon Pork to slam the door firm shut, which deed was quickly done, none of us caring to note whether the fisherman had previously removed his face from the frame or not.

'Abs and French,' cried Willis again, and the whole party of us laughed heartily.

'But there are so many absent friends,' said Little Elmlea sadly, her shyness quite overcome for a moment.

'Indeed there be,' agreed Mr Rickety, agreeably. 'But that reminds me – where did I put those missives?'

And from somewhere deep within his raiment he drew – not without some searching, and a great deal of difficulty – the two

Christmas cards, which were now gently steaming.

'Read them to me, Elmlea. My learning is not so learnéd as yours, and I should like to hear you speak out the words.'

Elmlea blushed a little and glanced toward Pork, who was opening walnuts for Mrs Gumboil by the method of placing four at a time between the toes of one foot, and then squeezing. The result was such a wonderful mingling of shell and nut as to keep Mrs Gumboil quite at a loss separating them out again.

'Yes,' said Pork, and, though it was but a single syllable, his meaning was clear enough.

'Very well then,' said Elmlea. 'The first is from Uriah Dump. He 'umbly wishes us a 'umdinger of a Christmas, and he hopes we will be 'umming a merry tune and not getting the 'ump.'

'There,' declared Mr Macabre, 'I knew that camels came into the matter somewhere.'

'Indeed,' said his wife. 'Although I cannot deprive myself of the belief that all Dump's fine words are nothing but humbuggery.'

'That may be so,' said Mr Rickety. 'That may be so, and I'm blessed if it ain't, but, nonetheless, I have a mind to indulge him. After all, the ass is a in-law.'

'The other card,' continued Elmlea, 'is from David's friend Mr Sneerforth. He wishes us the greetings of the season, and hopes that, although we are but poor, both in wit and wealth, and certainly not refined enough to appreciate the exquisiteness of his felicitations, we will nonetheless take some sort of crude pleasure from the time of the year. After all, he opines, regulation will occur in the most-accidental families.'

Mr Rickety was visibly touched. 'What a fine gentleman Mr Sneerforth is,' he declared, 'to take a moment of his precious time to write to the likes of us. Why, if I weren't so simple then I'm sure I would appreciate the sentiments something sumptuous!'

It seemed to me there was more to the note than that, but when Elmlea's eyes fell upon the remainder she blushed and put the card away in something that looked commonly like her bosom.

Had I but known then that she would later seduce Sneerforth, that she would ruin and abandon him, and that she and her father would be forced to emigrate to Australia; had I but known then that when Mr Macabre announced that 'Something will turn up' that very something would be the toes of both Pork and Sneerforth himself, drowned together but a handful of yards from where we kept such merry company; had I known any of that then, this might have been a considerably shorter book.

But, of course, I didn't know any such thing, so it isn't.

'God bless us every one!' cried Tinny Tom, who was immediately caught by the heel and thrown overboard for being in the wrong story. Mrs Gumboil, especially, was livid with him. But then, livid was her most favoured disposition. Which was, in itself, quite felicitous. Because, given her past, and taking her future, and allowing full consideration of her present, she was quite clearly destined to be happily livid, ever after.

DEREK'S *FIRST* LETTER TO
THE TRUNCHEONS

In 1994 Rev. Derek Bream, the vicar of St Just-near-Trunch, was laid up in hospital after an unfortunate incident with a passing lorry. Never one for idleness, and fearful that his flock might go astray without its chief crook, he wrote an uplifting message for the church notice-board. There it remained, unread, for several months. Eventually it was noticed by Mr Clerk, the Parish Clerk, who took it down and placed it amongst the Parish records. In due course, however, this much ignored missive was to become the first of a remarkable series of letters.

Life's like that, isn't it? Only the other day I was bicycling home from the Women's Bright Hour high-fibre bran-tub evening, when I ran into Len Kipper. And after he'd pulled me out from under his lorry, picked me up, and straightened my crossbar, he said, 'You want to look where you're going, Reverent Bream.' 'Call me Derek,' I was about to say, but then it struck me that he'd actually said something quite profound. For we all want to look where we're going, don't we? In fact, we're often so busy looking where we're going, that we forget to turn around, sometimes, and see where we've been. And then, when we do turn and see where we've been, Len, or someone like him, chooses that very moment to pull out of a side lane in front of us. And immediately all thoughts of where we've been are knocked aside by Len's lorry, and we can't even remember where it was we were going in the first place.

Let me ask you a question. Is there a Len's lorry in your life? I know there is in mine. It's big, and black, and has 'Len Kipper – Abstract Painter and Decorator' written on the side in bright green letters. And, do you know, I think the maker of Len's lorry was the maker of us all. I think He put Len's lorry here to stop me fretting about where I've been and where I'm going, and to make me jolly well think about exactly where I am.

You see what I'm saying, don't you? We are none of us quite sure where we've been; and we really have no idea where we're going; but we do at least have the comfort of knowing where we are. We are under the Len's lorries of our lives. So the next time you wake up thinking 'Where am I?', and you look up and get a splash of sump oil in the eye, just remember this: if The Good Lord had meant you to be anywhere other than exactly where you are, He'd have given Len Kipper driving lessons!

MY BOOTIFUL MAWTHER

as told by Sid Kipper

The same story may appear in a number of forms. This one was originally a musical, written by that prolific Norfolk librettist Andrew Smethurst. It's original title was Educating Greta, *but after threats of legal action from Miss Garbo, it was changed to* My Bootiful Mawther – *'mawther' being a Norfolk word for a woman.*

Smethurst also wrote the smash hit show East Side Story, *which older readers will probably be familiar with. If you haven't been privileged to see it, perhaps I might offer you a brief outline. Set in the tough East side of Kings Lynn, it follows the feuding of two local gangs, the Crabs and the Swedes. It begins with the Crab girls performing a Norfolk 'Flamingo' Dance, and singing:*

> *'I want to be in East Anglia,*
> *Far from Torquay in East Anglia,*
> *Nowhere to ski in East Anglia,*
> *Sing out of key in East Anglia!'*

Then one of the Swede boys sees something in Crab territory that he simply must have. Rather than grab it quickly and get away, he can't resist

bursting into song – this being a musical, after all:
>'Manure, I've just seen a load of manure,
>And suddenly I feel, I must go fetch my wheel
>Barrow!'

And so he gets caught by a Crab girl, who tells him where to go. In song, of course:
>'There's a place for you, a time and a place for you;
>But its not here, and its not now,
>So best you go, and hold your row,
>Somewhere, somehow, Somerset!'

But that's not this story, and I don't want to give the whole plot away. Go and see the show for yourself if you get a chance. I will tell you that it ends in a typically Norfolk fashion, in that everyone lives happily ever after, and none of them ever speak to each other, ever again.

Back to the story in hand. My Bootiful Mawther has two features of particular interest. Firstly, in performance it gives Sid an opportunity to demonstrate his not inconsiderable acting talents (although that doesn't come over so well on the page, of course). And, secondly, Sid seems to be completely unaware that it ever had any musical content at all.

Bert Baker had a wine bar. He wouldn't sell it in his pub under any circumstances. Because the Embalmers Arms in Walcott was a proper, old-fashioned sort of pub. And when our story begins Bert was down in the cellar, watering the beer. He did that because he believed in saving his customers from the evils of drink. That, and making a profit.

Upstairs, Norman Nobbs stood at the bar, nursing a half pint of something. He was waiting until the time came when his wife would let him back into the house, due to it being a Friday, and therefore Women's Quiet Night In in that part of Norfolk.

Farmer Hicks and Ruby Slipper were in the corner, playing cards. He was playing 'Beggar my Neighbour', and she was playing 'Old Maid', so the scoring was quite complicated!

And our heroes, 'Pigmy' Leon and 'The Professor', were sitting at their usual table, near the door. Of course, those weren't their real names. They were nicknames. Pigmy's real name was Leon Sea, and The Professor's was Mark Wide. But they got their names by the basic rule of clever nicknaming. You see, Pigmy was six foot three and built like a brick privy, and The Professor had once got the bottom score of minus three out of ten in a mental arithmetic test at school, more years ago than anyone who got less than seven out of ten in the test could calculate.

So, like I said, all was peaceful when the door opened, and in came a strange woman. She wore a brand new waxed jacket, shiny green gumboots, and a headscarf with horseshoes on. Not real horseshoes, you understand. They were printed ones. Otherwise when she shook her head to disagree she'd knock herself out, and forget all about whatever it was she'd been disagreeing with.

But she didn't shake her head. She did something even more amazing. She opened her mouth. And out came a most peculiar sound. It sort of sounded like English, but not how they spoke it in Walcott. You could recognise some of the individual words alright, but put them together and they made no sense at all.

'Oh, I say,' she said; 'How pahfectly quaint! How absolutely authentic!'

Well, all the regulars stared open-mouthed at this strange noise. Except for The Professor, but I'm coming to that. Because just then the stranger spotted Bert Baker popping up behind the bar. Well, he never liked to let a customer get away. So she went straight over to him and said: 'Tell me, my good man – I take it you are Mine Host. So, tell me, may one acquire a capuchino in your charming hostelry?'

Well, Bert couldn't understand a word of that. So he looked at The Professor for a translation. Because The Professor had been to London. Oh, it was only the once, and purely by accident, obviously. He'd simply forgotten to get off the train at Stowmarket, due to lack of ebriation.

'I reckon,' The Professor told Bert, in proper Norfolk, 'I reckon she want a corfee.'

'Well,' replied Bert, in the same tongue, 'if she want a corfee, wha's she doin' in a pub?'

'Buggered if I know,' said The Professor.

Well, the woman looked puzzled for a while, but not for very long. That wasn't her way.

'I say,' she said, 'I mean, it's simply sooper to hear your vernacular, but I'm afraid I don't quite follow the meaning.'

The Professor translated for Bert: 'She say as how she like the way we mardle, but she can't foller it.'

'I aren't surprised,' he responded. 'Arsk her if she want suffin' proper to drink, or can I get on with my wuk?'

13

'Sartenly,' said The Professor. 'Bert asks if you require some sort of an alcoholic beverage, or can he return to his duties?'

'Oh, I say!' exclaimed the woman. 'How frighfully clever; you're bilingual. But what luck – you're just *exactly* the sort of person I've been looking for.'

And with that she forgot all about the coffee, pulled up a three-legged stool, and joined Pygmy and The Professor at their table. She made herself as comfortable as she could, which wasn't all that comfortable, because the stool was actually supposed to have four legs. And then she launched herself into a little speech.

'You see, it's this wise. I moved into the village a few weeks ago, and of course it's absolutely delightful and so on, but I don't feel that I am quite fitting in. It's not that people won't talk to me. Quite the opposite in fact. Many of them even shout. It's just that I cannot understand a single word of what people say, although I think some of them might be inviting me to count their fingers. So, as you seem to understand both English and whatever passes for a language in these parts, I would like to engage you to instruct me in the local idiom.'

'What she want?' asked Pygmy.

'She say she want me to larn her to talk proper,' replied The Professor.

'That you won't,' said Pygmy. 'I'll bet you ten bob you don't.'

'Awright, yer on. When I're finished with her I'll pass her off as a lucal at the Stalham Shew!'

'Bless!' said the stranger. 'Why, it's almost musical. But tell me, what have you and your charming companion concluded?'

'I'll do it,' replied The Professor. 'We'll start tomorrow.'

It was just her good luck that Pygmy didn't understand her when she called him charming. Of course, he would never have hit a woman, but he'd certainly have born a grudge.

A week later The Professor was beginning to have his doubts. Well, not so much beginning as nearing a conclusion, to tell the truth. Oh, she was keen enough, alright. She tried really hard. For instance, she'd been to the rummage sale, and bought herself a new outfit of old clothes. But even then he had to explain to her that most people didn't tie binder twine round their ankles unless there was a real threat of something running up their legs. However, there was one good sign. She had at least changed her name from Dominique, which not only sounded posh but also foreign, to

Domie. Just now he was giving her what they call a vocal exercise.

'So, say arter me: "The doo in Koo fall nooly on the foo."'

She had a go. 'The due in Kew falls newly on the few.'

The Professor despaired. 'No, no, no! It's not "due"; it's "doo".'

'Deeoo.'

'Well, thas a bit more like it. Go agin.'

'Deeoo. Deeoo. Doo.'

'Thas it. Alright, go on. Do the whul thing.'

So she did. 'The doo in Koo fall nooly on the foo.'

The Professor sat up with a jerk. 'She're got it,' he cried. 'Blass bor, she're got it!'

'The doo in Koo fall nooly on the foo,' she repeated.

'Awright, so where do the doo fall?'

'On the foo; on the foo.'

'And where's them duzzy foo?'

'In Koo; in Koo.'

And with that she got up and started dancing round the room, almost singing: 'The doo in Koo fall nooly on the foo,' like she was gone out.

'Well,' said the Professor to himself, 'now we're a-gettin' somewhere. Though I'm buggered if I know where it is!'

Two more weeks went by, and now it was the eve of the Stalham Show. Pygmy and The Professor were sitting, drinking, at their usual table in the 'Travellers Vest'.

'Best you have your ten bob ready,' said Pygmy. 'I'll be havin' that orf of you tomorrer.'

'That you on't,' replied The Professor. 'I'll pass her off as a Norfolk mawther, and you'll have to swaller your own wuds, just you wait and see.'

Bert Baker offered his fourpenny worth. 'She're bound to put a foot wrong somewhere. That take a lifetime to larn Norfolk. Longer, if yer a slow larner.'

The Professor wasn't bothered. 'Well, we'll see, sharn't we? I're larned her all I know, and now she're got goin' she're took to it like an owd sow to mud. I'm confidently quiet.'

There was a pause for thought. It was soon broken by Bert Baker, who'd run out of material. 'What did she do afore she come hare, then?' he asked.

'I hud as how she used to be a flower seller,' said Pygmy.

'Well, tha's not whully right,' said The Professor. 'As a matter of fact she wus the top boss at Bartam Mills, which is a grit old company down London way. They reckon they supply flour all over the shop.'

'Are you narvous about tomorrer?' asked Bert.

'That I in't. And if I was, well, I'm now goin' out the back for a bowels match, so that'll take my mind orf it, even if it was on it, which it in't!' And he spent the rest of the evening on the bowling green, just like he'd said he would.

And so the day of the Stalham Show dawned. Of course it was raining, because it always rains for the Stalham Show – that's traditional. Nobody can work out whether the rain knows when the Show is on, or whether the organisers know what the weather will be when they fix the date. But it always rains for the Stalham Show.

Pygmy and The Professor picked Domie up on the Stalham road, so they could go to the Show together. The Professor had a surprise up his sleeve. He'd entered Domie for the Norfolk Dialect Competition, or, as it was known to one and all, 'Mardling Lucal'.

It was a cunning plan. You see the Dialect Competition was always the opening event of the Show, and he knew that if she did alright in that she'd be home and dry. Or away and wet, given the place and the weather. As a sort of insurance he'd let it be known that she was his cousin from the other side of the Broads who suffered from a speech impediment.

Well, when they got there the crowd was milling around, singing a song about how wonderful they all were, but that was nothing unusual for Stalham. The Professor led Domie straight to the registration table. She'd changed a lot. For a start, she'd lost her snooty manner. And she'd learned to walk with a proper Norfolk slummock, which is hard to describe, but you'd know it if you saw it. Nobody gave her a second glance, which, of course, meant she'd passed the first part of the test. Now came the second part.

'Wass yer nairm?' asked the clerk.

'Thas Domie,' she answered, word perfect.

'Right you are, Domie. An' what you goin' in for?'

'I'm a-goin' to do the Norfolk Talking cerstificate.'

'Awright. So wha's yer piece?'

'I'm doin' "Boadikippa".'

'Well that'll be nice for us orl, I'm sure. We'll corl you when we need you.'

And, before very much longer, entries were closed and the

competition was opened. Well, there were all sorts of pieces, performed by all sorts of people. Why they all went in for it nobody knew, because the competition was always won by a bloke who came over from Catfield every year and was never seen at any other time. But they still went in for it, anyway. A young boy did 'A pome called "The Bor Stood On The Bunnin' Deck".' A middle-aged woman gave them 'Wuddswuths Daffs'. And a very shy man performed '"Wha's Owed To A Greek" by a bloke called Ern.' At least, they thought that was what he performed. They couldn't actually hear any of it due to his very shyness.

And so it went on, until there was only Domie and the bloke from Catfield left to go. Well, it was the bloke's turn next, and up he got, and did what he always did:

'This here is by a bloke called Tom Gray, and thas called "An Allergy Writ in a Country Chuchyard", though I don't know what country that was in. Here go:

The curfoo toll the knell of partin' day,
The lowin' hud wind slowly or the lea;
The ploughman humwood plod his wary way,
And leave the wuld to darkness and to me; silly bugger.'

And as soon as he'd finished, people began to pack up their belongings to go. Because they all thought they'd heard the winning entry, as usual. But they were stopped in their tracks by a voice that rang out in tones of pure Norfolk. It was Domie, of course.

'I'm a-goin' to do you a bit from "The Song of Boadikippa", by T. S. Idiot:

In the town of Nooton Flotman,
By the shinin' Elsie Waters,
Up the crick without a paddle,
Sat a slummockin' great mawther.
She're the Queen of orl Iceni.
With her was the mighty hunter,
Known to orl as Higher Puchase,
He say 'I will lie with Boadi,
I will get my skinside inside'.
She say, "I should bloomin' cuckoo".'

And so on, for quite a long time. But the time didn't seem to matter. Because the audience, the judge, and all the other competitors were completely entranced. All except for the bloke from Catfield, who'd already gone home, leaving a forwarding address for them to send his prize. But, of course, he didn't get any prize. The prize went, by the unanimous vote of the judge, to Domie.

Well, it was a total triumph for The Professor. He got his winnings from Pigmy double quick, and then the three of them couldn't wait to get back to Walcott to celebrate in the dry.

'Get me to the pub on time,' cried The Professor.

'Yis,' said Pigmy, 'I feel pretty much the same. An she'd better come an all – I're grown accustomed to her fairce.'

'Come you on, Domie,' said The Professor. 'We'll drop you orf on the street where you live.'

Well, Domie just smiled. Then she sighed. And then she declared to one and all: 'Now, wouln't that be lovely?'

And, for some totally unknown reason, I feel like the story ought to finish on a song. But it can't, of course, because for the life of me I just can't think of a single song that would suit.

DOT KIPPER'S HANDY
HOUSEHOLD HINTS

Although Sid is clearly the family's literary genius, he is by no means the first Kipper into print. His mother, Dot, was published some years ago by the local firm of Sodder and Roughton. Her Book of Handy Household Hints, *subtitled:* All What The Newly-Wedded Wife Need To Know About Womens' Things, *and now sadly out of print, was something of a bible for many young brides in the area. Some of it is now startlingly out of date, or even bizarre. Take her advice for the wedding night: 'Just let him get on with it, while you lie back and think of Ringland'.*

But Dot's plain, no-nonsense approach to cookery is a breath of fresh air in today's welter of sun-dried tomatoes and unripe avocados. So let's hope these recipes will bring inspiration to a whole new generation of young wives.

EGG SOUP – This is a very rich and satisfying soup, what is economical and never fails.

METHOD – Just take one egg per person and pop them in a saucepan, but take care you don't pop them too hard, or you'll crack the shells, and that will spoil the broth. Now, put in just enough cold water to cover up over the top of the eggs. Put the pan on the range and sing the Egg Boiling Song, which should take exactly four minutes and a half. Then you just fish out the eggs and serve the soup before it gets cold.

TIP – You can dry the eggs off after, and use them again as often as you like.

THE UGLY SISTERS
from E. Sopp's *A Bunch Of Fairies*

Some scholars say that there is, at root, only one basic story, on which all others are based. On the other hand, the saying has it that there are two sides to every story, so that surely means there must be at least two basic stories. And then there's the other side to each of those two, and so on. So really there must be an infinite number of basic stories, of which all the ones we know are just a sample.

Mrs E. Sopp specialises in the telling of the other side of the story. In works such as Jack, The Giant Murderer *and* The Terrible Deeds of Handsel and Gretel *(where two greedy children label a poor old woman a witch, slay her horribly, and then proceed to eat her out of house and home) Mrs Sopp was always concerned to set the record straight.*

Here, in The Ugly Sisters, *she gives us a fresh insight into the real truth of that sickening goody-goody Cinderella.*

There were once two ugly sisters, which, as you'll know if you did your sums at school, is equal to twice one ugly sister, or four ugly half-sisters. And they were known to one and all as 'The Ugly Sisters'.

Of course, nowadays, many people say that you shouldn't call other people ugly. They think you should ignore the fact that the sisters were horrible to look at, and call them something else, such as 'ornamentally challenged', or 'differently lovely'.

But if I did that, then there wouldn't be any story for me to tell. I wouldn't be able to explain why people screamed and ran away whenever they saw them. Besides, the sisters were actually quite proud of their ugliness. They thought it was the thing that made them stand out from the crowd. Although, strictly speaking, it was more the thing that made the crowd move away in a hurry, leaving the sisters standing out on their own.

And when I say that they were ugly, I don't simply mean that they failed to conform to some fashionable idea of beauty. I mean they really were ugly. So ugly that you might easily have mistaken them for men, dressed up as women. Especially as one of them had a large luxuriant moustache, and the other had a wonderfully hairy chest. So ugly, in fact, that nobody ever bothered to even find out their names.

Now the two sisters spent most of their time in a large kitchen, along with a pure, innocent, wide-eyed girl called Cinderella. Cinderella was somewhat retarded, and still believed in magic and Fairy Godmothers, and the like. So, clearly, she had to be looked after for her own protection, and out of the kindness of their hearts the sisters found her simple things to do, such as raking out the cinders, which is how she got her name. (The other thing they let her do was gut fish, which is how she got another name. But she didn't use Salmonella very often.)

And they were all just getting on with their ordinary lives when one day they received an invitation from the Handsome Prince, who lived in the fairy castle a little way down the road, opposite the greengrocers. The Ugly Sisters read out the note to Cinders.

'Dear Ugly Sisters,' they read, 'I am having a Grand Ball next Thursday week, and I do hope you will be able to attend. There will be champagne and dancing and a posh buffet with vol-au-vents, and the like. Please do come, and wear your best.

Signed, Charles Charming, Prince.

PS: please do not bring that soppy, skinny, wet-looking Cinderella, as she would only be an embarrassment. If you ask me, she's anorexic.'

Well, Cinderella wasn't sure about the PS regarding them not bringing her along. In fact, if she hadn't been so pure and innocent she might have suspected that the sisters had made that bit up, and that they didn't want her coming along and showing them up. For she was indeed kind, and gentle, and if she'd been scrubbed up she might have been quite beautiful, in a rather slender sort of a way.

'Ah, well', she sighed, 'I couldn't have gone anyway, because I've got absolutely nothing to wear.' Which, if it were literally true, meant that if she had gone to the ball she'd have shown everybody up, to coin a phrase.

Well, the days and the nights passed by until the afternoon of the Prince's ball finally arrived. The Ugly Sisters spent hour upon hour getting ready. They washed themselves all over. They curled their hair (but not the moustache or the chest hair, because they were naturally curly). They powdered their faces and blew their noses, and vice versa. They dressed up in their very best clothes, and put on lacy bloomers.

And the result was a minor triumph. Lo and behold, now they didn't look really ugly at all. Now they just looked extremely unattractive. And Cinderella, in her old frock, which was tattered and torn in just such a way as to make her look all the more lovely, could only look on wistfully as they put the final touches to their primping and preening with a spokeshave, and a pair of pliers.

Finally they were ready, and they set off for the ball. But not before giving Cinderella her instructions.

'Make sure you keep raking those cinders,' said the first sister. 'We'll be checking them when we get back.'

'It's for your own good,' said the second. 'The work will keep you warm.'

'Oh dear,' thought Cinders. 'If I could only stop all this raking we might actually have a fire to keep me warm.'

How the evening dragged for Cinderella. Oh, how she longed to be at the ball. She thought about the sisters, and all the glamour and the fun they would be having. She thought about Prince Charming, who she'd once seen from a distance as she came out of the greengrocers. Local gossip had it that he was the answer to a maiden's prayer – especially if the prayer was that she wouldn't be a maiden for much longer.

But what was the use of dreaming? she thought. She'd never get to meet him. She wasn't even going to the ball. And, just as she thought that, there was a flash, and a loud sort of a 'ping!' and, as if by magic (which was no illusion, because it was by magic), a piece of paper appeared in her hand. And on the piece of paper was a pre-printed message, with her name filled in in golden ink. It said:

Dear Ms Ella,
At this point in the story, your Fairy Godmother would normally appear. She would then proceed to turn a pumpkin

21

into a coach and some white mice into horses, magic you into a beautiful dress, and send you off to the ball.

However, following recent cuts in Fairy Land, necessitated by the funding of our new Fairy Godmother Customer Liaison Department, I have to inform you that our transformation budget has been overspent, and we cannot supply any more such services in this financial year.

I trust you are not too disappointed, and apologise for any inconvenience this may have caused. If I may be of any further assistance please do hesitate to ask by visiting our web-site at fairygod/youdoallthework.com. Should you not have access to the internet, hard cheese.

Yours faithfully,
Fairy Godmother Customer Liaison Department.

And it was signed by someone apparently called 'Ms Illegible Squiggle'.

Cinderella was still puzzling over what it could mean when the note magically burst into flames. She quickly dropped it into the hearth, where it made a quantity of new cinders that had to be raked.

'Ah well,' thought Cinders, 'it's the thought that counts, I suppose.' And she was still raking out the cinders when the clock struck twelve, and shortly thereafter the Ugly Sisters returned, carrying a huge pumpkin.

Cinderella asked them about their evening.

'Well, it was all pretty boring really,' said the first sister, peeling off her false eyelashes with a pair of mole grips. And the second sister, slipping out of her size thirteen stilettos, said: 'That's right. About the only excitement was at midnight, when somebody had a stroke.'

And then they began moaning that they hadn't been able to get anywhere near the Handsome Prince all night.

'He was surrounded by beautiful princesses the whole time,' said the first sister, running her fingers through her stubble.

'Yes,' said the other, scratching her behind, 'you know the sort – bright eyed young things straight from finishing school. Still, at least we didn't come home empty handed. We found this pumpkin outside the greengrocers. So when you've finished the raking, Cinders, you can make it into a pie.'

And with that the two sisters went to prepare themselves for bed and finish their toilet (and, in this case, that last word should definitely not be pronounced with a French accent).

Well, they'd not been long gone when there came a loud rap at the door. Something like this:

'Well open right up and let me in,
'Cos here I come, I'm the Handsome Prince!'

So Cinders opened the door, and said, 'Excuse me, would you mind not shouting? It's enough to wake decent people up. Not that there are any decent people asleep here. I mean, the sisters may be asleep, but they're not decent. I'm decent, of course, but I'm not asleep. In fact, come to think of it, you might as well make as much row as you like.'

And as she paused for breath she took the opportunity to have a good look at him. Well, she thought, he certainly lived up to his reputation. He was tall, and dark, and handsome. He had dreamy blue eyes, and he was dressed in a tunic that showed off his manly features perfectly. He had hair that demanded to be stroked, lips that insisted on being kissed, and a bulge in his tights that looked like it probably wouldn't take no for an answer either. And in his perfectly proportioned right hand he held a glass slipper.

'May I ask you to try this on?' said the Prince, yawning in a fetching sort of way. 'Sorry to bother you and all that. It's just a routine enquiry.'

But Cinderella was looking in horror at the slipper.

'Golly gumdrops,' she said. 'You don't expect me to try that on, do you? Why, the glass might break, and then I'd cut my poor little footsie-wootsie!'

'Your poor little footsie-wootsie!' mimicked the Prince, rather cruelly. 'You know, that's all I ever get. I'm fed up to the backside with innocent, wide-eyed types going on about their footsie-wootsies. Why can't I meet some big, rough girls for a change? Like those two who came to my ball, for instance. Of course, I couldn't get anywhere near them for soppy drips like you, all mooning about and fluttering their eyeballs. I tell you, it's enough to make a handsome prince take up fox-hunting.'

Well, just then the two sisters popped their ugly heads round the door to see what all the noise was about. And as soon as the Prince saw them he let out a loud cheer. 'Hoorah,' he cried, 'It's the pair that I saw from afar. And now that I see you close up I can tell that you're even bigger and rougher than I thought. You're just my type. Why don't you come with me at once, and live with me for-ever in my fairy castle?'

'Well, now, we can't both marry you, can we?' asked the first sister, hastily adjusting her bosoms.

'Anyhow, I saw him first,' said the second sister, tightening her jock-strap.

'Marriage?' said the Prince with a charming little laugh. 'Who said anything about marriage? That was the last thing I had in mind. Anyway, that side of things is not really up to me. I mean, I expect my advisers will sort that out. They'll pick some wet-looking thing with lots of hair and child-bearing hips, no doubt. She'll be part of my royal duties, but that needn't take long. For the rest of the time it's you two I really want. Come, let us tarry no longer, and be as rough with me as you like.'

Well, the Ugly Sisters needed no second bidding, and ran off excitedly to get their duffle coats.

'Excuse me,' said Cinders, who had been ignored throughout this exchange. 'What about me?'

'You?' said the Prince. 'Why, I'd quite forgotten you. Well, you can come along if you must. I suppose you might be useful. You can live with us and rake out the ciders. We've got fifty-two rooms at the fairy castle, with an open fire in every one.'

'Well, it's promotion of a sort, I suppose,' said Cinderella, won-dering if she might be able to make herself more ugly so as to gain his favour. 'What do you think, Buttons?'

'Buttons?' said the prince. 'Who on earth is Buttons?'

'Oh, no one,' answered the first sister, coming back into the room and lighting her pipe.

'That's right,' said the second, pulling on the balaclava she wore when going out, so as not to frighten children. 'She's always talk-ing to items of clothing. Sometimes it's her socks, sometimes her shoelaces. Now it's her buttons.'

'A most interesting case,' mused the Prince, linking arms with the sisters, and setting off for the fairy castle. 'It rather reminds me of a wicked Queen I used to know. She was always talking to her mirror. I'll tell you all about it at the palace, while you two pleasure me with some wet-and-dry paper and a smoked haddock.'

And that's exactly what they did.

But that's another story. As for this one, well, it's nearly over. It only remains to be said that the Prince and the Ugly Sisters lived in sin happily ever after. And Cinderella lived with them. Until the day she got married to her buttons and consequently, for her own protection, had to be put away for good.

SHIP FASHION AND BRISTOL SHAPED
– the maritime memories of Albert Kipper

Albert Kipper's reminiscences have long been out of print, and many would say deservedly so. Because the fact is that hardly any of the published book was actually written by Kipper himself. It was outrageously altered by his editor, who seemed to find filth, depravity and innuendo in every other word.

Since then the original manuscript has been rediscovered in the Coote Memorial Museum, and Rev. Derek Bream (no mean scribbler in his own right) has been instrumental in having a limited edition published in its original, unexpurgated form. Because Derek, of course, sees only the best in everything.

For this publication I have concluded each of four extracts with a suitable song from Albert's other book, Shanties Of The Seven Cs.

Number One – First Lieutenant

Some of us sailor boys has a saying. We say that the sea is like a mistress. And so it is. Well, it's just like a mistress I once had. That was Madge Wimpole. The sea is exactly like Madge. It's cold, it's wet and, just when you think you can get a bit of kip, all hell breaks loose. So haul to, you bilge rats, and I'll tell you how I first came to take to the salty sea.

It was the year of our Lord eighteen hundred and ninety-four, when first I ran away to sea. And I never looked back, I can tell you. I didn't dare look back, as a matter of fact, for I had a furious husband breathing down my neck. I had a lovely neck in them days, and lots of it, some said.

Now this husband, he weren't irate about what I'd been doing with his wife. Far from it. He reckoned I was doing him a favour, by saving him the bother. Although to tell you the truth it was no bother at all. But I've learned, since then, that you never gets something for nothing. Never. And, if you do, then you always pay for it in the end. Because I've sailed the seven seas in my time, I have. Well now, that's not exactly right. That would have been unprofessional. I've always sailed them in someone else's time, as a matter of fact. Because you should never give something for nothing, neither.

Which is exactly what this husband I was telling you about reckoned. He thought that, in exchange for what I did to his wife, I ought to let him do the same to me, if you'll excuse the directness of a rough mariner. And such weren't to my particular taste, for all that I had boyish good looks and a lovely long pigtail.

Some of us sailor boys has a saying. We says that a sailor is like a woman. And so they are, some of them. Many's the cabin boy, with rosy cheeks and slim hips, that turned out to be a maiden dressed up as a man, chasing after her own true love who's been sent off to sea by her cruel father. Why, I was one myself when I first started out. Until, by chance, my lily white breast was spotted. And that can be a nasty thing, a spotted breast, miles from land and far from any doctor. That was after I got promoted from ship's cat, of course.

But I'm getting ahead of myself, like a chaplain in a whore-house. I had no choice but to sign on the first ship that would have me. And I soon found out it was a cruel life at sea. By the end of my first watch I was crawling on my knees, and only too glad to take to my hammock. But for all my tiredness I couldn't sleep easy there. Because as the newest recruit, I was only allowed to tie up one end of the hammock. It was a tough life on the spumey spray at that time.

But for all of that they were great days. They don't make days like that no more. Nor nights, neither. Why, at night you could lay on your back and see the stars, if you'd a mind. I didn't have much of a mind, but I could still see them, none the less.

Now, a lot of people wonder how us sailors used to spend our time, out there on the mighty main. Well now, you needn't let that detain you. There was always plenty for a crowd of rough sailor boys to do. Why, there was lashing, and whipping, and keelhauling, and many such ways of whiling away the weary weeks. Some favoured lashing, and some preferred whipping, but I myself had a partiality for the cat. It always reminded me of home, somehow.

Some of us sailors has a saying. We says that a cat is like a woman.

They're both soft, they're both warm, and they both want regular feeding. But you must never forget that they've both got claws.

Anyhow, that's how I came to take to the watery waves, and sometime I'll tell you more about it. But now the wind's up, and my bilges need pumping, and I expect you've heard enough from old Albert for now.

Some people say that I'm like a woman, but I say no. I say I'm more like a ship in a storm. I'm on the drink, rarely upright and always searching for port. So, if you don't happen to have a bottle about you, I'll bid you a sailor's farewell.

Breasting The Waves

I'm only a poor girl, but I've been treated bad;
Six months have I courted a young sailor lad.
With his oar in the rowlock he fair takes my heart,
Then hoists his Blue Peter, and to sea does depart.
Well, if I was a blackbird I'd whistle and sing,
I'd chirp, and I'd chatter, and that sort of thing.
From dawn in the morning, to last thing at night,
Till it drove him stark raving, and serve him quite right!
I love him, I love him, with love so profound;
I pant for his lusts, and the other way round.

My love's tall and handsome in every degree,
With bells on his fingers and rings in his knee.
With his mast in the crow's-nest he calls me his dear,
Then he fires the maroon, and soon he isn't here.
So if I was a seagull I'd fly overhead. I
Would practice my aim, now, until it was dead-eye.
And if he should point at me there with his rifle,
Why then I'd fire first, and he'd soon get an eye-full.
I love him, I love him – it couldn't be worse –
But if he'll breast the waves, then I'll do the reverse.

My love said we'd marry when he did return,
But he's just signed on for two more years I learn.
With his plank in the gangway he swears he'll be mine,
But then he goes off with his mates on the brine.
Oh if I was a parrot I'd fly 'cross the sky,
Until my love's ship on the sea I did spy.
From hiding I'd call 'Who's a pretty boy then?'
Until he grew nervous of all of the men.
I love him, I love him, whatever he do,
Oh, it's hard to be good; and the contrary too.

Now my love's returning all on the next tide,
And soon he will make me his own charming bride.
His gear in the locker he surely will stow,
And once he's in my quarters I won't let him go.
If I were a woodpecker I'd fly to the strand;
I'd find my love's tug as she waited there, and
I'd peck holes in her stern, I'd peck holes in her bow,
Singing 'Let's see you go off to sea again now!'
I love him, I love him, as he will discover;
If he bawls for his tug, why then I'll do the other.

UNDERWOOD'S MILK

by Augustus Swineherd

*This piece seems to have been heavily influenced by one of Swineherd's
closest literary friends, Thomas Dylan. Dylan often visited St Just in the
1950s, spending many an evening carousing in the Old Goat Inn. Nobody,
however, can remember him drinking milk!*

*Underwood's Dairy closed in 1964, a victim of competition from larger
firms, whose economies of scale, electric vehicles, and more rational delivery routes proved too much for the old way of doing things.*

First voice: Underwood's milk goes to every dwelling in the
village. Every hovel, every hut, every hall, hostel and
habitation.

Second voice: It goes to Lord Silver-Darling's awesome, Arcadian abode. To the Barbel's big, brown building. To the Misses Mackerel, in their cosy, careful, clean-as-a-new-pin cottage, where they ogle the milkman, Wally Whiting, through curtain like cobwebs.

First voice: It goes to Dorcas Dabb's dank, dingy doorstep, and Edward Elvers' elevated eerie. To the fine, flinty farm house, where Farmer Trout calls out 'Don't be a prat, Wally, I've got twenty Jerseys of my own', and Wally replies, 'Yes, it is cold out, isn't it?'

Second voice: On he goes, crissing and crossing the village like a spinning spider, with his pair of pallid ponies, nobly named for distant heroes, Pericles and Testicles. On to the great, grey, greasy Goat Inn, where Ernie Spratt lies snoring, snoring, snoring, dreaming of treble twenties and twenty trebles, and on to Widow Hake's huge, haunted house, where she lies dreaming, dreaming, dreaming of Ernie Spratt.

First voice: And on, and on, as he ventures from the Vicar's righteous residence, to Jenny's semi, all spick and span and spotless, and then to Miss Terrington's tiny tenement, where she sleeps soundly with her many lovers, two up, two down.

Second voice: And, as Wally dutifully drops his very last pint next to the Zimmerman's zestful zinnias, the village begins to waken and rise, as if in reluctant rehearsal for the second coming.

First voice: When Winnie Whiting welcomes Wally with warming Wincarnis she chitters and chatters, for all the world like a little linnet, as she hops from table to stove, from stove to cupboard, from cupboard to window and then, before he can stop her, she flies out of the open casement, over the meadow and on to her perch, thirty feet up in the holly tree. 'Good thing I bought that ladder off George Kipper,' thinks

Wally, only to remember that George Kipper had borrowed the ladder back again, the very same day.

Second voice: 'Mrs Whiting's up the tree again,' mouths Maureen Mackerel to her sister Marjorie. And they both watch wondrously, as Winnie wraps her arms around herself, and fluffs out her aprons to keep warm. 'I wonder if she's a little red-breast,' muses Marjorie, and they laugh, and laugh, at the thought of those two huge, scarlet breasts, proudly pouting. 'If she stays up there long in this weather she'll be more of a blue-tit,' murmurs Maureen, and that sets them both off again, so they cannot stop, even when the Vicar comes round for tea and crumpets, in his bible-black cassock, his winter-white woolly, and his bottle-green shoes. 'You'll feel better if you get it off your chests,' ventures the Vicar, but that doesn't help matters one little, bitty bit.

First voice: And so, as the villagers begin to pick up Underwood's milk from off their doorsteps, they greet each other with merry mirth.

Second voice: For this is a marvellous, magnificent, midwinter morning.

First voice: A bright, breezy, brand-new beginning.

Second voice: Another ding-dong Doris day!

THE ROMANCE OF RUMPLED
STILTSKIN O'BUGGER
as told by Sid Kipper

This is a story with a most unusual ending, and not just because nobody seems to live happily ever after. However, I do hope you'll wait for it and approach the end from the usual direction.

Of course, the ending of stories is a study in itself. Some have morals. Some have punchlines. Some tie up every last loose end, while some, like this one, just seem to peter out. It's almost as if the storyteller doesn't want to wake his listeners up. That's not the case, of course. What is happening is that the storyteller is leaving open the option of a sequel.

In the county of Norfolk, in the village of Frogshall, there once lived a miserly old miller. Now he wasn't just stingy, or a bit tight, or careful. No, he really hated to have to spend any money for any thing. He was so mean that he used to save his nail clippings, just in case they came in handy for something. And the last time he bought a drink for anybody – well, it would have been the first time as well.

He kept all his gold in a sock, and all his silver in the other one, which made walking quite a challenge. And what with his tight-fistedness and his peculiar gait, everybody thought he was a bit strange. And even though he ran a water mill he was known to one and all as 'Windy'.

His wife had left him years ago because of his stinginess. But she'd left behind her a beautiful step-daughter who was called Acappella, because she was always unaccompanied.

And, to be frank, she looked likely to stay that way, because she didn't get out much. Windy made her spend all her time on her knees, scrubbing the floors, picking up the spilled grains of corn one at a time, licking the hearth clean, and so on. And even though she never asked him to buy her nice things like clothes, or shoes, or food, he nevertheless moaned all the time about how much she cost him to run.

And that might have been the end of the story. In fact, it probably would have been, if Windy hadn't gone out drinking one night in the Under Arms. It was a rotten pub, but he liked it because the beer was cheap. And, throwing caution to the winds, the old miser went on a wild spending spree, and bought himself a second half of mild. It loosened his tongue. 'That girl,' he told everyone in the pub, 'she's always costing me money. She's always wanting something. One month it's a new scrubbing brush, the next it's knee pads. Why, before I came out she was having a cup of tea, and she'd only just had one, yesterday. I tell you what: she could spin gold into straw, that one.'

Nobody disagreed with him, but then again nobody agreed with him either. They'd all heard it all before. All except for the stranger in the corner, who was very small and rumpled, with rather prominent ears. He went so far as to buy Windy a third half. Well, unused to such copious quantities of drink the old miller ended up loosened all over, slumped on a stool at the bar, repeating over and over again: 'She could spin gold into straw, that one.'

And that might have been the end of the story. But somehow Windy's words came to the ears of their local King (they came to all the parts of his body, actually, but only his ears could hear them). Now, if it had been one of your average Kings it wouldn't have mattered in the slightest. Kings in those days tended to specialise. King Charles was mainly interested in spaniels. King Cole was chiefly concerned with pipes and bowls, and fiddlers three. So it was just a matter of bad luck that they happened to be subjects of King Midas.

Because Midas had a bit of a problem. You see, everything he touched turned to gold. And, to be quite frank, the novelty was beginning to wear a bit thin. His castle was getting cluttered up with gold sandwiches, gold toilet paper, gold chambermaids' bottoms and the like. Well, when the little bloke with pointed ears told him about Acappella's unusual talent he thought she might just be the solution. He went to see the miller, and quickly found out why he was called Windy. So he stood upwind of him, gave him a gift of 24 gold carrots, and said, 'One would have your daughter's hand in marriage.'

'That's all very well,' said Windy, 'but how can I tell which one it is?'

'No,' said Midas, 'you misunderstand me. I am One.'

'Oh you are, are you?' said Windy. 'I'd never have guessed. Still, that means you'd have no use for her yourself, I suppose.'

But eventually King Midas made Windy understand that he wanted to marry Acappella.

Windy still wasn't sure. He still had his reservations. 'I mean, what's in it for me?' he asked.

'Well,' said Midas, 'One could touch a few things for you, One supposes. And you'd save an awful lot on knee pads.'

Well, that clinched it, and very soon Midas and Acappella were wed. In a grand carriage the King took his new Queen to the Palace, where they had a meal and saw the show. And then he drove her to his castle.

And that might have been the end of the story. But it wasn't. Because then, without even pretending to offer her a cup of coffee, or asking her if she'd like to slip into something a little bit more comfortable, he dragged her straight up to a bedroom, high in a tower. And it was full of gold.

'Right,' he said, 'We want this lot spun into straw by the morning. Then We'll have it all burned.'

Of course, being a King he could get away with a bit of straw burning. I mean, if you or I was to try it the Parish Council would be round with a court order before we'd blown the match out. But Kings and the like can just ignore the law if they want. And if you don't believe me, try hanging around Sandringham for a while. Anyhow, His Highness was talking.

'Spin it into straw and then We'll have it burned. Meanwhile One will be visiting One's mistress.'

And do you know what? Well of course you don't; that's why you're reading this! On her own wedding night poor Ackers was left all alone, locked in a strange room, with only a pile of gold for company. But the truth was she could no more spin gold into straw than Cyril Cockle could get Farmer Trout's horse pregnant. Well, it's a stallion, you see.

And Acappella was so forlorn that she just cried and cried.

But then, through her tears, she heard a cry from below. So she went to the window and looked down and out, and there was a handsome Prince, calling up to her.

'Rapunzle, Rapunzle,' he cried. 'Let down your hair.'

And she called back 'Hold your row and bugger off! There's people up here trying to spin gold into straw.' And he said, 'Sorry, wrong tower,' and she went back to her weeping.

And that might have been the end of the story. But just then she heard a cough, and she looked up, and she saw a rumpled dwarf.

'Who are you?' she said.

Well, the dwarf drew himself down to his full height and said, 'I am called Stiltskin – oh, bugger!'

'That's a funny name,' said Acappella, though she could talk. 'Are you one of the Gimingham O'Buggers?'

'Never mind all that,' said the dwarf. 'Listen – I can help you. Because I can spin gold into straw.'

'Oh,' she cried, 'please, please tell me that you can.'

'Well I just did,' he replied. 'But before I start, there will be a price.'

'I rather thought there might be,' said Ackers, starting to unbutton her blouse. 'And I suppose you'd like it up front, as well?'

'That won't be necessary,' he said, averting his eyes. 'And please put those away or you'll catch your death. No, my price is your first-born son!'

'Well,' said Acappella, rebuttoning her blouse with a certain regret, 'that seems very reasonable. But wait a minute – isn't that sexual discrimination? I mean, what about my first-born daughter, eh? Wouldn't she be equally good? If you ask me, not being carried off by dwarves is exactly the sort of thing that keeps women on their knees!'

But the dwarf said he was Adam Ant, and in the end she had no choice but to accept his price. So he got to work, and by the morning he'd spun all that gold into straw.

Now that day Midas was out kinging until the afternoon, but when he got back he personally examined the straw, which, of course, immediately turned back into gold again.

'Never mind,' he said. 'If she can do it once she can do it again' (which, coincidentally, is exactly what the Seven Dwarves said when Snow White came to stay).

And Midas had Ackers brought to him, and he said, 'We are very pleased with your work last night, and One has decided to allow you to do some more. Meanwhile, One will be seducing a peasant girl.'

So once again Ackers was locked in the room full of gold, and once again the dwarf came and spun it all into straw.

And so it went on. Days turned to weeks, and weeks turned to months. There was no way to stop it. And in all that time Midas never laid a finger on Acappella. Which was probably just as well, considering his affliction.

And Acappella found that she still had to spend most of her

time on her knees, working at dwarf height, passing him the gold and bailing up the straw. And this went on night, after night, after night, until they were both bored limp with it.

And that might have been the end of the story. But then Acappella fell pregnant. Now how that happened I don't know, seeing as how she spent every night in a locked room with a load of gold and a dwarf who wasn't interested. Maybe the butler did it.

But the dwarf soon noticed the flushing of her face and the swelling of her belly. And he said, 'I trust you've remembered our little arrangement about me getting the first born son. Although I am obliged by the Federation of Dwarves and Allied Diminutives to say that if you can guess my name I have to let you off.'

'Well,' say Acappella, 'that's easy enough. It was in the story earlier. How did it go? "The dwarf was Adam Ant". That's your name.'

'Wrong,' cried the dwarf, gleefully.

'But it was in the story!'

'Well, you don't want to believe everything you hear in stories. Now you've only got two more guesses, one each for the next two nights.'

But no sooner had he gone than Acappella realised that she did know his name. He'd told her the first time they met. So the next night, when he asked her, she said straight out, 'Your name is Stiltskin O'Bugger.'

Well, this time the dwarf was even more gleeful. 'Fooled you!' he said. 'You'll never guess it', and that left Acappella really worried. Because now she'd only got one more guess, and no idea at all about what he was called.

So by the next next night, when he asked her his name for the last time, Acappella had reached her wits end, which wasn't an especially long trip. 'How the Dickens should I know?' she cried, which only provoked the dwarf to start a little dance of glee. 'I've always been hopeless at guessing dwarves' names. I mean – Gordon Bennett – it's totally impossible!'

And the dwarf froze in mid dance. 'Who told you my name?' he demanded.

And Acappella saw a gleam of hope. 'What, you mean you're called Gordon Bennett?'

'Don't be stupid,' said the dwarf.

'Dickens, then?'

'I'm called Totally Impossible. My mother was Totally, and, according to her, my father was Impossible.'

And the dwarf was not best please. In fact, he stamped and he swore and he ranted and raved, and generally got himself into a right tizzy.

'Blast,' he said, 'I've spun my fingers to the bone for you, and now I shan't have my proper reward.'

But then, gradually, he calmed down again. It was almost as if he'd only been pretending to be angry. In fact, it was almost as if in some way he'd known all along that she would guess his name at the last attempt.

And another thing: Acappella didn't seem especially excited about her close escape.

'So,' she said, 'what happens now, Mr Impossible?'

'Call me Totally,' said the dwarf. 'Well, I suppose I'll just carry on the spinning until something else comes up. Not many people want this sort of work doing nowadays. I mean, I had to go out of my way to set this job up. What about you?'

'Well, I fancy a bit of a change, really,' said Ackers. 'I'd like to do some stand-up, especially after all the kneeling I've been doing. Or maybe something in the Wicked Stepmother department, though I'm a bit young for that, yet. Anyhow, I'd have to remarry first. Until then, I suppose, I'll just have the baby and bring him up. By the way, what did you want him for?'

The dwarf shrugged, looking a lot taller now. 'Oh, I never wanted him at all. It's just part of the story. Personally, I can't stand babies. Horrible squalling things, if you ask me. By the way, who's the father?'

'They didn't tell me. Not relevant to the story, apparently.'

'Typical.'

And with that, and since they was nothing much else to do, the two of them went back to spinning gold into straw.

And that might have been the end of the story.

Well, as a matter of fact, that is the end of the story.

PETER PAIN
(THE MAN WHO WOULDN'T GROW UP)
by Augustus Swineherd

You may be wondering about the sheer range of writing attributed to Augustus Swineherd. Surely, you might think, these cannot all be the work of the same man. And, to save you all that wondering and thinking, I can confirm that they are not. In fact there have been Augustus Swineherds since 1784, when the first of them received a pension for life, which, due to a loophole in the contract, proved to be hereditary. Further details of this succession of Trunch Laureates can be found in Prewd And Prejudice, *by the same authors and publisher.*

This story, from the current Augustus Swineherd, is based on observation of a genuine individual from the Trunch area. His real name has been disguised as it cannot be used for legal reasons. However, there's nothing to stop it being used for literary reasons, so I can tell you that it's Pete Pain. So perhaps the disguise is not all that successful, anyway.

There is a place where time seems not to pass. A place where change is something you get when buying a pint, and then only if you insist upon it. And the name of that place is North Walsham.

Here lived Peter Pain. Or, as he called himself, 'Pete, er... Pain', because he wasn't exactly what you would call articulated. He was known to all his neighbours as the man who wouldn't grow up. Now that sounds quite romantic, don't you think? It sounds as if he might be a lot of fun. Well, so he might. However, the trouble was that Peter was 32 years old, and married, with three children and a mortgage to be responsible for.

His wife, Bel, was every bit as bad. They were a hopeless pair. So much so that their children, Wendy, John and Michael (who they called kids, even though they were not at all goat-like) had to be grown up for them. They had to get Peter and Bel out of bed in the morning, make sure they washed behind their ears and ate their breakfasts (and not vice-versa), and send them off to work. There had been a nanny for a while, but she'd left, because the Pains simply weren't grown up enough to look after employees. They had treated her like a dog.

Of course, Peter wanted to be grown up for certain things. He wanted to be grown up enough to buy alcohol, especially if it came in a fancy bottle and didn't taste difficult. And, as for intimate relations – well, he definitely wanted to be grown up enough for those. So much so that he'd demanded his conjugal rights long before he and Bel had actually been conjugated! But, generally speaking, Peter Pain was totally childish.

Like a child, he was keen on games. He didn't actually want to play any games himself, because that would have meant exerting himself, and going out when it was raining. So the games he liked most were football games, which he watched on the television down at the Darling Arms. And there, also watching, would be a lot of other childish men, just like him.

Like a child, Peter hated to lose. So he wasn't grown up enough to support his local football team, Nor Wal Wands, because they weren't especially successful. So he supported Man U, which is short for Mannington United, even though Mannington was miles and miles away, and he'd never actually been there. And the reason he supported them was that they always won everything, so Peter never had to be manful enough to accept defeat. Or, more to the point, he never had to fly into a tantrum, and wreck the Darling Arms, because they lost. So, in a way, that was probably just as well. Now, given what I've told you about him, and taking what I'll tell you in a moment or two, you'd think that somebody would have taken Peter to one side and told him to grow up, wouldn't you? But it wasn't as simple as that. Because it wasn't easy to tell Peter Pain anything. When he was out he spent all his time with other men who didn't want to grow up, so of course they wouldn't tell him. When he was at home he watched television programmes which were presented by people who's job it was not to grow up, so of course they didn't tell him, either. And if anyone should catch him out and about, and somehow persuade him to take his headphones off, then he'd do what he always did when anyone tried to tell him anything he didn't want to hear. He'd put his hands over his ears, screw his eyes shut, and shout out 'I can't hear you' until they gave up.

Like a child, Peter loved toys. And he had lots of them. There were mobile phones, personal stereos, video games and, biggest and reddest and shiniest of them all, his precious car. But, also like a child, he was for ever getting fed up with his toys, and wanting newer and shinier ones. So then he would use his favourite toys of all, which were his credit cards.

Except that they weren't just toys. Not at all. They could perform real-life magic. You could pass your card to someone, for just a few seconds, and in return they would give you almost whatever your heart desired. Just as long as your heart desired something which could make a profit for someone else. And you didn't have to pay for it at all. Of course, Peter knew, deep down, that you really did have to pay for it, later. But he only had a short attention span, so he could easily pretend to himself that you didn't.

Well, this couldn't go on for ever. Because the credit-card debts were building up. And the children were getting old enough to be embarrassed. They were tired of being seen with him and Bel, who insisted on going into hamburger shops, drinking milk shakes through a straw, with a lid on so that they didn't spill any. The children wanted to stop having to be so responsible, and have their own childhoods. And his parents were getting worried, because they were getting older, too. They were wanting to enter their second childhood, when they could grow old disgracefully, but they couldn't because Peter still hadn't got out of his first. So they weren't able to lay down the burdens of life, take up playing bowls, and splash out wildly on a stair lift, so they could ride up and down together all day. Eventually it got to the point where everyone decided that something simply must be done. And everyone decided, for some reason, that Peter's behaviour was a matter for the Vicar.

Now the Vicar was quite mature, and very serious, and extremely keen on all things to do with being adult. Except for adultery, that is. He had a long think about things, and decided that it would be best if he had a solemn chat with Peter. So he invited him to the Vicarage, sat him down, and gave him tea and biscuits. And, while Peter was looking about for a straw to drink his tea with, the Vicar nipped round behind him, and tied his hands behind his back. That way, you see, Peter couldn't put his hands over his ears and not listen. And then the Vicar gave Peter a grave, grown-up talking to, like this: 'I am reminded of 1 Corinthians, 13:11: "When I was a child, I spake as a child, I understood as a child, I thought as a child: but when I became a man, I put away childish things. For now we see through a glass, darkly." What do you say to that, Peter?'

Well, to be frank, he'd lost Peter as soon as he used the word 'spake'. But Peter did manage to latch onto the bit about glasses.

'Ah, now,' he said, 'That don't apply to me, your Reference, 'cos

I don't, like, you know, drink out of no glass. I take it by the neck. You know, straight out of the bottle.'

'I see,' said the Vicar, thoughtfully. 'And, tell me: does this bottle have a teat on it?'

Now you need to know something. You need to know that, for all his childishness, Peter Pain was not stupid. In fact, he had a perfectly good brain. It was just that most of the time he preferred not to use it. So Peter understood the significance of the bit about the teat, alright, and he didn't like it one little bit. He used his brain, for once, and told the Vicar that if he didn't untie him, immediately, he would be pressing charges for unlawful imprisonment. Which meant that the Vicar was forced to let him go. He said afterwards that Peter was the best argument for youthenasia he'd ever come across.

So, although I said that it could not go on any longer, it nevertheless did. Peter Pain just carried on as he'd carried on before. Will he ever grow up? Or will he, perhaps, end up in prison, with all the other lost boys? Well, you're about to find out. Because Peter Pain was about to have an awfully big adventure.

Now, Peter, for all his faults, was a very optimistic sort of person. For instance, he didn't think there would ever be a rainy day, which is why he didn't bother to save for one. Again, he always thought of a glass as being half full, rather than half empty – even if his next act was invariably to empty the glass in one swallow. He probably thought that he would live forever. Which meant that Peter was at risk from anything which might be regarded as foolprone. Foolprone is the other side of foolproof. Whereas foolproof means that a thing is always safe, even from idiots, foolprone means that a thing is generally safe, but there'll always be some idiot who manages to get into trouble with it. These are the people who get caught in booby traps.

Now, there's a foolprone bend in the back lanes, on the Southrepps side of Northrepps. It doesn't trouble most people. They have the imagination, given that it is a blind bend, with warning signs, to think that there just might be something coming in the other direction. And, because of that, they drive with caution. But, of course, Peter Pain didn't. He assumed that if he couldn't actually see anything coming around the bend, then there must be nothing there. So when he sped round that bend one day, as fast as ever he could, he was totally amazed to see a massive Ferguson tractor coming towards him, smack bang in the middle of the lane. And he hadn't the first idea what to do about it. Oh, he wished and he wished, as hard as anybody could wish, but somehow he just couldn't do what he wanted, which was to fly from the car, second to the right, and straight on till morning. And the tractor just got bigger and bigger, and bigger, until everything suddenly went very dark for Peter Pain.

He was saved by his fluffy dice, which cushioned his forehead when he finally did succeed in flying, clean through the car windscreen. I say he was saved, but by that I simply mean that he didn't die there, and he didn't die then. He was rushed to hospital (oh, how he would have loved the sirens and the flashing lights) where he then lay, month after month, dead to the world, in a deep coma. The hospital did everything they could to cure him. As well as all the clever medical sort of things, they also played him his favourite music, which was essentially childish music, of course. He liked a nice, simple rhythm, and some nice, simple words about love and stuff.

And they asked some of his favourite people to record personal messages for him, and Chris Evans and Keith Chegwin were kind enough to oblige. They even put his favourite alarm clock, which was shaped like a crocodile, beside his bed, so that he could hear it ticking. But nothing they did seemed to have any effect.

Bel visited him, and sat by his bedside every day. Of course, she found that very difficult, because she couldn't rely on her usual distractions. She couldn't listen to her personal CD player properly, what with Peter's music playing, and Chris Evans and Keith Chegwin talking, all the time. And, horror of horrors, she was forced to switch off her mobile phone when she was in the hospital.

So she very soon got bored. In fact, after a while, she got desperate. As a last resort she actually took to reading some of the magazines that were left lying around, for just that purpose. Now, Bel had never really tried reading before. Oh, she'd learned to read at school, of course, so she knew the how of it. But she'd never really seen the why of reading. Because you didn't need it, did you, in the real world? For instance, the places where they ate had pictures on the menu, so you didn't need reading for that. And the things they liked all had logos on, so you didn't need it for them. Some of their toys did come with instruction leaflets, but they never bothered to read those. Which might explain why they broke half of them, long before they ever got them going properly.

So it was a surprise to Bel when she discovered that she quite liked reading the magazines. In fact, she came to look forward to sitting by Peter's bedside, leafing through them. She read all about pop-stars, and celebrity funerals, and how to redecorate your house with sea shells, and so on. She found out what her horoscope was three years ago, and how to cook endives. But eventually there came a day when she'd read every single magazine that the hospital had. All that was left was a newspaper. And I mean a real newspaper. Not the sort that are barely distinguishable from the magazines. I mean the sort that take some effort to read, not least in handling the grown-up sized pages.

Bel only picked it up because there was absolutely nothing else. She only intended to see if there was anything in it about film stars. But, by the time she put it down again, her eyes had been opened. She had discovered that there were things going on in the world that were not reported in *Hello* and *OK!*

Well, there was no going back. One thing led to another, as it so often will, and eventually Bel began calling in at the public library on her way to the hospital. She claimed that she only got the books to read out loud to Peter, to keep his mind active. But, really, it was her mind that was active. So she read, to Peter, all about geography, and history. And then she told him about philosophy, and science, and all sorts of grown-up things. And, as time went by, what with her reading all those books, Bel somehow grew up. One day she was still a childish adult, and the next she was a real, mature, grown-up. It's a very fine line, you know, and one that cannot be seen with the naked eye.

And, not long after Bel had grown up, Peter finally came out of his coma. He just opened his eyes one day, and said, loud and clear, 'Hello, Tink' (it was what he always called her) 'I could murder an Indian.'

Well, you can imagine the excitement, what with nurses and doctors being called, and the children being sent for, and kissing and hugging, and so on. And everyone assumed that when Peter had spoken those first words, about murdering an Indian, he had been asking for a curry. Which, of course, he couldn't have, in his condition.

It was only as time went on that they found out the truth. They discovered that while Peter had been in the coma he'd been living in some sort of a dream world, on a magical sort of island, where he really did murder Indians! Or, as Bel called them, having read about such things, 'Naive Americans'. And also on the island were Pirates, and Mermaids, and all sorts of childish, fanciful things. Peter said it was a theme park, called 'Never-Never Land'.

And the tragic thing about it all was that Peter missed his island, terribly. He wanted to go back there, and he didn't get better at all. He even begged the doctors to hit him over the head, in a medical sort of way, so that he could return. But, of course, they wouldn't, because that would have broken their hypocritical oath. And so, as the truth slowly sank in, Peter grew more and more depressed.

He got so low that it was touch-and-go for a while. Peter got weaker and weaker by the day. Eventually he had sunk so far that he took no more notice of his surroundings than he had when he'd been unconscious. He didn't even notice Bel when she came to visit him, every day, just like before. She had her books for company, of course, but she didn't want to read to herself in case Peter felt ignored. So she took to reading aloud to him again.

And one day, not a special day, she was reading, to Peter, about Captain Cook. She was telling him all about Cook's voyages, and his explorations, and so on. Though she was really reading it for herself, of course. In fact, she got so involved in the story that she quite forgot where she was. So it came as quite a shock to her when Peter suddenly sat bolt upright and cried 'Captain Hook! Tell me more about Captain Hook!' Bel explained, gently, that it was not Captain Hook, but Captain Cook, that she had been reading about.

'What did he do?' asked Peter. 'Did he have a mortal fear of crocodiles?' No, she said, but he did have a lot of adventures. And she told him about some of them. Well, that was it. He simply loved those stories. And from that moment on he grew better by the day. Soon he was as keen on books as Bel was, and after a while it became clear that he had actually begun to grow up, too. It took some time, of course. It was a while before he happily started a book which didn't have lots of pictures. But Peter slowly recovered his health, and painfully achieved adulthood. He gradually grasped that he was responsible for himself and his place in the world. And that he was also responsible for his children, and his parents.

They were all delighted, of course. His mother and father went straight out and signed up for an evening class in basket weaving. And Wendy, John and Michael, finally released from being all serious and sensible, immediately started drinking, taking drugs, and hanging around street corners, getting into trouble. And in due course Peter left his job at the estate agents, Conman and Shyster, and got a proper, grown-up job, as an author. And his most famous and successful book of all was a magical story about some children, and an island, and Indians, and pirates, and I don't know what else. But don't worry – he wrote it in a most adult way.

So, now time has passed in North Walsham, after all. And since Peter has finally grown up, I think we can safely leave him to live happily ever after. Except to add one thing. We must always remember that, no matter how grown up we may be, every single adult among us still has a child within them. And that is why, every year, Peter and Bel take a holiday, nearly always to an island, where they let their inner children come out to play for a week or two.

PIERING OUT TO SEA
as told by Sid Kipper

Unusually, this is one of Sid's stories which can be tested for truth. It's hero, Jimmy Kipper, made many hundreds of appearances on the Music Hall, for some of which he was actually paid. And, after some research, as far as I can tell, Sid may here be breaking the habit of a lifetime and telling it exactly as it was.

For the interest of the reader I have inserted some of the evidence I found into the text, in the form of 'bill matter' – the pithy descriptions of an act that used to appear on the old music-hall posters.

Cromer Pier was the place where my great uncle, Jimmy 'Am-I-Boring You' Kipper, made his name – which was really James anyhow. 'Jimmy' was what they call a stage name, although I never knew that stages had names. Except for Wells Fargo, perhaps. And semi-final, I suppose.

Anyhow, Jimmy was totally stage struck all his life. If he'd been alive today he would have been 139 years old. But that's not the point. If he'd been alive today he would have put on costume and make-up before he opened the fridge door. He tried no end of ways of making it to the top. Before the events I'm going to tell you about, he'd done just about everything.

He tried plate-spinning (*James Kipper – the Spin Doctor*), but he couldn't afford to keep buying new plates, although people were actually very impressed by his dancing-on-broken-china act. It was just that he didn't mean to dance. He only did it because his soles were worn thin with failure.

He tried ventriloquism (*Jimmy and Algy – Which One is the Dummy?*). He used to do a routine where he sang a song while the dummy drank a glass of water. But after a bit all the metal parts that worked the mouth of the dummy rusted up, and it ended up with Jimmy moving his lips while the dummy's were stuck in a hideous grin, which was a novelty, but not a very entertaining one.

He tried escapology (*Jim and Maisey Kipper – Hoping to Get Away for the Weekend*). They used to do this death-defying thing where his beautiful assistant used to be chained up in a tank of water, and he had to get her out before the piranha fish were released. As a matter of fact they didn't always defy death, which partly explains why he had five wives. Well, it was cheaper to marry them than to pay them, although it did cost a few bob to change their names to Maisey.

He tried magic (*Professor Kipper – Makes Audiences Vanish*). He used to borrow things like watches and cigarette cases from members of the audience, then make them disappear. He was very good at that. Some people reckoned he was the best in the business at the disappearing. But the flea in the basement was that he could never get them to reappear again. That was because he hadn't got a clue where they'd gone to. I reckon he should have had a word with his third beautiful Maisey. You see, as soon as he gave up magic she divorced him. And although she didn't get a penny from him, she somehow went on to live a life of luxury, with a gold toilet chain and everything.

He tried knife-throwing (*'J Kipper Esq. – He Aims to Please'*). That was in the time of his second beautiful Maisey. He used to stand her up against a board, and then blindfold himself and throw knives into the board. Of course, being blindfolded, he couldn't see what happened. What happened was that as soon as he put the blindfold on she used to hide behind the board for her own protection until he'd thrown all the knives. Then, as Jimmy was slowly and dramatically taking off the blindfold and turning to the audience for applause, she used to whip round to the front of the board again and rearrange the knives to look like narrow misses of where she was standing. Jimmy could never understand why the audience weren't very impressed. He certainly was.

He tried fire-eating (*'J. F. Kipper – the Singeing Sensation!'*), but he could never keep it down.

He even had a go at the sand dance (*'Monsieur Kippèrre – a Touch of Eastern Promise'*), but got fed up with having to sweep up after himself.

No matter what Jimmy tried, audiences always ended up laughing at him. So in the end he decided to go with Flo, and he took up comedy (*'Jimmy "Am-I-Boring You" Kipper – Reaching New Depths'*). Well, they certainly stopped laughing at him then, I can tell you! As a matter of fact he was the only English comic who went down just as well at the Glasgow Empire as he did everywhere else.

But I was going to tell you about Cromer Pier. Now, on the end of Cromer Pier is a theatre – the Cromer Pavilion. Well, no, that's not quite true. Right at the end of the pier is the lifeboat house and slipway, but next to that, on the landward side, is the theatre. (During the war they took the middle out of the pier to stop German nuns parachuting on to the end and invading Norfolk. Then they had to put some of it back so the lifeboat men could get to their boat to rescue our own nuns who'd been shot down.)

This theatre was where Jimmy was appearing when he made his name. Now this confuses a lot of people (not all of them, of course, because some of them are confused already). A lot of people think that if you appear on the pier then you must be a pierrot. What do they know? Pierrots are singers on the beach, and they're called pierrots to distinguish them from the beach buoys, which is what they use to tie the crab boats up to.

Anyhow, about Cromer Pavilion. I've performed there, of course, because I appear at all the major venues. But for Jimmy it was a big break. I mean, he'd never appeared on a pier before. The nearest he'd got to it was doing Punch and Judy on one of the groynes, because if you did it on the beach you had to pay for a licence. But his agent had got him a summer season on the pier by editing some press notices for him. It's a common practice. You just cut out the bad bits. That's why they're called cuttings.

For instance, he quoted the *Trunch Trumpet* as saying 'Jimmy Kipper is really good', which he got from 'Jimmy Kipper is really no good at all'. From the *Cromer Clarion* he got 'The aisles were full of people rolling with laughter' ('The aisles were full of people rushing to get out. I was rolling with laughter at their expressions of desperation'). His finest achievement came from the *Hunstanton Huzzah*: 'Kipper is simply the best, funniest and finest act I have seen this season' ('Kipper is so bad I won't favour him with further mention. I simply don't know why he bothers. The best thing he could do would be to shoot himself on stage. That would be the funniest and finest thing he could manage. If someone doesn't act soon I might even do the shooting myself. He is the worst thing I have seen in all my life, never mind this season').

CROMER PIER PAVILION
is proud to present
Jimmy
'Am I Boring You?'
Kipper
(with Guest Appearance by Cromer 'That Sinking Feeling' Lifeboat.)
also featuring

Rosie	**Rex**	**Bertie**
'She's blooming'	**'Mother's boy'**	**'Chapped-cheeks'**
Nice	**Oedipus**	**Bloggs**
(Plant Impressions)	**(Big in Bungay)**	**(Master of Mirth)**

Parts in all seats. Prompt finish assured.

That's how Jimmy got the job, and it was the making of him. He made his name on the very first night of the summer season of 1897. Now, being the first night, things were a bit disorganised. But he got up there and did his act, which went down just about as well as usual – that is to say, like a stone. And to end up he went into his big finishing number:

All the sailors hate a nice girl, all the sailors hate a star;
All the sailors hate a nice girl –
Well, you know what nice girls are.
Passion killing, quite unwilling, and tastes you can't afford;
So when the fleet's ashore they prefer the girls who roar
'All aboard, all aboard!'

But he never got that far. You see, in those days, they didn't just stand on the stage and sing. They used to move all over the stage while they did it, from side to side, back to front, corner to corner. That was to make it more interesting, by offering the audience a moving target. But this being the first night, and a bit disorganised like I said, someone had accidentally left the stage trapdoor open. And Jimmy hadn't noticed.

He did have one bit of luck, because the tide was in. So when he fell he had a soft landing. And, being a real trouper, and knowing that the show must go on and on, when he came up the third time he carried on singing the song. The band nipped out and played over the side of the pier, and both the audience came out to watch, and Jimmy was going down really well as he slowly drifted out to sea, singing his song.

Until, that is, someone decided to launch the lifeboat for him. That was where his luck ran out. Because he was just passing the end of the slipway at the time. So the next thing he knew he woke up the following morning in Cromer cottage hospital, with a lifeboat shaped hole in the back of his head. He opened his eyes, and there at the end of the bed he saw the theatre manager. And the manager just looked at Jimmy and said, 'We'll keep it in!'

So Jimmy did it every night for the whole of that summer, and they slipped the lifeboat men a few bob to do the big finish. All except for the last night of the season. They didn't bother then because they didn't need him back. That's when Jimmy went on his Dutch tour, as a matter of fact.

His act became so popular that soon he was one of the biggest draws in the country – at places with piers, of course. He was very popular with theatre managers, because if they put him on last then the audience all cleared out double quick to watch the big finish. After a bit the audience started to leave as soon as Jimmy came on stage, because that way they could get the best view of the finale and avoid his act into the bargain. And, of course, there was no question of an encore, which meant they could fit another house in.

But, sure enough, it all ended in tears. You see, eventually people worked out that they could see the highlight of the show, without the risk of having to sit through Jimmy's act, if they never went into the theatre in the first place. Huge crowds used to hang about at the end of the pier, waiting for him to pop out. So he lost all his work, because nobody paid to go into the theatres.

Poor old Jimmy. His name was all unmade again. It was all rather sad after that. He used to go down to the end of the pier at Cromer, stand on the handrail, and try to get people to pay him a halfpenny to jump off and sing. Then the theatre people told him to push off from their end of the pier, so he went down to the landward end to do it. But he forgot that the tide doesn't always reach that far.

In fact, if that family of three from Leicester hadn't broken his fall, he wouldn't have been here today to tell the tale. Which, of course, he isn't. So, in a very real sense, they all got squashed to death in vain. And none of them lived happily, ever again.

London Spurning
as sung by Jimmy Kipper, and his descendant, Sid

> She was poor, but she was honest;
>   well that's one of nature's laws.
> If you're poor you must be honest,
>   if you're honest you'll be poor.
>
> So she stayed both pure and modest,
>   quite untouched, like morning dew;
> Goodness knows I tried to touch her,
>   but she'd studied ju-jitsu.
>
> Then she left our little village,
>   leaving me in want and grief;
> While she sought for fame and fortune,
>   cold baths were my sole relief.

By the time she got to London
    she had lost her honest name;
To be frank she never missed it,
    but she prospered all the same.

For she very soon discovered,
    virtue's easy, but it's flawed;
And it's no good being upright,
    if you're hoping for reward.

Now her beauty brought her fortune,
    and her art, it brought her fame,
As for due consideration,
    she lost her name time and again.

Soon this simple country maiden
    with the swells was seen abroad;
Taking tea with all the Ladies,
    sharing breakfast with the Lords.

Then she met Sir Percy Hardwick;
    just Home Secretary is what.
In the House he was Right Honourable;
    in the tool shed he was not.

First he loved her, then he loved her,
    then he loved her once for luck;
Then he left her empty handed;
    wasn't he a rotten pup?

For it's the rich what gets the pleasure,
    and the wealth, and the acclaim.
It's the poor what must provide it;
    and it's always been the same.

Standing on the bridge at midnight,
    she cries 'Farewell, blighted love';
There's a splash, a scream - Good Heavens!
    I believe she's pushed him off!

When his body it is landed,
    there's a note pinned to his frock;
She had writ, in neatest writing;
    'How's that for a short, sharp shock?'

London spurning she departed,
    and returned to me again;
Now she lives a life of chastity,
    ain't it all a bloomin' shame?

For it's the same the whole world over,
    there's no change where'er you roam;
It's identical everywhere you go,
    so you might as well stay at home!

DEREK'S *SECOND* LETTER TO
THE TRUNCHEONS

*In 1998 Derek Bream was invited to spend a year as a sort of missionary to
the whole county of Norfolk. He toured all over, meeting people both
ordinary and extraordinary. He also had a regular guest spot on Radio
Norfolk, each Sunday contributing his 'Thought For The Day' (which was
known around the radio station as 'Soup of the Day').*

*Being a committed environmentalist, Derek was determined to recycle
his work, and thus he continued his thought provoking series of letters to
his home parish.*

Life's like that, isn't it? Only the other day I was ambling through
Ashwicken when I realised that I didn't know a single person there.
Nor any married people, come to that. And then I had one of my
little flashes. I suddenly knew why. It's because I am a stranger.
Because, in fact, I have been sent to tour Norfolk, from the village of
St Just-near-Trunch, in a sort of a missionary position.

So let me introduce myself. My name is the Reverend Derek
Aluitious Bream, but you can call me Derek. I've been given this
task as a sort of sabbatical peripatetic, to bring Norfolk the word.
Not that you don't have some very powerful words of your own, of

51

course, as the good people of Ashwicken were only too quick to demonstrate.

And that set me to thinking. For we all have our words to say, don't we? Some of us have five letter words, and some of us have three letter words (the people of Ashwicken, incidentally, seem to fall squarely between those two camps). But often we're so busy telling people our own words, that we don't take the time to listen to theirs. And, of course, they're too busy telling us their words to listen to ours. So all those words are being spoken, but none of them are being listened to.

I was so struck by this that I immediately decided that I should devote this, my first broadcast, to listening to your words. But then the technical chappies pointed out that I wouldn't be able to hear you, because this is the wireless, of course. And the wireless, they told me, is a one way street. So, although my words can travel towards you, and turn left, or right, try as they might (and I'm sure they do) your words can never go against the traffic and come to me. You, in fact, are the listeners, and I am the broadcaster. But I am not, like the countryman of old, broadcasting ears. Rather, I am broadcasting to ears. And the oats I shall be sowing are my words.

But I want to receive some of your oats, too. So, I shall be travelling around Norfolk on my mission, listening to other people. Why, this very week I shall be visiting the good people of Blakeney (not neglecting any bad people who may live in that fair town). And next Sunday I shall be back here, on the wireless, to share my thoughts with you again.

But do you know my thoughts at this very moment? I sincerely hope not. But then, if The Good Lord had meant you to know what I was thinking right now, He wouldn't have invented the guidelines on taste and decency.

SIR WAYNE, THE GREEN KNIGHT
as told by Sid Kipper

Are you sitting comfortably? Well, never mind, because you can always get some ointment for that later. But, before you do, I'm going to tell you the story of Sir Wayne, The Green Knight.

Now this is a very ancient story. It comes from right back before the Romans arrived in this country. I don't know if you had the Romans round your way, but where I come from they were a proper nuisance. They wanted everything to change, just to suit them. That's typical of incomers, of course. We still get the same today. But the Romans were the worst, because they had such strange habits. They wanted all the men to wear skirts and sandals, and everyone to take baths, and worship Diana. Of course, none of that was going to catch on around my way. And the proof of that is that, even to this day, very few of our men wear skirts and sandals, hardly anybody worships Diana, and nobody takes a bath unless it's absolutely unavoidable.

We did our best to resist the Romans. Well, my lot did. My lot were the Iceni, who you may have heard of. They were led by a very famous ancestress of mine, perhaps the most famous member of the Kipper family until me, a woman by the name of Boadikippa. Now she was known for any number of things. She fought against the Romans, she set fire to London (which is why it's called The Smoke), and in her spare time she invented the combine harvester. Well, with such a leader the Iceni were clearly invincible.

The other people who were living round our way when the Romans came were the Celts. You could always spot them, due to their habit of painting themselves blue with woad, and then running around without a stitch on. I don't know why they did that. I suppose it was just a fashion thing. Come to think of it, skirts and sandals would probably have been an improvement. But they never got the chance for that.

You see, when the Romans came the Iceni did the decent thing. That is, they fought against them, and nearly all got wiped out. So I suppose you'd have to say they were vincible, after all. But the Celts didn't hang around for that. They all boldly went West, out of the way of the Romans, led by their King, Caractacus. So they didn't help us fight, and they didn't nearly all get wiped out.

It was quite a bone of contention with us at the time, I can tell you. It still is, as a matter of fact. Because we've got long memories where I come from. We haven't forgotten the Celts all boldly going off West like that. As a matter of fact, we only forgave them for it a few years ago. And then blow me if they didn't all start boldly coming back East again, bombarding us with all their Celtic culture, and their Celtic music, and so on.

Well, as a matter of fact, we're fed up with it. So I've taken it upon myself to promote the Icenic culture, because that's our heritage, and it's just as good as any of that Celtic stuff. And one of the ways I'm promoting it is by telling the story I'm going to tell you now.

This is it. The story of Sir Wayne, The Green Knight.

Long ago, in the nightmare time, the ancestors walked upon the earth. And they walked upon the grass, and upon the rocks, and upon anything else that got in their way for that matter. And the world at that time was young, but nevertheless old enough to know better.

And in that time there were witches, and witch doctors, who looked after the witches when they were ill, which was often enough, because they kept inflicting diseases upon each other. And there was no C of E.

And, in those far off days, men were men, women were women, wishes were horses, and beggars could ride.

And at that time, in the land of the Iceni, there lived a good knight of great stature. And his name was Wayne. He was known, short, fat and wide, for his valour, his virtue, and his truthfulness. He was a green knight, which means that he was kind to animals, he knew the ways of the woods, and he always recycled his beakers.

The story starts one night, when Wayne was fast asleep. And while he slept he had a mighty dream, full of signs and poor tents, and that sort of stuff. But when he awoke – well, when he awoke he couldn't remember a thing about it. So Wayne thought that he'd better set off on a great quest, just in case that was what the dream had been about.

So he packed a wicka basket. In it he put his magic crystal, a love philtre, and a clean hanky. He also took some dried rhunes, which were all that he had to sustain him on his journey.

Nobody knew where Wayne was going. Nobody knew why he went. Nobody cared, as a matter of fact. They were just glad to see the back of him. Because, being so green and virtuous, he was always trying to stop them doing things, such as eating meat, wearing fur, and hunting wild boar with dogs.

Of course, Wayne didn't know where he was going, either. He didn't even know which way to go. But, nothing daunted, he took his rod in his hand, and he cast about him. And lo, his rod pointed and showed him a lay line. Which was the way Wayne went. And the lay line led to a tor, which stood, at that time, in a far and strange land, which nowadays is known as Peterborough. And there, at the tor, he found a sword, embedded in a stone. And a passing raven told him that whomsoever should pull the sword from the stone would be the true Queen of England. So, with one mighty heave, Wayne pulled the sword clean out of the stone. And he looked, and there, in the sword's shining blade, he saw a reflection. It was a reflection of the future. He saw lords and ladies, all in glittering carriages. He saw a prince, with mighty ears. He saw a princess, having her toes sucked in some strange ritual. And seeing all that he changed his mind, and straightway returned the sword to the stone. And this was a sign – a sign that Wayne's stature was increasing. And he knew that his quest was not yet at it's end.

So he cast his rod about him again, and it showed him another lay line. Which was the way Wayne went. And in due course (just as it had been foretold by the wise woman who practised cup and saucery, or the reading of tea leaves) it led him to a circle of grate stones. And in each of the grates there was a fire. And over each fire hung a bubbling pot. And in each pot was a potion. And a passing blue tit told Wayne that he must choose a potion. It told him that all but one of the potions were terrible poisons, which would kill him in agony. It told him that only if he were of sufficient stature would he choose the one safe potion. And Wayne thought about it. He thought about it for a whole night and a day. Then, being made wearisome by all that thinking, he fell asleep, and he had another dream. And this dream he remembered. It told him that he must go directly to the circle, and drink from the one pot that didn't have 'poison' written on it in big, red letters. So that is what he did. And lo, his stature increased yet further.

And Wayne took his rod, and he sought, and he found another lay line. Which was the way Wayne went. And, after many days' journey, the lay line led him to the mouth of a sacred cave, which was guarded by a huge, fearsome, fire-breathing dragon. And a passing shag told Wayne that he must slay the dragon, for it was defiling the cave, and having a terrible effect on local property prices. So henceforth Wayne approached the cave, and he called out to the dragon: 'Dragon! My name is Wayne, and I have come to slay you!'

And the dragon stuck it's head out of the cave, and it laughed. It laughed and it laughed. 'Slay me?' said the dragon. 'Oh you do. But tell me, little man, exactly what are you going to slay me with?'

'Well,' said Wayne, who was now rather wishing that he'd kept the sword from the stone. 'Well,' he said, kicking himself for not having carried off one of the potions which was poison. 'Well,' he said, desperately trying to think of something to do. 'Well, I shall slay you with the simple sword of truth, and the trusty shield of British fair play.'

And the dragon laughed all the more at that, as anyone would, hearing such nonsense. 'Little man,' it roared 'don't make me laugh so much. You'll be the death of me.' And as the dragon carried on its chortling, Wayne looked desperately in his basket for something to help him. And his hand fell upon the magic crystal. So, as he was desperate, and as he had nothing anything else to try, he held the crystal up to the dragon, and he cried, 'Take that!'

Well, the dragon looked at the crystal, which was quite small and rather unimpressive, and it said, 'Take what? If that's the biggest rock you can find to throw at me, then you had better prepare to be toasted, little man.'

But Wayne held his ground, because he was a hero, so he had no choice in the matter. 'This is no ordinary stone,' he declaimed. 'This is a magic crystal.'

Well, of course, that changed everything. When the dragon heard that, it took a sharp intake of breath; but, as it was just getting ready to breath fire at the time, it roasted itself inside out, and instantly fell to the ground, self-basted. And Wayne had slayed the dragon. All the people ran to him and thanked him for their liberation. And they told him there would always be a home for him amongst them, even though it would cost him a bit more now, what with the way property prices had gone up so suddenly. But Wayne thanked them for their thanks, and said no, because he knew that he must go on with his quest. And then he set off immediately, pausing only to have his picture sketched with his foot on the dragon's neck and his crystal held aloft. And this was yet another sign of his increasing stature.

And so Wayne cast about for the next lay line. Which was the way Wayne went. And eventually it led him to a place where his rod pointed straight to the heavens. And he knew from this that his quest was finally nearing its end. And here, beside a clear flowing stream, he beheld a young damsel, sitting astride a unicorn. And Wayne wondered, and he thought that was a funny way to sit astride a unicorn. For the unicorn was lying on its back, and the damsel was sitting upon it's head.

And a passing great-crested grebe told Wayne that it was written in the stars that he would woo the damsel, and that she would fall in love with him.

But Wayne hesitated. Because, for all that he was truthful, and valiant, and virtuous, he had no experience with damsels. He knew only that damsels were strange. Damsels were different. And they usually wanted rescuing before you had a chance of getting anywhere with them. In fact, the truth was that Wayne had no experience with women at all. Because a knight has to keep himself pure, and not think of such things.

But Wayne, at that moment, was thinking of very little else. He was thinking of things that women had and men didn't. Of things concealed in frills and flounces and furbelows. Of things that went bump in the night. And all these things made Wayne feel weak at the knees, and light in the head, although in between those areas everything was fine. More than fine, in fact. He looked in his basket for help, and there he found his clean hanky. So he blew his nose, loudly, on that, and then he looked in the basket again, and his hand fell upon the love philtre. And he took that out, and downed it in one. Suddenly he felt fine all over. And just at that moment the young damsel called out softly to him, and, without quite looking directly at Wayne, beckoned him to approach her.

So, henceforth, Wayne walked up to the young damsel, who was passing fair, but still on the right side of it. 'What is your name?' asked Wayne, and the unicorn said, 'Dick. What's yours?' But then the damsel turned, and he looked into her eyes, and he was lost. He forgot the unicorn, and the stream, and even the great-crested grebe.

'My name,' she said, 'is Lebam.' Which is, of course, Mabel, backwards. And, emboldened by the love philtre, Wayne quothed, 'Lie with me, Lebam.'

'Ah,' she said, 'but in truth I cannot lie with you. For it is written that, before any man may lie with me, he must first perform three great feats. He must pull the sword from the stone, he must choose the potion which is not poison, and he must slay the fearsome, fire-breathing dragon.'

And Wayne smiled a little smile. Then he smiled a bigger one. Finally he smiled a huge leer. And he quoth: 'Lebam, I am that man. For I have been there; I have done that; I have got the amulet.'

'Then,' said Lebam, 'we shall lie together, and our two bodies will merge as one.' So they lay together all that night, and Wayne's stature increased, again and again.

And the earth turned, and the moon waxed, and the moon waned, and in due course Lebam's loins bore fruit. First they bore two plums and a banana. Then she hit the jackpot with three melons. And people came from miles around just to see.

And then, finally, Wayne completed his journey. He took Lebam with him and they went back to his home in Norfolk. But they didn't go in a straight line, like the Romans did. No, they took the Icenic route. Because there's an old Icenic saying, which, as a matter of fact, we share with our Celtic brothers and sisters. And it goes like this: 'If the Gods had meant us to walk in straight lines, they would never have given us alcohol.'

HOW THE COYPU DUG HIS GRAVE
from the St Just So stories, by Rudyard Kipper

The late Rudyard Kipper was one of Sid's second cousins. In Norfolk this need not be a particularly close relationship, however. Indeed, half the county are related this way. The other half are just friends of friends, enemies of enemies, friends of enemies, and so on.

The St Just So stories were Rudyard's one real success. Whereas some of his other efforts, such as Plane Tales from the Carpenter, *were frequently dismissed as rather childish, these stories were actually meant for children. So, it is a cruel contradiction that they are often thought of as almost grown up.*

How The Turkey Got His Gobble *has already been printed in* The Ballad Of Sid Kipper, *but a host of other tales remain for Sid to plunder.* Why The Cuckoo Lost Her Nest, Where The Heron Stuck His Beak, *and* When The Rabbit Got It's Oats *all spring readily to mind.* How

The Coypu Dug His Grave *is the very last story of the collection. Indeed, it was the last thing Rudyard ever wrote, rising from his deathbed to commit it to paper in his distinctive Kipperplate hand.*

The coypu is a large South American rodent, imported originally for its fur, which accidentally escaped into the wilds of East Anglia. In 1989, when this story was written, it was being hunted into extinction by the sinister forces of Coypu Control, because it was destroying the banks of Norfolk's rivers. Rudyard was strongly opposed to this policy, because he hated authority, and he loved coypu-paste sandwiches.

The story having been finished, Rudyard went back to his death bed and died. Sadly, the same fate very soon overcame the last Norfolk coypu, although not in bed, of course.

Not so long ago, oh best Beloved, and not so very far away, the Coypu was welcome almost everywhere in the county of Norfolk. For he was sleek, and he was handsome, and he was charming and cheerful, and always very kind to his mother. And everyone, oh best Behaved, was glad to have him pass by where they lived. And, just so long as he kept passing by, he was loved and lauded by all his fellow creatures.

The trouble came, however, when the Coypu decided to stop his passing by, and start some settling down. Because nobody actually wanted the Coypu to live next door to them. 'I'm sorry, Mister Coypu,' they would say. 'That spot is taken.' 'What a shame, Mister Coypu,' they would declare; 'I've decided not to rent it after all.'

Because, you see, the Coypu was the very busiest of bodies. But not in the way, oh best Berated, that you might think. Not in the way of being lewd and lustful, and licentious. No, not in that way at all. The Coypu wasn't interested in that sort of thing, except for once a year, during the mating season, and that is none of your business or my business, or anybody else's business. That is a matter for Mr and Mrs Coypu, when they are best Betrothed.

For the rest of the year what the Coypu was interested in was digging. He liked to dig and dig, and dig. Indeed, his body was so busy that once he'd started to dig he simply didn't know how to stop. And the place where he liked to dig the very best of all was in the banks of a river.

It was not any particular river, oh best Begrudged. It could be any of the wonderful waterways of Norfolk. Such as the yattering Yare, which impales the county to it's very heart. Or the wide and watery Waveney, which guards the county from the outlandish peoples to the South. It might be one of the rare rivers of the West, such as the Great Ouse, or the Hundred Foot Drain, which flush the fruitful Fens. It may be the tiny Tud, the giddy Glaven, the narrow Nar, the Tiffey or the Wissey or the Burn, or the Thet. And that is not to forget, oh best Befriended, the wavy, wiggly Wensum, which wanders as it pleases through the middle of Norfolk. It could be any of those, because all the rivers were as one to the Coypu.

Now you can, and I can, and everybody else can surely see where the problem lay. It lay in the fact that there was every chance that the Coypu, and his busy body, would dig, and dig, until the whole county of Norfolk was flooded, and watery, and wet, and all of the creatures were damp, and dank, and dismal.

So all the creatures of the county got together, and they had a deciding. And what they decided was that somebody would very definitely have to have a strong word with the Coypu about his digging.

To choose who it should be they eenied, and they meenied, and they minied and they moed until only one creature was left. And who should that be, but the Grey Squirrel? Nobody, oh best Bewailed, because it was the Grey Squirrel!

Now the Grey Squirrel seemed a very good choice to one and all, because she was a cousin of the Coypu's. And, of course, and although it may not be polite to say so, and even though I'm sure that they were each very fine creatures in their own ways, it has to be said, nevertheless, that they were both foreigners.

Now, both being foreigners like that, you might think that the Squirrel and the Coypu would be friends. But the truth is they were not. You see, the Grey Squirrel thought herself rather superior, because she came from the North of America, which was the land of the free and the home of the braves; where seldom was heard an encouraging word, and the skies were all cloudy and grey. On the other hand the Coypu thought himself somewhat supreme, because he came from the South of America, which was the home of the pampas and, I dare say, the mampas; where the sun always shone and the beef was all corned, and nobody cried for me, Argentina. So even though they were both foreigners, and cousins, and family and all, they were really not the very best of friends.

But nevertheless, and notwithstanding, the Grey Squirrel still set off to find the Coypu, because that is what had been decided.

She had been told to look for him high and low, but she very much suspected that she would find him low. Because that was where he did his digging. Did I tell you about the digging? I'm sure I did, oh best Betrayed.

And the Grey Squirrel hadn't looked far around the bright, brave Broads when she came across the Coypu. He was doing what he always did. And you know, and I know, and everybody else knows what that was. He was digging, of course.

'Hello, cousin Coypu,' said the Grey Squirrel. 'Now tell me, what is it that you are digging?'

The Coypu didn't stop his digging to reply. 'Oh, you know, cousin Grey Squirrel. I'm digging whatever it turns out to be.'

'I see,' said the Squirrel. 'So, tell me, how do you know where to dig?'

'Oh, you know,' said the Coypu. 'I dig wherever it happens to be.'

'I see,' said the Squirrel. 'And how will you know when it is finished?'

'Oh, you know,' said the Coypu. 'I'll know because it will have been dug enough.'

'I see,' said the Grey Squirrel, although the truth is that she didn't see at all. She didn't understand digging. She thought it was hard work, and dirty work, and not at all the sort of thing a superior creature should contemplate.

The Coypu, it must be said, thought that swinging through the trees, and playing hunt the nuts, and so on, was skittish, if not down-right Scottish, and therefore not at all the sort of thing a supreme creature should contemplate, either.

'I have been sent,' said the Squirrel, 'to ask you to stop your digging.'

'Indeed,' said the Coypu, digging on, undeterred. 'And tell me, whatever would I do if I stopped digging? Because, you know, and I know, and everybody else knows that I am a very busy body, and must have something to do.'

'Well,' said the Squirrel, who hadn't really thought about the matter, 'perhaps you might take up a hobby.'

'And what,' asked the Coypu, still digging as if his life depended on it, which, perhaps, it did, 'what sort of hobby might a Coypu take up?'

The Grey Squirrel hadn't really thought about that either, but she told him of many fine hobbies, such as the collecting of stamps, the spotting of trains, and the breeding of newts.

'But, tell me,' said the Coypu, who by now had dug himself almost out of hearing, 'do any of those hobbies involve digging?'

Well, the Squirrel considered the matter. She thought of the stamps, and the trains, and the newts, and she finally had to admit that they did not.

Well, by now the Coypu had dug so very deep that his voice had become extremely faint indeed. The Grey Squirrel had to strain her ears to hear him, and even then she could only just catch his reply. And his reply, oh best Berated, was this: 'Then they don't sound like suitable hobbies for a Coypu at all.'

And those were the last words that any of the creatures of Norfolk ever heard from the Coypu. Because the Coypu had dug so very, very deep that he had dug himself all the way back to his home in the South of America, where he stayed and lived happily ever after, and dug the Panama Canal.

And the county of Norfolk went back to how it had been before, which was calm, and quiet, and distinctly un-dug. All except for the Broads, that is, which had been dug many years before, just enough, thank you, and not too much.

And from that day to this the Grey Squirrel has been allowed to stay in Norfolk, as a reward for ridding it of the Coypu. Although, of course, if they ever found out that the Coypu had actually got rid of himself, oh best Bewitched, they might, and you might, and everybody else might feel very differently about the matter indeed, might they not?

DOT KIPPER'S HANDY
HOUSEHOLD HINTS

CHOCOLATE FINGERS – This is always popular with kiddies, which is more than you can say for a firm clip round the lug, though I dare say that would do them a sight more good.

METHOD – First buy some chocolate, because there won't be any in the house due to Sid having eaten it all. Then melt it over a low heat. You can use a tall heat if you must, but then you'll have to stand on a chair to be able to see when the chocolate has melted. Then you just pour it into a bowl, and let people dip their fingers in and suck it off.

TIP – If you don't want to catch something nasty, make sure you have the first dip.

THE GIMINGHAM IDIOTS' PLAY
as performed by 'Partners in Crime'
(Sid Kipper and Dave Burland)

This piece of rustic drama is clearly very old because mumming or mystery plays of this sort were invariably the property of the various guilds and trades, such as Grocers and Nightsoilmen, and it's many years since Idiocy was recognised as a trade. But at one time it was an honourable enough calling, involving a long apprenticeship and a jealously guarded body of expert knowledge. Nowadays, of course, anyone can be an idiot, as Sid and Dave regularly demonstrate.

I've got Sid to write some introductory notes, by providing him with the relevant headings.

Introduction:
There's loads of Robin Hood stories from Norfolk. Mostly they feature Robin of Foxley, who used to ride round Wicklewood Forest with his merry band, which included Big Bad John on lute, Eleanor Dale on piano, and Errol Flynn on drums. Robin did the lead vocals,

like me. But in this story Robin is on his own, so don't worry about any of that.

There was also Maid Marion. Now, if she thought we'd believe that she really was a maid, when she spent all her time in Wicklewood Forest with a bunch of lusty men, she must think we're all as thick as two short plankton! So I reckon 'Maid' was just one of those names that don't necessarily mean what they sound like, such as Earl Hines, and Duke Ellington. And Dick Tracey, I suppose.

This version of the play has been cut down so it can be done by only two people: Robin Hood and the Notif of Sheringham. I've put in some instructions about what they should do, what we theatrical people call 'staged erections'. Otherwise you wouldn't know what was going on half the time.

Staging:
You can stage the play if you must, but it's only short, so you really ought to be able to do it all in one go.

Characterisation:
Robin Hood is always good. He's cheerful and jolly, and always joking, and jesting, and indulging in innocent horse-play. I reckon if he was real he'd get on your nerves something chronic.

The Notif of Sheringham is always bad, and he hates just about everyone, but most especially Robin Hood. He doesn't think horse-play is much fun unless the horse gets seriously injured in the process. As for joking and jesting, his idea of a punch line revolves around a real punch. So he's always trying to come up with ways of making Robin Hood the but of his jokes. However, it always turns out that the only but is the one in 'but Robin had the last laugh', although everybody knows that he who laughs last is a bit slow, and has only just got the point.

Normally I play the goody, and my Partner In Crime, the famous folk-singer Dave Burland, plays the baddy. It saves a lot on the acting.

Costume:
Dave and me find you can get away with just wearing a funny hat, but if you really like dressing up then here are some guidelines.

Robin Hood always dresses in a good colour, which is Lincoln green. It's a sort of green which was only ever found in Lincoln.

Plus wherever Robin Hood happened to be, presumably.

The Notif of Sheringham wears black, which just goes to prove how bad he is, because everybody knows that wearing black is just an excuse for not washing your clothes as often as you should.

Anyhow:
Anyhow, that's enough pre-ramble. Let's get on with the show.

(Enter Robin Hood and The Notif of Sheringham riding imaginary horses. Unless they can afford real horses, that is. Imaginary camels left over from the Nativity Play won't do.)
Both sing *(to the tune of the song from the Gimmingham Idiot's Play):*
>Come Ladies and Gents, and the rest of you too,
>We are mummers from Mummerset to entertain you
>With wisdom and wit, with action, also
>Gratuitous violence and innuendo.

(They stay on the stage, even though you'll find that they're just about to say they're coming in! It's just how we do things in the theatre.)

Robin: In comes I, bold Robin Hood,
>It's no coincidence that my name rhymes with good.
>My merry band laugh at danger and fret,
>They giggle at hazard, and chortle at threat.
>Why, only this morning Big Bad John broke a bone;
>They're still laughing so much I had to come on my
>own.
(You'll find you have to force the words to fit sometimes. A jemmy might come in handy.)

Notif: In comes I, the Notif of Sheringham.

Robin: The what?

Notif: The Notif of Sheringham.
>I hate Robin Hood and his band of hyenas,
>And today I'll take him and his grin to the cleaners!
>A most cunning plan I have put into place;
>That jackass will laugh on the other side of his face.

Robin: *(questioningly)*
Far be it from me to query and pry,
But why do they call you the Notif, asks I?

Notif: *(answeringly)*
You'd like to know that, I surely don't doubt;
Just get on with the play and you'll soon enough find out!

Robin: Maid Marion fair is held hostage, I fear,
In Sheringham Castle, so I'll go there and free her.

Notif: Not if ... I have anything to do with it.

Robin: My derring I'll do, and if they should catch me,
I'll buckle my swash, and with one bound be free.

Notif: Not if ... I can help it.
(You can see why nobody liked him much!)

Robin: Alright, alright, your point you have made;
Now it's I must tell you to get on with the play.

Notif: At Sheringham Castle I've only to wait,
Certain that Robin will come to my bait.
For I have Maid Marion, just like he said,
Stripped to her petticoat, and tied to a bed.

Robin: Now, now, that's a lie! I'm certain, you see,
I could never persuade her to do that for me.
It's impossible.

Notif: Not if ... you know what you're doing.

Robin: Then I'll hide myself in a cart-load of hay,
And smuggle myself into the castle that way.

*(The Notif answers wearily. You can either achieve that by acting, or do it
like Dave does and just stay up late the night before.)*
Notif: Well now, Robin Hood, you could do that I s'pose;
Get straw in your ears, and hay up your nose.

Then I'd have to hold an archery match,
Which you'd have to win, so I'd have you snatched.
Then you'd escape, and run round the castle,
Till we had a fight. Why not save all the hassle?
It's a tedious tale, which I'm bored of somehow.
Why not cut to the chase, and have the fight now?

Robin: Alright, alright, I'll call his bluff;
Come and have a go, if you think you're hard enough!

(Both get off their horses, real or imaginary. Robin practices a lot of flash moves, then faces the Notif and calls out 'On guard' – which is English for 'En garde'. They touch swords, nose to nose, at which point the Notif whips out a knife in his other hand and stabs Robin in the back. He falls to the ground, usually making a meal of it if I have anything to do with it. [Then again, if that's all too complicated for you, just have a fight. But make sure the Notif wins, otherwise the rest of the play will make even less sense than it does already.])

Notif: *(to the audience, if any)*
You can call me a bounder, a cheat and a cad;
That's one of the pleasures of being totally bad.
Speaking of which, now that he's not so bold,
I'll go and ravish Marion, before she gets cold.

Robin: *(Who's not dead after all, otherwise he couldn't get up and speak, which is what he does.)*
Not if...

Notif: *(interrupting him)* Yes, what?

Robin: *(ignoring him, which is easy to do when it's Dave)*
Not if courage, and valour, and quickness of wit
Can overcome evil, and make bad men submit.

Notif: I thought you were dead, by my own hand harpooned;

Robin: Not at all, not at all; it was just a flesh wound.

(They start circling round each other, although it would be a lot easier if one of them stood still if you ask me.)

67

Notif: But hold, Robin Hood, must we enemies be?
Someone could get hurt, and it might just be me!
I'm not totally bad; be not quick to condemn;
I'm kind to young women before I ravish them.
You don't understand, power makes me alone,
And besides, I come from a broken home.
(Of course, he doesn't mention that he was the one who broke it.)

Robin: Now you're not all evil, I understand that;
You were kind to your dogs when you fed them the cat.
But there's one thing you do I could never ignore,
And that is your wickedness in taxing the poor.

Notif: I do tax the poor, that's perfectly true,
But I couldn't do that if it wasn't for you!

Robin: If it wasn't for me? Explain that, concisely;
I am the one gives them money –

Notif: Precisely!
They'd have nothing to tax, but for all the cash which
You give to them, after robbing the rich.

Robin: So if I killed you, then they wouldn't be poor.

Notif: And they wouldn't need you and your men any more.
Whereas if I killed you, we could all be at pax.

Robin: But then, my dear Notif, you'd have no-one to tax.
No, there's only one way that this striving can cease;
We must both kill each other, and leave everyone in peace.

Notif: Well, alright – if you're sure.

Robin: I am.

(They run each other through and both die. You'll find it's a lot more comfortable to die on a chair, especially if you have to wait a long time for the applause. It also helps to make you visible when the corpses start talking again, which Dave and I always do with this bit we've added on.)

Notif: Is that the end, then? I thought I was going to ravish Marion.

Robin: Yes, but this is the two-handed version. We haven't got a Marion.

Notif: Well, we could ask for a volunteer from the audience.

Robin: I tell you what, we'll ask later. For two volunteers.
Let's just do the final number; I'm fed up with being dead.

Both get up and sing (*to the tune of the other song from the Gimingham Idiot's Play*):
So Ladies and Gents, and the rest of you, too,
We mummers from Mummerset have entertained you.
We now would be grateful for whatever you gave us,
In cash or in kind, or sexual favours.

(*They both wait hopefully for a while, then exit, disappointed. At least, that's our experience.*)

SHANTIES OF THE SEVEN Cs
as told by Sid Kipper

Now, my Uncle Albert was a sailor. You'd know that if you'd ever met him, because he'd have told you. He was especially known for his wooden leg. He always had it with him. It used to come in handy for things like planting spuds, propping the door open, and getting cobwebs out of awkward corners (although if you ask me you should let sleeping spiders lie. You'll get a lot less trouble with flies that way). Who the wooden leg belonged to we never did find out.

And *Shanties Of The Seven Cs* was a book of sea songs he wrote when he retired from the smuggling.

What Albert used to smuggle was brandy. Now, he wasn't daft. He knew that the Exercise men were looking out for people trying to smuggle stuff into England. So he fooled them by smuggling the brandy out of England and into France. You see, there was a big demand for brandy in France, due to so much of it being smuggled out to England. That's why brandy casks were made so solid – they used to go round time and time again.

Of course, you didn't get such a good price in France. But that didn't bother Albert, because he never paid for it in the first place. So he sold it to the French, who sold it to smugglers, who smuggled it back into England again. And Albert spent the proceeds on drink.

And it all worked perfectly well for many years. But all good things must come to an end – except for the Archers, obviously. What happened was that they got a new chief Exercise man round our way. He was called 'Gov' Guppy. The 'Gov' was short for Governess. He was called that because he was strict but fair, and he always made the other Exercise men put their toys away before they could have their supper. Of course, that meant that there was a time each evening when all the smugglers knew that the Exercise men would be busy. So that's when they did their smuggling.

As well as that, just to be sure, the smugglers-in used to pay the Exercise men to look the other way. Now before Gov came they didn't actually bother. They stayed in the pub and just didn't look at all. But Gov wouldn't have any of that. He said that if they were being paid to look the other way, then that's exactly what they would do. So they did. They looked the other way, and that was when they spotted Albert.

Well, they waited till Albert had moored up, and then they boarded his boat. They asked him lots of questions, like where he'd been and what he'd been doing. Then they searched the boat from bow to stern. But they couldn't find anything, and they couldn't get a straight answer out of Albert. The only thing they found was a very ripe cheese which Albert had got for one of his lady friends, who reckoned it disguised the smell of his feet.

Albert was in luck, really, because the cheese duty had only been lifted the month before. But that all meant that there was not a thing the Exercise men could charge Albert with. But Gov Guppy had taken against Albert. He said he didn't like the look of him. Well, he wasn't the first to say that, as a matter of fact, so it was water off a duck's arse as far as Albert was concerned. But Gov had got it into his head that if Albert wasn't guilty just at that particular moment, he was definitely guilty in general. And he swore there and then that he'd get Albert, if it was the last thing he ever did. Well, he swore wrong, as a matter of fact, but we'll come to that in due course.

From then on they stopped and searched Albert time after time, but always when he was on the way in, so, of course, they never found anything. So then they came up with a plan. They decided it would be a lot easier to set Albert up than to catch him. So when they knew he was due to make a trip they hid some brandy on his boat, so they could discover it when he came back. But Albert found it first, and he sold it to the French.

Well, when he came back they were waiting for him. One of them went straight down below, and without even bothering to do any searching he immediately called up 'Gov, you'd better come and look at this.' So Gov Guppy got hold of Albert, took him down below, and pointed dramatic-like to where they'd hidden the brandy. 'So-ho,' he said. 'And how do you explain that then, Kipper?' Albert looked, and of course he worked out what had happened straight away. So he just said 'Explain what?' And then Gov looked, and, of course, there was nothing there. Well, that got him really riled. He stomped off the boat and once again said that he'd get Albert if it was the last thing he did.

And then he did the last thing he ever did. As it turned out it wasn't getting Albert. It was tripping over Albert's wooden leg, fall-ing overboard, and drowning. That was three things, of course, but it all happened so quickly it felt like one.

Well, there was an enquiry, of course. There was some suspicion that Albert may have been involved, giving that it was his leg that Gov tripped over. But Albert explained that he hadn't been wear-ing it at the time, and he was cleared of all blame, but officially warned about leaving loose limbs lying about.

After that the other Exercise men became convinced that Albert must be a seriously dangerous criminal and, bearing that in mind, they decided to leave him severely alone in future. But Albert didn't know that, and he thought he would be under closer tabs than ever. So he decided to give up smuggling as too dangerous. He cut out the middle man and drank the brandy himself.

And that's when he wrote *Shanties Of The Seven Cs*. And if you're wondering about the title, it helps to know that the Seven Cs were all ports on the Norfolk coast which began with the letter C. Let me see, from North to West that's Caister, California, Cliftonville, Cromer, Cley and Kings Lynn. Well, they weren't so fussy about spelling in the old days. Nor counting, come to think of it. It made life a lot easier.

DEREK'S *THIRD* LETTER
TO THE TRUNCHEONS

Life's like that, isn't it? Only the other day I was bicycling through Blakeney, continuing my mission to the people of Norfolk. I've decided to call it Mission Possible. After I'd been thrown off the quay for preaching to the seagulls, I entered a local hostelry to take some refreshment. I walked up to the bar and addressed the very pleasant barmaid, who seemed to be missing several buttons from the front of her blouse, and wore a badge saying, 'I'm Randy – have a nice day.'

'How do you do,' I said. 'My name is Reverend Derek Bream, but you can call me Derek.'

'What's yours?' she replied. And do you know, I realised that she'd served me better than she could ever know. Because it came to me, there and then. Just what is mine? Is my dear wife Bridget mine? Certainly not. Bridget is very much her own woman. Are my daughters Briony and Brenda mine? Well, yes, I hope so. But then again no, not really. In fact, I am reliably informed that Briony is nobody's, whereas I gather from various people that Brenda is, in fact, anybody's.

So just what is mine? Well, in a slightly real sense, that doesn't matter, does it? Because, as a Christian, I believe that what's mine is yours. And, of course, vice versa, if you'll excuse my Greek. After all, the Almighty doesn't say to Himself, 'I'll create this tree, and it will belong to Derek,' does he? No, he does not. Nor does he declare, 'I'll make this sheep, and it will belong to Kevin Kipper.' Indeed, if he says anything at all of the sort, he says, 'I'll create all the things on land, sea and air, and they'll all belong to Lord Silver-Darling.'

But even his Lordship must admit, I humbly suggest, that his family is only the custodian of these things. He is but flesh. And then that last, rather worldly, word brought me out of my reverie. And I realised that my eyes were focused in concentration on that area of Randy's anatomy revealed by those missing buttons.

Just at that moment I felt a hand upon my dog collar, and immediately found myself being propelled towards the door by a large man, who declared that Randy was his, and that he knew how to deal with the likes of me.

72

And as I landed on the pavement with a bump, I realised something. I realised that if The Good Lord had meant us to fly, he would certainly have given each and every one of us a large, rough man, exactly like Randy's friend, to launch us.

THE DIGRESSION OF THE
THREE GRUFF BILLY GOATS
as told by Sid Kipper

There has long been an association between the village of St Just-near-Trunch and goats. It is surely no coincidence that the pub in the village bears the name of the Old Goat Inn, if only because pubs are rarely named by coincidence anyway. For many years the village boasted a large goat market. It didn't actually have one, but it certainly used to boast it. And the local hand-made, wholemeal, unpasturised goats cheese, Slimeswold, is deservedly feared.

So it is hardly surprising to find a story from St Just with three goats as the central characters – albeit that, there being three of them, one of them is slightly to the left of centre and another slightly to the right.

This is a story about what happened long, long ago and far, far away – which is just another way of saying you can't check whether any of it is true if you ask me.

So – long, long ago and far, far away there were once three Gruff-Billy goats. There was Slightly Gruff-Billy Goat; Pretty Gruff-Billy Goat; and Extremely Gruff-Billy Goat, and they were all brothers. Of each other, as a matter of fact.

So, one day – I think it was a Wednesday, because it was early closing, but then again it may not be early closing on a Wednesday far, far away. Or it may be now, but it may not have been long, long ago. Anyhow, I do know it wasn't a weekend. It was just a normal grazing day for the Billy goats.

So, one day – oh, by the way, because they'd all been christened Gruff-Billy by their parents Mr and Mrs Goat (Billy and Nanny to their friends), they were known to all and sultry as Slightly, Pretty, and Extremely. Now that made Pretty almost as gruff as Extremely, because it's not very nice being called Pretty when you're not.

73

Especially if you're a bit dim and keep thinking you might be made into a pickle at any moment.

So, one day – well, actually, by now that day had passed, what with it being early closing and so on, and now it was the next day, which I think was a Thursday. I'm sure it still wasn't the weekend, which come to think of it means that the day before couldn't have been a Friday, so it's even more likely it was a Wednesday. Though by no means definite.

So, one day, Slightly Gruff-Billygoat said to Pretty and Extremely, 'I say chaps, I'm jolly well fed up with this meadow. I think I'll go over the wickety-wackety bridge for a bit of a graze where the grass is greener on the other side.'

So that's what he did. He went crip, crap, crip, crap, over the wackety bridge. Well, that's to say he started to go crip–crap, but as he approached the middle of the bridge a horrible thing hauled itself into his path and, without any sort of formal introduction, launched itself into a tuneless, rather tasteless song:

'I'm a Trog, Fol-de-rog
And I'll eat you for my dinner.'

'I rather think not,' said Slightly, quite unraffled. 'As a matter of fact I think you'll find it's far too early for dinner. I think you'll find you mean that you'll eat me for your luncheon. It's a frequent enough mistake amongst common creatures like yourself.'

Well, the Trog was so amazed by what he said that it simply stood aside and let Slightly pass by to the other side where the grass was greener.

A little while later Pretty Gruff-Billy goat said to Extremely, 'I say, old fellow, I'm jolly well fed up with this meadow. I think I'll go over the wickety-wackety bridge for a bit of a graze where the grass is greener on the other side.'

So that's exactly what he did. Well, it's exactly what he started to do. He went crip, crap, crip, crap, over the wackety bridge. And guess what? Before he'd got to the middle, and without a bring and buy you're leave, up came the singing Trog again:

'I'm a Trog, Fol-de-rog
And I'll eat you for my dinner.'

Well, Pretty eyed the Trog with interest – although not very high interest. More the sort of interest you'd get from my uncle George if you were lending rather than borrowing. 'A Trog?' said Pretty. 'Well now, tell me, my good fellow, what might a Trog be when it's at home?'

'It might be much the same as it is when it's away,' said the Trog, grumpily. 'A Trog's a thing that lives under bridges, and jumps up and eats passing billy-goats.'

'I see,' said Pretty. 'And is that a good job then?'

'Not too bad,' said the Trog, 'though I have to admit the food's not up to much.'

'And tell me, my good Trog, just how long have you been Trogging?'

'Mind your own business,' was what the Trog wanted to say. But, although he was perfectly aware that he was as good as any jumped-up, lardy-dah Gruff-Billy Goat, he was somehow mesmerised by Pretty, who stood there so calmly, with his hooves clasped behind his back. So all he could do was to meekly say: 'As long as I can remember, your Goatship.'

'Well, it's been very nice talking to you,' said Pretty, 'but I must get on. I've got some important grazing to do.' And with his nose in the air he marched on, straight past the Trog, and into the other meadow where the grass was greener.

Now that only left Extremely Gruff-Billy Goat. And although he didn't tell anyone, because there was no one there to tell, he too decided to cross the wickety-wackety bridge to join his brothers. So that's what he went to do. He went crip, crap, crip, crap, and all that old crip. And up came that old Trog again, bold as bras.

'I'm a Trog, Fol-de-rog
And I'll eat you for my dinner
– and don't try any clever stuff.'

Well, Extremely looked the Trog up and down in a snooty way, and eventually he said: 'Pray, tell me, what sort of a song is that?'

'It's my Trog song,' said the Trog.

'I thought as much,' say Extremely. 'I take an interest in the music of the common people. I believe the song may be related to one I collected from a troll down in Somerset. What do you think?'

Well, the Trog wasn't accustomed to thinking, so he just stared at Extremely and said nothing. If Extremely had studied the common people better he'd have realised that the Trog was getting fed up to its back teeth, which is a long way on a Trog. But Extremely just carried on as if nothing was about to happen.

'Mind you, I have to say that, all in all, I think I still prefer 'Love Is All Around'. Do you still do that one?'

Well by now the Trog was getting pretty aeriated – by which I don't mean he was getting Pretty aeriated, because Pretty was grazing in the other field where the grass was greener. Anyhow, to tell the truth, what with dealing with all these posh goats, the Trog had got more than pretty aeriated. In fact he'd got extremely aeriated. No, that's just as confusing. Let's just say the Trog had got ever so aeriated – which is nothing to do with the goats' Auntie Everso-Billy Goat, who isn't in this story at all, so I won't mention her.

So, let's keep it simple. The Trog was aeriated, alright? All of a sudden he lost his grip. He jumped up and down, and he shouted at Extremely in a very vulgar manner. 'Never mind "Love Is All A-blooming-round"!' he shouted (only I've cleaned it up a bit). 'Never mind that,' he said. 'If you aren't careful I'll do "Wild Thing" in a minute. But first, I'm going to eat you up.'

And that's exactly what he did.

Which just goes to show that it's not always easy or wise to be a critic. And the Trog settled down under his bridge without another sound, except for the occasional belch, thinking that was the way to deal with poncey goats, and he'd showed him a thing or two, hadn't he?

And not quite so long, long ago, but just as far, far away, there were now just two Gruff-Billy Goats, plus a full Trog.

And some time later Slightly said to Pretty: 'I say old thing, where do you think Extremely's got to?'

And Pretty replied, 'I really have no idea. I suppose he must still be on the other side of the wickety-wackety bridge, where the grass is not as green.'

'Ah, now I think you're mistaken there, brother. It's a well-known fact that the grass is always greener on the other side.'

'What – even greener than here?'

'Of course – that's the other side, isn't it?'

'Well, yes.'

'And there's grass there isn't there?'

'Indubitably.'

'Then I rest my case.'

And that kept the two brothers ruminating for the rest of the afternoon – which, after all, is what goats are really good at.

And they all lived happily ever after. Which, come to think of it, means they must all still be alive today. So if you've got any questions about it don't bother me – just go far, far away and ask them.

SHIP FASHION AND BRISTOL SHAPED
Number Two – Masters and Mistresses

Some of us sailor boys has a saying. We say that a woman is like a violin. And so they are. They can both make sweet music. They can both be nicely curved, with holes in just the right places. But they always comes with strings attached. So haul up a hammock, and let me tell you about my experiences with masters and mistresses.

Now when you're contemplating a long trip you wants to make certain as to have a good master. A bad master can blight a sailor's life worse than the scurvy and the pox put together. That's what we call the purvy, and no laughing matter.

Now you can choose a two-master or a three-master, but, before you sign your papers, make sure she's sound as nine-pence, and right as a bell. For that ship's going to be your home, and your house, and your outside privy and everything else for months on end, far from land.

Some of us sailor boys has a saying. We says that a ship is like a soccer team. Some of them are top of the league. Some achieve mid-table respectability. And some are fighting relegation. Only when a vessel gets the drop she don't come back up again next season, if you take my meaning. So it's best to get a transfer before then.

But as well as a good master you wants to have a good mistress or two. And you need mistresses with mattresses. Because a sailor boy can get mighty lonely when he's out on the briony, month after month, being tossed from side to side. So when he's in a foreign port he wants his home comforts, so he does. Even though he's not at home. He wants his pipe warmed, and his slippers lit, and something warm and soft to lay up alongside of at night. To put it bluntly, like the bluff sea-farer I am, he wants a woman. Unless, of course, he wants a man. Some sailors have fancies in that direction. Not me, though. So I've had to fight for my honour a few times, I can tell you. Well, I just have, haven't I?

Some of us sailor boys has a saying. We say that a tar should have a girl in every port, and a port in every girl. But we're wrong, of course. He only needs girls in the ports and ports in the girls he actually visits. Otherwise there'd be a lot of spare going spare, if you take my meaning. Or even if you don't.

I've had some women, I can tell you. Let me see, there was Val

Paraiso in Chile, Ann Twerp in Belgium, Winny Peg in Canada, and Mable Thorpe in the bushes. And that's just some of them. There was a widow woman in America called Mrs Sippi, who used to open me with welcome arms whenever I was in port. And then there was a brothel keeper in the South of France called Ma Seilles. She'd be down on the dockside to pick me up as soon as I landed, and she wouldn't let me go until I'd sampled all of her wares. I was glad to get back to the ship alive.

Some of us sailor boys has a saying. We say that a sailor is like a pair of breeches. And he is, too. He has his ups and downs. He gets washed, once in a while. But most of the time he's just doing his best to hold everything in.

But that's enough salty stories for now. If I haven't said more than enough, then I've probably said just about the right amount, and we'll say no more about it. So I'll bid you farewell, and thank you kindly if you'll cast me off and give me a shove off the shore.

The Sailor In Diss Dress

Now hear me wail my woeful tale,
    of painful education;
How I got hurt by a dockside flirt,
    who'd nothing in moderation.
She said 'You are a bold Jack Tar',
    which took me quite aback, then;
How'd she know Ma and Mr Tar
    had christened their son Jack then?

'Now I've just come from sea,' says me,
    'My purse is packed with plunder.'
When she heard that she grinned like a rat,
    and said 'Well now I wonder;
Perhaps you'd care my bed to share
    and spend a night of passion?'
Says I, 'Aye aye, I'd like to try,
    for I've been on short rations.'

'But first,' she say, 'a jest we'll play
    if you'll oblige me, maybe;
If you put on my petticoats
    we'll dress you like a lady.'
I soon agreed because, you see,
    you must remember this, Sir;
To promenade dressed like a maid
    is my idea of bliss, Sir.

For it's all very fine, on a ship of the line,
    to show your manly powers,
But you have to hide your gentle side,
    and interest in pressed flowers.
So I got in her crinoline,
    the rest was not forgotten,
And when I passed the looking glass
    I fancied myself rotten.

Now we went round Great Yarmouth town,
    I danced with all the sailors.
And my night was made when I got engaged
    to a big Norwegian whaler.
Well all went fine until such time
    as my old tank was full, Sir;
For I couldn't clear my pumping gear
    for satin, silk and wool, Sir.

So there was I with me skirts held high,
    not thinking of flirtation,
When that way came my fiancee,
    demanding consummation.
Well it's no fun to have to run
    when you're bursting for relief, Sir,
And not so soft with your dress
    ripped off by a lecherous whaler's teeth, Sir.

I managed to cling to my under-things
    as I sped down Regent Street, Sir,
Where I was proffered a number of offers
    by half the bloody fleet, Sir.

That dockside tart she broke my heart,
    and left me in this mess, now;
She stole my purse, but what was worse,
    I miss that lovely dress, now.

MAY TO Z
Sid Kipper's handy alphabetical
guide to May customs

In the rural England of yesteryear, May was the month of rising sap, thrusting shoots, swelling buds, and stirring blood. For the farmer it was the start of the growing season. For the young and unmarried it was the time for pairing off, and outdoor courting. For the seasoned countryman, like Sid Kipper, it is still an opportunity to bamboozle everyone with trivia, most of which he seems to have gleaned from the mobile library.

This material was originally broadcast as part of Trunch Wireless's May Day celebrations in 1998, and rebroadcast four days later on Radio Norfolk.

May Apple – this is the fruit of an American tree, so it's of no interest to us at all.

May Balls – in Cambridge, it seems, May Balls are held in June. And they reckon they're educated! I learnt better than that at Knapton Academy. Obviously they should be called June Balls. Although, come to think of it, I used to know a girl in Dilham called June Balls, so I suppose that could have been confusing. I mean, if someone had said 'We're holding June Balls', people might have thought it was a kidnapping! Then again, I suppose they'd only have said that in Cambridge, and there she'd be known as July Balls anyhow.

May Bells – the widely feared sound of Trunch Mixed Morris. At this time of year they come out of hiding and generally make a nuisance of themselves.

May Bird – the Whimbrel, which, according to one book, is not to be confused with the Curlew. Which I never have. Although, now it's been put in my mind, I probably will.

May Blossom – is another name for hawthorn. Which seems strange to me, because hawthorn actually comes out in April. Except in Cambridge, I suppose.

May-Bug – the cock-chafer beetle. Well, you can see why they'd want to give it another name. On the other hand you'd think they might be more concerned about getting treatment.

May Bull – in the old Celtic calendar (which had pictures of young women, one for each month, playing fiddles and dressed only in woad) May 1st and October 31st were the two most important days of the whole year. Because those were the days when the animals came out for the summer, and went in for the winter. You can see why that would be important. I mean, if you got them the wrong way round you'd be in real trouble, because it would be six months before you could put it right again.

The May Bull would be decorated up, and lead all the other cattle out. It was traditional, if you met them on their way, to raise your hat and say 'Hello, May Bull'.

May Bush – is another other name for the hawthorn. Except in Cambridge, where it refers to the Monkey Puzzle Tree.

May Cup – this held the potent festive drink. If a young person didn't find a companion during the May Day celebrations, they blotted it out by drinking from the May Cup. People used to say 'He didn't get anyone, so he's gone to May Cup his mind.'

May Day – has a number of meanings (although I can't find out the actual number). For instance, it was supposed to be the day that Robin Hood died, having Mayed Marion. Some say he was buried in Wighton. Well, that's as May Be. I'll tell you one thing, though. He definitely wasn't buried in Cambridge, whatever they say.

From 1890 to 1977 May 1st was called Labour Day, and everyone had a day off. Which means they'd misnamed it, if you ask me. Nowadays we have the May Day bank holiday instead, which can be held on any date you like, except May 1st.

May Dew – this is collected early on May Day morning. It's supposed to be good for the complexion, apparently. This leads to 'May Dew Jump', where you tip some of it down the back of someone's neck, in order to give them a bottom like a baby's face.

May Ewe – the May Ewe was a bit like the May Bull, only a lot more sheepish. It was the biggest, cleverest sheep in the flock, and would lead out all the other sheep for the grazing on May Day. In America they call it a Bell-Wether, and I dare say they do the same in Cambridge.

81

May Eye – this is when you eye up members of the opposite persuasion, before the pairing off on May Day. This usually starts well in advance. About May 2nd the previous year, in fact.

May Fair – in our village this is held in August, in order to ensure a day off for rain during harvest time. We probably got the idea from Cambridge.

May Flower – is the name given to a number of flowers, such as the Cowslip, or Lady's Slipper. Anything slippy, I suppose.

It was also the name of the first ship that went to America. My relation, Abraham Kipper, sailed on the second ship, the June Flower. Mind you, he wasn't best pleased. The bloke who sold him the ticket swore it was a return.

May Fly – this is used in fishing. It also means to leave the village suddenly, as a result of the consequences of May Day.

May Hap – a hap is 'a covering', apparently, so you can work it out for yourself (except in Cambridge, where you probably can't).

May Hem – the May Hem is all to do with the May Queen, which we haven't got to yet due to alphabetical order. It's the hem of the May Queen's skirt, and the first three young men to touch it on May Day become May Kings, who in some places are known as May Ji. I'll leave you to guess where.

Being a May King gives you certain privileges, and, naturally, everyone wants to be one. So, as the May Queen appears at dawn, all the young men rush, and fight, and push, and shove, to touch the hem of her skirt. And that's why it's called May Hem. Of course, once the three Kings have been decided there's no special reason for touching the May Queen's hem. After that any girl's hem will do, and they grab hold of those hems and won't let go for anything. That's known as Hem Lock.

May Kin – these are in-laws, acquired at shot-gun weddings in the Autumn, when the results of the May Day activities can't be hidden any longer.

May Kit – all the young men carry what they call their May Kit. It contains all the things you need for the May Day revels. The two most important things in the modern May Kit are vitamin pills to keep you going, and what I think they call condominiums. Of course, in my day we were a lot more traditional, although the stuff in your May Kit did much the same things. The two important things then were a cod's liver (for the oil), and a sworn statement that you were nowhere near St Just on the day in question.

Mayniac – this is someone who goes crazy about the May Day celebrations. Except in Cambridge, where they have Lunatics instead. And lots of them.

May Nuts – my book says that May Nuts is a corruption of May Knots. But it doesn't say what May Knots are, so I don't see the point.

May-on-Naze – a small village halfway between Ross-on-Wye and Eccles-on-Sea.

May Pole – everyone knows about the maypole, so I suggest you ask them.

May Queen – the May Queen in our village was selected by a panel of judges called the Queen's Bench. First they chose the Queen, and then two attendants. The three of them were then rounded up, and locked away until dawn on May Day. You know the rest. Or you should do, because I already told you.

May Sons – or, to give them their full title, the Three May Sons. This is a highly secret group of people in St Just, which consists of Lord Silver-Darling, Ernie Spratt and the doctor. They have their secret meetings every third Thursday, at half-past eight, in the back room of the Old Goat Inn. If you want to know what they talk about I can't tell you, because I can't remember. But don't worry. Just go into the front room of the Old Goat and you can watch the whole thing on the security camera.

They're all the children of old 'May' Monkfish, who used to come to the village every year to do odd jobs. Where he came from, nobody knows. Probably Cambridge. He used to work free of charge for some of the local women, in return for you know what – if you know what I mean. They called him 'May' because that was the time of year he used to arrive. He didn't have a fixed time for departing, but when he did it was always in a hurry. And the May Sons were all born on the wrong side of the blanket. Still, they were conceived with no blankets at all, so I suppose that was progress, in a way.

May Songs – you get lots of these from different places. There's the Southrepps May Song, the Haddiscoe Maypole Song, and so on. They're really for old people, who haven't got the energy for the more interesting activities on May Day.

May Tide – years ago this referred to the purchase of the annual box of washing powder. It ensured that everyone's underwear was clean at least once a year.

May Tree – yet another other name for the hawthorn. They were obsessed, if you ask me.

May Tree Arc – an arc, or arch, of hawthorn branches. Except in Cambridge, I suppose, where it's probably something stupid like an old woman!

May Tricks – impractical jokes, to keep the younger children amused, such as making an apple pie bed with real apple pies.

Mayweed – Stinking Camomile. Or, in Cambridge, something a good deal stronger, I dare say, like Mary Joanna.

May Zing – that special feeling which you only get on May Day. Some people get completely carried away with it all. Like Simon Smith, who got so excited one year that he took off all his clothes and cavorted about nude. There was a song written all about it, called 'Simon Smith and his May Zing, Dancing Bare'!

May I Go Now Please? – the request of someone who's had enough of going on about May, especially as it's only March, the pub is open, and the mobile library is about to leave.

NO ROOM AT THE GOAT
(the Christmas story for tiny tots)
by Uncle Derek Bream

This piece was originally a drama, most memorably performed by Sid and his alleged father, Henry, as part of their 1988 Christmas tour. Sid's joint portrayal of the two main characters was a revelation, especially in Norwich, where the screen was accidentally knocked over during one of his many quick changes. Henry was perhaps a little overstretched in his playing of all three wise men, as well as all of the shepherds, but he did his best, and audiences were kind enough not to laugh.

Now the work re-emerges as a children's story. In preparing it Derek took advice from Mrs Fry, the retired headmistress of Trunch Bored School, who gave him two simple rules of writing for children: 'Start from where the children are, and explain anything they might not understand.' I think you may see the influence of that advice in what follows. And as the particular children Derek had in mind were those in St Just-near-Trunch, then that is exactly where he started.

You know the Old Goat Inn, don't you? Of course you do. It's where Daddy goes instead of coming to church on Sunday mornings, before he goes home and falls asleep in his dinner. Well, that's where my story is set.

Of course, when I say 'set' I don't mean it's gone hard. This is not a hard story at all. No, I mean that the Old Goat Inn is where my story happened, so I suppose I might just as well have said that in the first place. And this is how my story starts.

Mr Chippy the carpenter was very, very sad because he didn't have a job. Now, in those days, an order had gone out that all people who didn't have a job had to get on their bikes, and go out and look for work. So Mr Chippy set off on his little yellow bicycle, with his very good friend Tracey perched on the handlebars. And as they pedalled along they sang their special pushbike song:

Little pushbike, little pushbike, with your rusty wheels,

Little pushbike, you look just like the way I feel.

Now Tracey was about to become a mummy at any moment. And when somebody is about to become a mummy, everybody else always wants to know who helped her to make the baby. Especially if, like Tracey, they're not married. But Tracey couldn't tell them. Now that wasn't, as sometimes happens, because she didn't know. And it wasn't because it was Mr Chippy who had helped her to make the baby, because it wasn't. He and Tracey insisted that they were just very good friends. No, it was because the baby had been made by magic. Isn't that exciting?

Now, some poor children have never met their fathers. As a matter of fact I know that some of you have never met your fathers. And some of you think you've met your fathers but you haven't. But the special thing about Tracey was that she'd never met the baby's father, either!

You see, Tracey was what we call a virgin, which is someone who has never made a baby. But she was about to have a baby anyway. Well, that's a bit of a puzzle, isn't it? And the answer to the puzzle is that God had put the baby into Tracey's tummy, without her ever having the chance to say no. Of course, nowadays we know that's a very bad thing, but God didn't know any better at the time, so we'll just have to forgive him, won't we?

So there we have them, Mr Chippy and Tracey, riding along on his little yellow bicycle, singing their special song. Well, they rode and rode, until after a while it began to get dark. By now they were very, very tired, because it was long past their bedtimes. In any case, Mr Chippy didn't have any lights on his bicycle, and we all know that it's very naughty to travel after dark without any lights on our bicycle, don't we? Well, we do now.

So Mr Chippy stopped peddling, and he and Tracey looked around, and they saw that they were outside the Old Goat Inn. And they decided to stay there for the night. So Mr Chippy called for the landlord, who is the person who runs the Inn, and is responsible for the disgusting state of the lavatories.

When the landlord came Mr Chippy said, 'Have you a room for the night, for me and my very good friend Tracey?' Although I'm sure he really meant two rooms, one for each of them. Otherwise we'd have to wonder about them saying they were just very good friends, wouldn't we?

And what do you think the landlord said? Well, yes, if it had been the real landlord of the Old Goat Inn he probably would have said 'Bugger off!' But this is a story, remember. So what the landlord said in the story was, 'There is no room at the Goat. We don't do bed and breakfast any more. Not since that couple from Thetford stole all the towels.'

'Oh,' said Mr Chippy in reply. 'Then perhaps you have a stable we could use?'

'Well that's just daft,' said the landlord. 'The stables were pulled down years ago. We've got a car park there now. You can sleep on that if you like, just as long as you don't use the Vicar's reserved parking space.'

Mr Chippy thought about that, but it didn't seem like a very good idea. So then he said, 'But my friend Tracey is about to become a mummy.'

'Well,' said the landlord, 'that's not my fault, is it?'

'No, it isn't,' agreed Mr Chippy. 'Mind you, it's not my fault either, come to that. But is there nowhere we could stay?'

'Well, as a baby is involved,' the landlord said, 'I suppose the Children's Room would be appropriate. You can sleep there if you like, on the pool table, just as long as you keep putting your twenty pences in the slot.'

So that's what they did. And much later, in the small hours of the morning, when all good children are tucked up in their beds, and after a lot of moaning and groaning, with Tracey pushing and Mr Chippy fainting, and a rip in the cloth on the pool table that the landlord never got properly fixed, the baby was born. But if you want to know more about the details you'll have to ask your mummies. Or your daddies, of course. If you know who they are. And the baby was wrapped up in swaddling bar towels.

Well, when the landlord came down the next morning he saw that all three of them were wearing haloes, which surprised him, since haloes weren't the craze that year at all. Because you'll notice, as you get older, that every year at Christmas there's a craze for a piece of silly head gear. One year it might be Santa Claus hats, another year it might be balls on stalks that waggle as you move your head. That year it was actually floppy reindeer's horns, but Mr Chippy and Tracey didn't seem to know that. So, as I said, they were wearing haloes, which are lights that shine around your head. They're harmless enough, as long as you make sure you use rechargeable batteries.

But back to our story. I think it is our story now, not just mine, isn't it? Well, I think it is. Now, in the fields around St Just-near-Trunch there were shepherds, watching over their flocks. Of course, when I say the shepherds were in the fields, they weren't actually out in the open, because it gets very cold in the winter and they weren't stupid. They were just a bit simple. So the shepherds were watching over their flocks by looking out of the living-room window, across to the barn, which is where the sheep were.

And an angel appeared to the shepherds. Now the best way to explain angels is to say that they're a bit like big fairies. Although, come to think of it, that might just as well describe Cyril Cockle, but never mind. This particular angel was called Uncle Gabriel. Now when they first saw him the shepherds were all sore afraid. Well, obviously they each had their own individual feelings, which is always important to remember. So, actually, while some of them were afraid, others were just sore. But Uncle Gabriel reassured them all, and told them to go straight away to the Old Goat Inn if they wanted to hear some good news.

Well, the shepherds needed no second bidding. Because they assumed the good news must be about the Inn opening early, and all the drinks being on the house. Which doesn't mean that the drinks were on the roof next door. Well, never mind what it does mean. Let's just get on with the story.

The shepherds did what they were told, and set off straight away for the Old Goat Inn. And, having crossed the road very carefully, looking right, and left, and right again, they came to the Inn, and went into the Children's Room. Well, Mr Chippy and Tracey were quite surprised to see them.

'If you want to play pool,' said Mr Chippy, 'I suppose I could put the baby on the Space Invaders machine.'

But when the shepherds saw the baby, and the haloes, and so on, they realised that this must be the miracle Uncle Gabriel had meant. And they all bent the knee. Except for one, who couldn't bend his knee because of a nasty accident he'd had when one of the sheep backed up suddenly and took him by surprise. And they all spoke humbly.

'I have come to see the tiny babe,' said one.

'Yes, so have I,' said another.

'I just came along to keep the others company,' said a third, 'but I might as well have a quick butchers' while I'm here.'

And the fourth one said 'Baa!,' because it wasn't just his leg that got damaged by the sheep backing up. But the others never mocked him about it because they were good, kind shepherds. Anyhow, they knew it could just as easily have happened to one of them.

'We were watching our flocks, when an angel of the Lord came down,' said one.

'That's right,' said another.

'I wasn't watching the flocks,' said a third. 'I was watching One Man And His Dog on the telly.'

And the fourth one said 'Baa!', as usual.

Mr Chippy made them all welcome, and made them a nice cup of coffee, which, frankly, rather disappointed the shepherds, given that they'd been hoping for free drinks on the roof next door. But when they asked if they could watch Tracey breast-feeding, Mr Chippy thought he'd better change the subject.

So he asked them, 'How was your journey, this dark night?'

'Well, the weather's not bad – we had a red sky,' said one.

'I was delighted,' said another.

'I wasn't,' said a third. 'I had five pounds on a white Christmas.'

And you can guess what the fourth one said.

'We wanted to bring a present,' said one.

'We were thinking about a lamb,' said another.

'Only you don't get lambs at Christmas,' said a third. 'So we got some Bernard Matthews Crunchy Lamb Fingers out of the freezer instead.'

'Baa!'

And with that the shepherds handed over their present, had another quick look at the baby, and then left to collect their subsidies.

Now, there came three men from out of the East. Which is to say, the village of Paston. Some people say they were Wise Men, but you have to doubt that, given that they came from Paston. Other people say they were Astrologers, but that's all superstitious mumbo jumbo, and there's no scientific evidence for it at all, although it's interesting to think that Jesus was a Capricorn, isn't it? Perhaps it's best if I call the men from the East 'Magi'. That's harmless enough, because most people don't know what it means, anyway. Although, to be fair, I should explain that Magi is the plural of Magus, which comes from the Old Persian language and means a member of an ancient Persian priestly caste, skilled in Oriental magic and sorcery. So I hope that's clear.

Anyhow, these Magi were following a star. And by 'star' I don't mean a Kylie or a Jason. No, it was a real star, shining in the sky. And the Magi followed it West until they came to Knapton, where they met a very bad man called King Horrid. Now, I know you'll find this hard to believe, but King Horrid didn't like little boys. Well, alright, some of you little girls can believe that easily enough, but King Horrid wasn't a little girl, was he? Well, I'm telling you: he wasn't.

When King Horrid heard that the Magi were seeking a little boy, he pretended to be nice to them so as to take advantage. Which just goes to show that you should never speak to strange men, unless you're actually related to them. And King Horrid told the Magi that they should come back and see him afterwards, and have some squash and a biscuit, and tell him all about it. Then he let the Magi carry on West, which they did, until they came to the Old Goat Inn. Well, the star came to a halt over the Inn, so the Magi went in, and there they saw the baby, along with Tracey and Mr Chippy. And they gave the baby three gifts, because it was his birthday: one gave him some talc; one gave him some deodorant; and one was even more generous: he gave him airline tickets to Egypt. This was so they could all fly, because the Magi had dreamed a dream that King Horrid was going to get up to no good.

And that's exactly what happened next. Mr Chippy and Tracey flew to Egypt with the baby, which meant they were all kept safe and sound, and away from any danger. So that was a happy ending.

Even if every other little boy in the area did get massacred, which wasn't very nice, was it?

And you might think that was the end of our story, but of course it isn't. As a matter of fact it's only the beginning. And if you'd like to find out what happened next, then you'll just have to come along and be one of St Just's Sunny Sunday Seekers again next week.

But, for the time being, we'll leave Mr Chippy and Tracey, and the baby, all heading for the airport on Mr Chippy's trusty yellow bicycle, singing some more of their special pushbike song. You can join in, if you like.

Little pushbike, little pushbike, journey's end is near;
They won't let a little pushbike on the plane, I fear.
Never mind my dear old chap,
Though perhaps you'll go for scrap;
We will see you by and by, behind that bike shed in the sky.
Little pushbike, little pushbike, with your rusty wheels,
Little pushbike, you look just like the way I feel.

The Lost Flock
by George Kipper

While drinkers watched the flock one night
The table seated round,
A devil of a swell came in
And rubbed his hands a-round.

Fear Not, said he, for mighty bread
Had seized his troubled mind;
Good tidings for my kind I bring,
And this shall be the sign:

The Old Ship Tavern, a la carte,
With lager and Bordeaux,
All neatly served on sewing machines,
By the Ship Trading Co.

And then a dining throng appeared
All ordering tasty snacks,
Put down their mobile phones, and thus
Addressed their joyful fax:

All glory be to food and wine
And Perrier and din.
But for the likes of me, I find,
There's no room at the Inn.

THE HEADLESS HORSE MAN
OF HAPPISBURGH
as told by Sid Kipper

Ghost stories have always been a great favourite in Norfolk. From Black Shag, the headless hound with eyes as big as saucers, to the many tales of Old Harry, who used to run a second-hand turnip business in Ormsby, they have been told and retold around the fire on long, dark, winter evenings.

Of course, to get the full effect you really do need to have an outside toilet. Because it's one thing, hearing such a story, to know that afterwards you will be able to go upstairs to a well-lit, centrally heated bathroom, and quite another to know you will have to venture outside into the cold and dark, with only a guttering candle between you and the world of spirits. In fact, under such conditions, the effect of the story is often to persuade the listener that they don't need to go, after all. Hence the expression 'scared shitless'.

It all happened one dark, moonlit night in Demon's Wood. Well, not all of it, actually. Some of it happened the next night, as a matter of fact, but we haven't got to that bit yet, so it's probably best not to mention it. Otherwise this could get rather confusing, whereas in actual fact it's actually all quite straightforward.

One dark, moonlit night Ephraim Kipper was riding home through Demon's Wood, just outside my little village of St Just-near-Trunch. Now old Ephraim was a bit of a man of mystery. For a start, he said he had a war wound, but insisted on never talking about it. For a carry-on he claimed to have a mistress, but was always much too discrete to mention it. For a finish, he lied about everything, but always swore it was the truth. So nobody really knew a single thing about him. Not for sure.

But that needn't concern us here. Because all that was pretty much behind him when this happened. Because when this story starts he only has twenty-four hours to live. But don't tell him that. Otherwise he might go and do something else entirely.

Ephraim was on his way back from the Jolly Undertakers in Knapton. He'd been drinking there because he was barred from the Goat Inn in St Just at the time. Well, actually Ephraim himself wasn't barred, but his horse was. So the horse had to go to Knapton for a drink, and Ephraim went with him, because otherwise he wouldn't get a lift home.

What had happened in the Goat was this. The horse had one pail too many one night, and one thing led to the other, and the landlord, Ernie Spratt, barred it until it apologised and bought the barmaid a new blouse. Well, the horse was far too proud to apologise, and it wasn't about to spend good drinking money on blouses, so it took its custom elsewhere. And it took its customer elsewhere, too, which was Ephraim.

So that's how Ephraim and the horse came to be riding home through Demon's Wood, late at night. Well, Ephraim was riding – the horse had to walk, of course. And that was when it happened. That was when they met the headless horse man.

They were just going along through the woods, minding their own gin traps, when all of a sudden the horse was startled. It reared up, and Ephraim was thrown off and dashed to the ground. As he lay there he looked up and saw the terrible sight which had frightened the horse. He saw an eerie, sort of see-through figure appear through the gloom. It was dressed in a long coat, and it had hoses on, and a ruffled neck, and an old tricornered hat with a big feather in it. But, most eerie of all, it was riding a big, black, ghostly headless horse.

Ephraim got to his feet. He'd have got to them sooner, but he had trouble getting his socks off. But eventually he managed it, counted to ten to calm himself, and looked the fearsome figure up and down. He stayed as cool as a gherkin, and called out to this frightful figure: 'Why have you exhibited yourself? What do you want with me?'

Now the spectre on the headless horse had some difficulty getting his mount to halt, due to the fact that the reins weren't attached to anything, what with the horse being headless.

'Well,' said the figure, after he'd eventually stopped the horse by jumping off and pulling it back by its tail. 'Well, you're a fine one to talk about exhibitions, what with falling off your horse like that. I might well ask you the same things. But since you mention it I'm here to haunt the ten-till-six shift.'

'By the cut of your costume' said Ephraim, by way of making conversation while he put his shoes and socks back on, 'you must have been doing it for centuries. I suppose you've put the willies up some interesting people in your time.'

'Not at all,' replied the figure. 'As a matter of fact I'm new to all this. I only started last Friday. You see, I was riding home from a fancy dress party in Happisburgh when the horse in front pulled up, all of a sudden. Then it all went black, and when I came to I was like this. As you can see, the horse came off worst, but now I'm dead, and I'm stuck here in this blooming awful costume which I only wore for a bet in the first place. I say, I don't suppose you've got a fag on you?'

So Ephraim took the hint and gave the fearful figure a fag. Well, he tried to give him a fag, but of course the figure couldn't get hold of it, due to only being half there.

'You've got a lot to learn about this haunting business,' said Ephraim, lighting the cigarette and smoking it himself. 'For instance, I've been with you for nearly five minutes and you haven't moaned or groaned once.'

'Well, I've moaned about the costume, haven't I?' said the figure, rather put out.

'I don't mean that sort of moaning,' said Ephraim. 'I mean terrifying people by wailing like a banshee, or howling like a werewolf. That sort of thing.'

'I wouldn't know where to start,' said the frightful figure, looking enviously as Ephraim took another drag. 'I was a tax inspector before all this happened. The only way I know to frighten people is by sending them final demands.'

Well, Ephraim said he didn't think that would do. He said he didn't think people would be especially frightened at being sent a note, even if it was see-through. He reckoned it definitely had to be something you could hear. And to show the frightful figure what he meant Ephraim flung back his eyes, threw his teeth out, and let fly an awful, echoing moan. Well, it was so terrible that it scared the pants off the fearful figure.

But when Ephraim had finished, and the figure had put his pants back on, the spectre carried on complaining as if nothing had happened. 'I'm doomed to wander these woods aimlessly forever,' he said. 'You see, rules is rules. The only way I can be released is if I can scare someone else to death. Then they can replace me. Still, I suppose I could practice moaning a bit.'

'Well,' say Ephraim, 'that's up to you.' He put out the fag on his shoe and turned to go, putting the stub in his pocket to avoid forest fires. 'It's been nice talking to you, but I must get on or all of the best game will have been poached. But I'll be coming this way again tomorrow, so if you're still about, maybe I'll see you then.' And with that – or without it – he mounted his horse and rode off.

Well, the next morning Ephraim got up as usual, and at first he thought the whole thing had been a dream. But then he found the fag end in his pocket. And since he didn't smoke he realised that the incident must have really happened.

He told several people about it, but they all assumed he was telling tales, as usual. Of course, he didn't help matters by adding all the usual bits to his tale, such as having the figure arrive in a flying saucer, and how Ephraim had personally beheaded the horse with his bare hands, and how it had aggravated his mistress's war wound, and so on. In fact, his last day was rather sad, really, since for once he had a true story to tell – albeit with some bits added on – but nobody would believe him.

So that evening he was ready for a drink more than ever – which was saying something, given that his nickname was 'Mine's-a-pint'. So Ephraim may have had a few more than usual before he set off home from the Jolly Undertakers that night. But how he set out isn't all that important – what's important is the fact that he never reached home. His horse returned without him, which set people to wondering what had happened to Ephraim. And in the morning, when they entered the woods to search for him, they found him, dead as a dormouse, in the middle of Demon's Wood, with a note pinned on to him where his pants used to be. It said 'Thanks for the moaning lesson.'

And that is how Ephraim Kipper become the Pantless Phantom of Demons Wood.

But the story does have a happy ending. You see, Ernie Spratt felt a bit responsible for what happened, so he decided to unbar the horse from the pub. And they all lived happily ever after. Except for Ephraim, of course, who was dead. But he wouldn't have lived happily ever after anyhow, because he was a miserable old bugger.

And the story has an unhappy ending too. You see, to this day, mothers in St Just-near-Trunch always warn their daughters that if they go into Demons Wood at night they must always be sure to keep their pants on.

More's the pity.

THE PIED BLOWPIPER OF KINGS LYNN
by Augustus Swineherd

Sid was forced to memorise this seemingly interminable poem at Trunch Bored School. He insists on it being included in this volume because, as he says, 'Once I've passed it on, then maybe I can forget it at last. Perhaps I can get it off my chest, and onto somebody else's.'

The blowpipes referred to are the Trunch Blowpipes, a local instrument of some renown, if not to say infamy. Their music is said to be an acquired taste, but, apart from those who play them, I have been unable to find a single person who has managed to actually acquire it. As to the blowpiper being pied, this does not mean that he was bi-coloured. The word here is a contraction of 'pie-eyed', or drunk. Sid – no mean blowpiper himself – assures me that this is the only way to play the instrument.

And so to the poem. It is Christmas Eve, and the town of Kings Lynn is being bothered by mischievous, excited children.

> Kings Lynn town's in Norfolk,
> Beside the famous Wash.
> The River Ouse, great and wide,
> Washes its wall on the Western side,
> A pleasanter spot you never spied.
> But, when begins my ditty,
> Many Christmasses ago,
> To see the townsfolk suffer so
> From children, was a pity.

95

Brats!
They snowballed all the dogs and cats;
They lost their gloves and tore their raiment;
Swore with many damns and drats,
And rode their bikes upon the pavement.
They knocked off all the policemen's hats,
Put holly in the old men's spats,
And altered all the thermostats.

Brats!
In and out like acrobats
They crept in every nook and cranny,
Over walls and under mats,
And all around poor frightened Fanny.
Until the Mayor decided that
Something really must be done
To put an end to all their fun,
And called his secretariat.

All day they met in council,
That snowy Christmas Eve,
With nothing to announce, till
The Mayor cried 'I believe
I've got it, now I clearly see,
How we might have some harmony.
We'll advertise a big retainer
And hire a children's entertainer!'

They sent the word both high and low,
To search for such a one,
Till striding up the Downham Road
Came Mrs Winkle's son.
'Bring out your brats,' this hero cried,
'And I'll soon have them pacified.
A tune or two from out my pipes
And they'll be good as gold.'

Brats!
All of them came to meet the man
Who said he'd make them sorry;

96

Dirty Dick, and Smelly Stan,
Ethel, Will and Horrie.
The piper then prepared to play,
Called all his concentration;
The brats themselves stood idly by,
Quite unconcerned, and nice as pie,
But that soon changed, you'll learn, as I
Continue my narration.

He piped and played with all his heart;
The pipes, the pipes were calling.
But clearly, from the very start,
It really was appalling!

'Rats!' cried the brats, as they covered their ears;
'Rats!' yelled the brats as their eyes filled with tears.
Until, as the pipes on and upward did soar,
Their delicate ears could stand it no more.
This carol of beauty and joy was bereft;
The brats all cursed and blinded and effed,
Then made their excuses, impolitely, and left,
And troubled the town no more.

So, duty done, you must agree,
The piper went to seek his fee.
But though, that very afternoon,
They'd asked him in, and called the tune,
And though he'd scared the brats away,
Nobody wanted the piper to pay.
And though, through Lynn, the piper roamed,
And though he knocked on doors pell mell,
Shouted at keyholes and hammered on bells,
Called, and cried, and yodelled, and yelled,
Nobody seemed to be at home.

And so the piper had no choice
But to pack his pipes, and save his voice.
He turned his back on Kings Lynn then,
Swearing never to return again.

Peace then, at last, on Christmas Eve;
The folk of Lynn could scarce believe.
No brats to give them furrowed brows,
And no more of that piper's row.

They sat a while besides their fires,
Then put on glam and glitter,
And to the Town Hall they retired,
None needing a baby-sitter.
They drank and danced till very late,
Thinking that this life was great;
Though Christmas Day was almost dawning,
They could have a lie-in in the morning.

And now you're thinking, I expect,
That everything was just perfect.
But truth to tell it all seemed queer,
They missed those awful brats I fear.
Unopened presents 'neath the tree;
No little smiles where smiles should be;
No-one to dandle on daddy's knee.
They realised then how much they missed them,
And if they'd been there, they would have kissed them.

But hark – the awful silence breaks.
What is that row, for goodness sakes?
It sounds like little running feet –
The brats are scampering up the street!

Brats!
They swept back into town just like
A tidal wave of noise might strike.
Up the streets and into the houses,
With mud on their knees, and tar on their trousers.
With fingers fast, and scissors swift,
They stripped the wrappings from the gifts.
They beat the drums, blew the trumpets,
Ate all the cakes, and pies, and crumpets.
They bit their Uncles and cheeked their Aunts,
Put glue in all the potted plants,
And answered all requests with 'Shan't!'

But after they had gone to bed,
To dream the morrow's mischief,
Then many a prayer of thanks was said
To many a dampened kerchief.
For now the folk of Lynn all knew
That happy ever after
Requires some pain and tantrums too,
As well as children's laughter.

And so once more may life go on,
And though they sometimes feel depressed,
By all the brats, and need a rest,
A single thought, and all's redressed -
'At least that bloody piper's gone!'

DEREK'S *FOURTH* LETTER
TO THE TRUNCHEONS

Life's like that, isn't it? Only the other day I was coasting through Cantley when I saw a delightful little chap, no more than six years old, fishing from the river bank. 'Hello Sonny,' I called out to him. 'My name is Derek. And what have you caught this fine day?'

'Snot Sonny,' he replied. 'Sabigail.'

I have to confess that I couldn't understand a word of what the little fellow said, apart from Sonny, that is, which, of course, I'd already provided him with. So I decided to try again.

'That's a jolly nice shirt you're wearing,' I said. 'Is it by any chance drip-dry?'

He looked at me thoughtfully for a while, and then got up to go.

'Go get mummy,' he said, and I felt a warm glow as I realised that I had made something of a breakthrough on the communications front. I looked forward cheerfully to having a few words with the little fellow's mother.

She was some time in coming, however. And when she did arrive she had with her two burly policemen, who insisted that I accompany them to the station. How kind, I thought, although my train was not actually due to depart for a full hour.

I have to tell you now that I missed that train. I also missed several more after it, as it was the police station to which I was escorted. There I was interrogated as to what had been my intentions in asking a young girl (for so it turned out she was) intimate questions about her apparel. It was only after they had talked for some time to my dear wife Bridget on the telephone that they allowed me to depart. In fact, they insisted on it. They refused to be satisfied until they had seen the train depart from Cantley station with me aboard it.

And as I watched Cantley pass out of sight I had a little thought. I thought how easy it is to be mistaken about somebody. You see what I mean, don't you? I was mistaken about Abigail, and the police were mistaken about me. And all because of one little word. And that little word is 'take'. You see, if you take then there is always the chance that you will mis-take. Whereas if you give, then you risk only misgivings, which aren't anything like as dangerous. Indeed, if I'd only had misgivings in Cantley then there would surely have been no mistake at all!

I shall certainly be more careful in future. But I shall also bear this in mind. If The Good Lord had meant us never to make mistakes, He wouldn't have provided a railway line to Cantley in the first place.

DOT KIPPER'S HANDY
HOUSEHOLD HINTS

RATATOUILLE – This is a big favourite in our house because it stops all that scratching and scrabbling in the roof.

METHOD – Take a rat or two, depending on availability. Gut, skin and joint them in the usual way, then soak them in stale beer for 57 minutes and 30 seconds, or thereabouts. Drain, add a chopped shallot, and fry gently in butter (you don't need to use the expensive stuff. I get I Can't Believe It's Butter from Mrs Dace's Corner Shop). Add some tomato, bits of baby marrow, and anything else trendy. Simmer until the vegetables are tender and season to taste. Serve hot or cold, or not at all.

TIP – For a leaner rat, get the cats to play with it for an hour or so before killing it.

THE BURNINGHAM BODYLINE
as told by Sid Kipper

Mention the words 'cricket' and 'Bodyline' in the same sentence almost anywhere in the English speaking world and thoughts will immediately turn to Australia and 1932. Not so in St Just-near-Trunch, however. Thoughts there will turn to an even more shameful episode which occurred a year earlier. Because it was then that St Just faced their old rivals, Burningham, in the final of the North Norfolk Tea Service.

This was the most prestigious competition in the area. Most of the others were played for as little as a cup, or a plate. The winners of the Tea Service, however, would not only be the toast of the county, but they'd also have the toast rack to put it in! But I'll let Sid take up the tale, in a tour de force of storytelling and oral history.

The Run Up

The 1931 final featured a number of famous cricketers. Of course, most of our players weren't famous before the match, but they certainly were after. There was my great uncle Albert, for a start. Being a seafaring man he used his wooden leg as a bat and fielded in the deep. For a carry on there was Arthur Haddock, who was a slow bowler. Well, he wasn't just slow – he was positively snail-like, actually. In fact, his only hope of getting a wicket was to catch the batsman having a nap waiting for the ball to arrive. He also had a lot of trouble with no-balls, which may or may not have had something to do with his party piece, which consisted of putting live ferrets down his trousers while he was wearing them.

On the Burningham side there were some people who were already famous. Best known was Douglas Sardyne. Now, he was hated and feared by everybody, especially his own team, because he was what they call super-silly-arse. They also had a demon fast bowler, the Reverend Harold Larboard. He used to have batsmen shaking in their boots at the very thought of facing him. In fact, a lot of them didn't face him, which may account for some of his success, because it's not easy batting with your back to the bowler. Especially if your boots don't fit.

And if Larboard didn't get you there was no relief, because he was backed up by three more bowlers, nearly as fast, and twice as ugly.

On the St Just side there was also the vicar, Reverend Aubrey Gudgeon. 'Gudgeon by name and gudgeon by nature', they used to say about him! Then there was my grandfather, Billy. Plus Cecil Salmon, of course, who was the village blacksmith. Huge great bloke he was. Augustus Swineherd wrote some lines about him once:

Under the standing chestnut tree,
The village blacksmith spreads.

Actually he wrote those lines more than once, because that was the chorus.

Swineherd also wrote a poem about our captain, the Left Honourable Fortescue West-Runton, but that one was unprintable (and I should know, because I've tried to print it). Now Fortescue was highly thought of in underwear. Him and his wife, Muriel, used to run a factory making foundation garments for women – or men, if they were inclined that way. The firm was called 'Bodyline Fashions'. All the women in the area used to wear them at that time of the day. There was something for everyone in their range. There was the 'Bismarck Indestructible 24-Hour Girdle', the 'Titanic Unsinkable Reinforced Bra', and loads of stuff like that.

Taking Guard
The story really begins when the St Just team held a meeting in the New Goat Inn. As well as the people I've already mentioned there were Lord Silver-Darling's two boys, Gilbert and Sullivan, who were down from Oxford (which shows how much they knew about geography in those days), and the village Bobby, who wasn't a policeman but a young boy called Bobby Bass who lived in the village. But, then again, the local policeman was there, too – although I forget his name. I do know his initials were P.C. No, I've got it, it was P. C. Clam. 'Clam by name and clam by nature' they used to say about him! And, of course, the landlord, Ernie Spratt, was there, although no one was sure whether he was there for the meeting or just because the meeting was held in his pub and he had to be there anyhow, whether he liked it or not, which he did, as a matter of fact, but that's not strictly relevant.

So that was ten of them. The eleventh one was the vicar, but he wasn't precisely in the pub. You see he'd sworn at a young age never to set foot in a public house, or 'The Dwelling of Beelzebub and his Lickspittle Minions' as he put it. Not like our vicar-before-last. He used to nip out for a quick one during the collection and, then, if

102

there was enough in the collection, he'd go back again for the other quart. But the vicar in this story is very important, because he had a lot to say at the meeting.

I know, you're wondering how that was, given all his swearing. Well, you see it was only his foot he'd sworn about. So he used to stand outside the pub in a sort of lean-to that Ernie had built for him, and poke his head and body in through the window. The barmaid kept topping his glass up for him, as and when needed.

That was Betsy, the buxom barmaid with the hourglass figure. She's important to the story, too. You see, when the meeting was due to start she and Uncle Albert were carrying on a bit – you know, what they call canoodling. Although I don't know why they call it that. I mean, if you tried that in a canoe I reckon you'd get your ardour damped good and proper. Anyhow, the Honourable Fortescue was getting fed up with them causing a distraction, because he wanted to get on with it. So did Albert, as it happens, so him and Betsy went down to the cellar to change a barrel. Meanwhile, old Fortescue announced that on Saturday they would be playing their old rivals, Burningham.

Of course, the team already knew that. So then he told them that Burningham had beaten them every time for the past six years due to all their fearsome fast bowlers, but, of course, they already knew that, as well.

So he called for ideas on how to avoid losing again, and the vicar chipped in at once. He said they could easily avoid it by calling off the match. Nearly all the others agreed and, after a bit of discussion, it went to a vote, and they voted nine to one in favour of calling it off (Albert wasn't there to vote, of course). But the captain's vote was the one against, and he said his was the casting vote, and he'd cast it, which was what counted because that was democracy and it overruled all the others. He was a bit of a dictaphone if you ask me. So then he asked for more suggestions. Well, P. C. Clam said he was thinking of wearing his helmet for protection, but old Fortescue said he didn't think much of that. He said he didn't believe the day would ever come when cricketers would wear helmets. They'd be wanting pads next.

Then Gilbert Silver-Darling said that his Dad had loads of old suits of armour up at the Great Hall that were surplus to requirements. He said they could borrow them to protect them from the bowling, plus they could polish them up, and that would have the added advantage of dazzling the opposition at the same time by reflecting the sun in their eyes.

Well, old Fortescue got on his high horse over that. He had two horses – a high one and a low one. To be frank, it was a bit of a nuisance him bringing them into the pub just for a cricket discussion. I mean, it wasn't as if it was a hunt meet or anything, although that was probably just as well, really, as then he'd probably have brought the hounds as well. Anyhow, he declared from the saddle that wearing armour would be downright cheating, and he wasn't going to stoop to that. He said he didn't mind a bit of fair cheating, but he refused to be downright about it.

After that everyone looked thoughtfully into their empty glasses, waiting for someone to come up with another idea or, even better, buy a round.

Meanwhile, down in the cellar, Betsy was showing Albert her gratitude for him broaching her barrel with his wooden leg. She moved into his arms, and said she didn't know if she wasn't going to swoon with all the excitement, and with that in mind would he mind reaching behind her and loosening her stays, purely for medicinal purposes? And Albert said he didn't mind if he did, if it would help her feel better. And she said it might well help him to feel better as well, and one thing led to the other, and the next thing the meeting upstairs knew was that Albert came rushing into the room waving a size 14 Great Eastern Ironclad Corset, shouting something about balls.

Well, as you can imagine, there was quite a kerfuffle. The vicar fainted, because he'd never seen a lady's underthings before. Old Fortescue was staring at Betsy, who'd followed Albert up from the cellar. She looked rather put out. She also looked a different shape. Without her corset she wasn't so much buxom as just big. The sands had all run out of her hour glass, so to speak. Gilbert Silver-Darling didn't know where to put himself, while Sullivan did, but he thought that this was neither the time nor the place.

But eventually things calmed down and Albert explained his idea. He said they could wear the underthings under their things for the cricket match, and fend off the fast bowling that way. And after some discussion, with everyone waiting to see which way the casting vote was going to go before they committed themselves so as not to fall out with the captain, it was unanimous.

So then Ernie Spratt asked the Left Hon. Fortescue what time they should turn up at the factory for their fittings. But Forty said there was a bit of a problem over that. He said all the undergarbs in the factory had been sold to an Arab Shriek who wanted one for each of his 57 wives, plus two each for his 1,001 knights. So he said it would have to be up to each man to provide his own garments. Then, since there was no any other business, he closed the meeting, and they all got down to some serious drinking.

The First Test
Of course, it was easier for some than for others to get their hands on lady's underwear. Some just got them off their wives or sisters, or the like. But it wasn't so simple for others.

Take Ernie Spratt. He wasn't married at the time, and his only sister was a Mother Superior. So he went round to see a young widow he was acquainted with. Well, she was just coming to the door when he arrived, because she was putting something out for the milkman. It was his cigarette as a matter of fact. So Ernie waited outside until the milkman had finished and then, when he'd gone, Ernie knocked on the door. And when she answered it he said to the widow, 'Look here, my dear, I'll come straight to the point. You've got something I want.' So she said, 'Have I indeed? And what makes you think I should let you have it?' So he said well, it wasn't for him, as such – it was more for the honour of the village. 'Well, that puts a different light on it,' she said. 'Why didn't you say that in the first place? You'd better come in.' So he went in, and she took him up to her bedroom, and straight away she took off all her clothes. Well, Ernie just grabbed her underwear and went straight back to the Old Goat, carrying it in triumph. Oh, he said she seemed to be a bit disappointed about something, like she'd wanted something in exchange, but, as he said, what would she want with an old pair of long johns with a hole in them, anyway?

And that was him fixed up.

It was even more difficult for the vicar. I mean, he couldn't just go up to some woman and ask her straight out for her underwear, could he? So he appealed for help in confidence to the Women's Bright Hour. Well, they went into a sort of a huddle and he assumed they were just discussing the matter. But then out of the huddle Mrs Dace handed him a set of pink frilly underwear, still warm. Well, he went as red as a beetroot. He didn't know where to put himself. He tried the cupboard, but he wouldn't fit. But after a cup of tea and a biscuit he cooled down, as did the underwear, and then that was him fixed up as well.

Of course, my Uncle Albert enjoyed searching for underwear so much that he collected six different sets from six different women.

Fast Bowlers

So, one way and another, come the day, all the team were fixed up with Bodyline underwear. Now, there were still one or two problems that had to be sorted out before the match. For a start, the horse which they used to roll the pitch with had died. Of course, a lot of teams prefer to use a roller, but we always used a horse, which was trained up specially. But on the morning of the match it died in mid roll and they had a hell of a job getting the carcass off the wicket.

Then the spin bowler, Arthur Haddock, arrived, and stuck two fingers up at the captain. He wasn't being rude. It was just that he'd had an accident with his ferrets and two fingers was all he had left. He said 'I'm afraid I won't be able to bowl very well with two fingers, skipper.' The Left Honourable looked him up and down sarcastically, and said, 'Well, that's a relief, then. I was worried it might have affected your performance.'

And that was when a big, black, shiny charabanc drew up, and out stepped the Burningham team. First came Douglas Sardyne, the captain. Then came Reverend Harold Larboard, their demonest bowler. There was a bit of bad blood between him and our vicar as a matter of fact. It went back to when they held a combined harvest festival for both churches. As it took place in our village, Gudgeon reckoned he ought to have all the collection for his organ, but Larboard reckoned that as no one from our village had turned up he should have it for his hassocks.

Anyhow, after him came four hulking great blokes. One of them was the driver, but the other three were the other fast bowlers. (I don't mean fast bowlers like they used to do at the hatters in North Walsham. They used to specialise in them. You could go in there in the morning and get your head examined, then go to market and buy a cow, and by the time you came back your bowler was ready. Of course, you didn't have to buy a cow. You could buy a pig. Or even a sheep – which is a very handy thing to do if you've got an odd sheep that needs evening up.)

But I digest. The three fast bowlers were 'Ripper' Ruddock, 'Cannonball' Nobbs and 'Whistling' Jack Smith. The last one was known especially for whistling the ball past your lugs. They used to say that if you didn't hear the whistle that meant it had hit you smack between the two of them.

Sardyne walked straight into the pavilion, marched up to Fortescue West-Runton, and sneered, 'Well, shall we get on with it, then?'

Old Forty stood firm. He looked Sardyne in the eye. 'Not at all,' he said. 'On the contrary. As a matter of fact I think we should get on with it right now. But wait – aren't there one or two little preliminaries we ought to complete? Things such as wishing each other luck and tossing a coin?'

But Sardyne was having none of that. He said, 'Look, we'll have plenty of time for preliminaries afterwards. Let's just get on with the thrashing shall we? We'd better bat first, otherwise the game will be over before the teas are ready.' And with that he sent his opening batsmen out to the middle, and took up a sneering position in the pavilion.

'Play'

So there was nothing else for it. St Just-near-Trunch took the field and battle began. Fortescue West-Runton invited Gilbert Silver-Darling to open the bowling. Gilbert replied that he was very sorry, but he couldn't possibly accept the invitation as he had a previous engagement. So then he was ordered to open the bowling, and that's what he did.

He didn't much like what he found when he opened it. He come trotting in to the wicket and bowled, just in time to see the ball disappear back over his head to the boundary. He always said afterwards that it was a good thing he wasn't a quicker bowler, because in that case he'd have got to the wicket that bit sooner and might well have been hit by the ball.

The next ball went for six and demolished the Gents lavatory, which didn't please Lord Silver-Darling as he was using it at the time. Burningham got 14 off the first over and then Cecil Salmon came on to bowl at the other end. He did a bit better than Gilbert – he only went for 13 runs, and he sort of got a wicket. Well, he was involved in it, anyway. Mind you, it was a bit of a fluke.

You see, Lord Silver-Darling had just got himself free from the wreckage of the Gents and came bursting on to the field to demand to know what was going on. So what looked like a certain six bounced off his head and lodged in my Uncle Albert's trouser turn-ups. Of course, Albert could have just caught it if he'd been wearing the trousers at the time. But, as it was, he quickly picked the ball out and claimed the catch anyway, and Cecil Salmon pointed his finger at the batsman, Brigadier Pratt, and shouted that he should get back to the pavilion. The umpire refused to give him out of course, but the Brigadier looked at Cecil's finger and said that he had no intention of staying where he wasn't wanted, and retired hurt with a stiff upper lip.

And that brought Sardyne swaggering to the wicket. Well, you could have cut the tension to the quick as he took guard, slowly looked around the field, and prepared to face his first ball. It duly arrived, and he drove it gently but stylishly into the covers. He was busy sneering at the bowler when the bloke at the other end called for a quick single. Well, that wasn't exactly Sardyne's way, so he went for a swaggering single instead, and was swaggered out by my grandfather for nought.

But after that it all went Burningham's way. And in what seemed to be no time at all, but must have been really, they'd scored 155 for two.

Well, when the Left Hon. saw the ball cross the boundary yet again to bring up 159, he realised he'd have to try some desperate measures. So he tossed the ball to Arthur Haddock.

Now, like I said, Arthur was a sort of spin bowler. Like I also said he weren't a very good spin bowler. For a start he was the sort who didn't actually spin the ball. But everyone else was fed up of bowling, so he got the ball anyhow. And that was when it all happened. Now, you may remember that Arthur had lost two fingers and a thumb to his ferrets, so he had some difficulty actually holding the ball. But he loved bowling, and he didn't often get the chance, so he decided to give it a go anyway. He ambled up, turned his arm over and then, having got his arm the right way up again, he bowled the ball. Well, whether it was because he only had two fingers, or whether it was because he didn't have the other two I don't know, but he found that now he spun the ball all over the place. In fact nobody could play him. And wickets started to tumble.

Of course, there was that bit of trouble with the umpire. You see, when Arthur appealed he used to throw his bowling hand straight up in the air, fingers spread in a dramatic fashion. Well, what with him only having the two fingers, that did lead to a certain amount of misunderstanding. But despite all that he took the last eight wickets for only seven runs, and, with a few byes, Burningham were 171 all out. So that left St Just needing 172 runs to win.

Putting On The Covers

So during the tea interval our side went to get into their underwear. Not that they weren't wearing any underwear before – this isn't that kind of a story, thank you very much. I'm talking about the Bodyline underwear: the ladies' fundamentals.

It was quite a sight in the dressing-room, because most of them didn't have a lot of practice in wearing women's underwear. So they were all too busy fighting with straps and bows, and hooks and eyes to wonder how come Cecil Salmon got into his like a flash and was able to help all the other players get into theirs. Nevertheless, it still took so long that they didn't have time to go for any refreshments.

Meanwhile, in the pavilion, the Burningham team were taking a leisurely tea. Douglas Sardyne was crowing. It was the only bird impression he did, but he was very good at it. He reckoned it would be a knock-over, which is somewhere between a knockout and a walkover. Or is that a walkout? Anyhow, he reckoned Burningham would win easily because of their non-secret weapon, which was all their fast bowlers.

They bowled what they called 'lug theory'. How they did it was like this – they used to bowl one past the batsman's left lug to get him worried. Then they used to bowl one past the right lug to get him even more worried. And then, when he was really worried, they bowled one into his ribs to get him retired hurt. And, of course, every ball was lightning fast.

Over And Out

Everything in Burningham was fast. They had fast bowlers, fast women and fast lanes. Whereas we were more specialised in slow, such as slow bowlers, slow learners and, at the match, slow handclaps. The slow handclap was for the batsmen, because the Burningham side had finished their tea and taken the field for the St Just-near-Trunch innings. The openers were late coming to the wicket, but eventually the first two batsmen came out, waddling a bit. They were Gilbert and Sullivan Silver-Darling, and it was Gilbert that had to face the first over from the fastest of all those fast bowlers, the deadly Harold Larboard.

Now Larboard held a lot of records. But, then, being a vicar, that was part of the job. And as well as the parish records he also held the Norfolk record for the longest run-up. He often used to have a chair put at the end of his run-up so he could have a rest from the walk back before bowling. That wasn't needed at St Just, because it wasn't a very big ground, so his run-up actually started in the pavilion and he could have a sit down there. So, off he went, back past the boundary, up the pavilion steps, and in through the door.

The tension was almost unbearable. Gilbert stood at the crease, trying to look brave, which is rather different from actually looking brave. The umpire called out 'Play', the pavilion door burst open and Larboard come rushing down the steps, cricket ball in hand. He tore towards the wicket getting faster and faster. The crowd held its breaths, as Larboard come up to the umpire, braked to a halt, and said, 'Pardon'. You see, he hadn't been able to hear what the umpire said for the singing of the St Just Women's Bright Hour Female Voice Choir, who were using the pavilion for their rehearsal. So the umpire said, 'What?' and Larboard said, 'I said what did you say?' and the umpire said, 'I said "Play".' And Larboard decided that, rather than waste all the effort of the run-up, he'd bowl the ball anyhow. So he sent down a gentle long hop, which Gilbert gratefully hit over the boundary for six.

Well now, that was probably a mistake. You see, before that Larboard had been feeling quite mellow, because he'd managed to get the bun with the icing on at tea, but now he got proper riled. He decided to lengthen his run-up. He went into the pavilion, out of the back door, and down to the end of Mrs Dace's garden. They had to put a bloke on the pavilion roof with a flag to pass on the umpire's signal. Well, the umpire signalled, the flag went up, and Larboard set off again, nostrils flared, arms whirling, feet pounding. He come on to the field, almost scorching the grass, thundering towards the wicket. He reached it, his arm started to come over like a catapult, and at that moment the umpire shouted, 'No ball!' You see, Larboard had left the ball in the pavilion. But so as not to waste all that effort the umpire lent him another one, and he sent down a gentle long hop, which Gilbert hit over the boundary for another six.

Well, now Larboard was really wound up. He'd never been hit for two sixes before. As a matter of fact he'd never been hit before. So he lengthened his run up again. He went through the pavilion, into Mrs Dace's garden, up the path and into her front parlour. Mr Dace had to stand at the kitchen window to tell him when the flag went up.

Up it went, and off went Larboard. Down the garden path, through the pavilion, over the turf, up to the wicket, all just as before. Except this time, when he reached the wicket, he tripped over the umpire. Well, he'd got bored waiting, and laid down for a bit of a nap. So Larboard tripped over him, the ball went up in the air, and arrived at Gilbert Silver-Darling as a gentle long hop. Well, Gilbert knew what to do with that, and he hit it for six again.

Well by this time Larboard practically had steam coming out of his ears. He lengthened his run up yet again. Through the pavilion, up Mrs Dace's garden path, through the house, out of the front door, up the road past the Post Office, and out on the Knapton road. And then – well, nobody knows for sure what exactly happened then. It seems he went so far that he couldn't find his way back. He was never seen again. Then again, they do say that to this very day he can still be seen running round Knapton with a cricket ball in his hand, asking his way to the Recreation Ground. It all depends on your point of view, I suppose.

After a while the umpires gave him up for Lent, and Sardyne finished the over himself. Gilbert Silver-Darling, out of decency and sportsmanship, played each ball gently back to the bowler, and that was the end of the first over. It had taken 52 minutes, and yielded 18 runs.

Getting The Runs

So now Sardyne called up another fast bowler – although some people say that six balls every 52 minutes isn't exactly rapid. Sullivan Silver-Darling was stood motionless at the wicket as 'Ripper' Ruddock came running in. In fact, Sullivan was fast asleep, because he'd had nothing to do for nearly an hour. So the bowler woke him up with a fast ball in the middlerift. But of course he wasn't hurt at all, because the underwear protected him. But there was also an added bonus: you see, the rubber in the underwear sent the ball flying off to the boundary for four leg byes. Of course, it wasn't actually his leg that the ball came off, but in cricket whatever the ball comes off is called a leg. That goes back to Victorian times, when it was considered rude to mention other parts of the body. It was rude to mention legs, really, but legs were a lot less rude than the really rude bits. Crotch byes would have startled the horses and made all the ladies faint.

So now St Just found out how the underwear stood up, although I could have told them that. It stood up because it had Sullivan Silver-Darling inside it.

And they started getting all their runs in legs byes off their corsets. Of course, they could still lose wickets. Gilbert Silver-Darling was the first to go. He was stumped. Now it's quite unusual getting stumped off a fast bowler, what with the wicket keeper standing all the way back near the boundary. But what happened was that the ball hit Gilbert on the shoulder, went straight up in the air, and fell to ground right next to the stumps. Gilbert realised that he was out of his crease and should be stumped, but he also knew the wicket keeper would never get there before he got back, so being a man of honour he stumped himself, appealed, and gave himself out. That's what you get with an Oxford education – no sense at all.

Anyhow, that brought my uncle Albert to the wicket. Now Albert was a classy batsman. And he didn't disappoint on this occasion. He played some fantastic shots with his wooden leg, in particular a thrilling square cut, and a delicate leg glance. None of them got anywhere near the ball, but that didn't matter because he missed with style, and he also got a couple of leg-byes off his underwear in the process. Of course, the sixth ball he faced did smash his wicket into a thousand tiny pieces, but, like he said, that could happen to anyone. And, anyhow, it was style that mattered.

So now it was 54 for two, and in came the Left Honourable Fortescue West-Runton. He called Sullivan Silver-Darling to the middle of the wicket for a conference. He said they had a real chance of winning the match, so he reckoned the two of them should go for it. Sullivan said alright, so that's what they did. They went for it. But as it was round at West-Runton's house they both had to retire from the cricket. Which meant St Just were effectively 54 for four.

So now two new batsmen came to the wicket: P. C. Clam and my grandfather, Billy. Now Billy was a bit of a hero in the match, because he was the only one other than Gilbert Silver-Darling to score any runs off the bat. Not that he meant to do it. As a matter of fact he'd come down the wicket to ask the policeman what he meant by arresting my uncle George for possession of a bicycle with intention to ride without lights, when a wasp attacked him. He swatted at the wasp with his bat, and that was just the moment when the bowler chose to bowl the ball. It hit the bat and flew over the boundary for six runs. Everybody leapt up and cheered. Well, everybody except for Lord Silver-Darling, who'd just got his portable commode set up, what with the collapse of the Gents earlier, when the ball smashed in through the canvas roof and knocked him off his pedestal.

Still, the leg-byes kept coming, and they'd got to 127 for four when they had a collapse. They didn't so much lose wickets as deliberately mislay them. First the policeman was given run-out when he tried to arrest the square leg umpire for loitering. Then Grandfather was out Handled Ball, although he always swore that he was only adjusting his abominable projector. Ernie Spratt was run in when Clam caught him stealing a run, and the blacksmith went 'something before wicket'. Well, he was so big the umpire couldn't see the wicket, so he didn't know which bit of him was before it. But the bowler assured him it would have hit, so he had to go.

Then Bobby was caught by his mother and dragged home by his lug for his supper. All that meant they were now 152 for nine, with no wickets left and 20 runs to get, with just the vicar and Arthur Haddock to bat. There was a close, breathless hush, I can tell you.

They'd got ten of the runs in leg-byes when old Sardyne looked at his watch, looked round the field, and sneered, 'That's it then, gentlemen. It's a draw, I believe.'

You see, they'd agreed to finish at so many overs, or 7 o'clock, and his watch said five past. But Arthur Haddock pointed and said, 'No, because we always go by the Trunch church clock.' So they all looked at the church clock, which said a quarter to seven. Of course, Sardyne didn't know that it had stopped at a quarter to seven years before. They only used to go by it when it suited them. If it suited them to get off early they went by the Knapton church clock, which was in the opposite direction. That one had stopped at a quarter past. Nobody knew a quarter past what, because the little hand had dropped off. Not that the bloke who's head it landed on thought it was particularly little, but that's another story, and to tell the truth I've got both hands full with this one.

Anyhow, they played on, until it was the very last ball of the match and St Just needed four to win. The bowler summonsed up his last bit of strength, came tearing in, and let loose a fearsome bounder. The vicar lifted his bat, and wiggled his hips to give his underwear the maximum chance. But it didn't hit his underwear. The ball hit him smack between the eyes and shot to the boundary for four. So St Just had won the match, and the batsmen were carried off in triumph. Well, the vicar was carried off in a coma, actually, but they propped him up in his personal lean-to outside the New Goat for the celebrations and nobody could really tell the difference.

Caught
But before that they had to get changed out of their cricket gear. Having lost the match Sardyne was forced to grit his teeth and do the decent thing. By which I don't mean that he took himself to one side with a loaded revolver and shot himself – he wasn't that decent. No, he simply went along to the St Just dressing-room to congratulate them on their victory. At least, they assumed that was what he said, because it's difficult to hear clearly when people talk through gritted teeth.

But when Sardyne had said whatever it was he said he looked around, and what he saw was the home team all changing out of their corsets. Well, he was livid. He declared that it just wasn't cricket, and was against all the rules. Fortescue said if it was against all the rules it must be cricket, otherwise the rules wouldn't apply. But Sardyne went straight to the umpires and logged a complaint.

The umpires went through the rule book, but they couldn't find anything specifically against the wearing of corsetry. In the end they had to appeal to Lords. Well, before long the papers were full of the scandal. The *Trunch Trumpet* said that cricket was dead, and the body had been buried and sent to Coventry. The *Manchester Guardian* said that all the players were cods, but that may have been a topographical error. They probably meant to say cads. Or possibly sods. The *Daily Telegraph* said they should all be hung, drawn and quartered to within an inch of their lives, and the *Times* said it was the end of civilisation as we knew it – which wasn't saying much as we never had much civilisation round our way in the first place. The *Daily Mirror* had a picture of Betsy the barmaid on page three, holding up her underwear in a strategic place.

Well, the come-uppance was that the St Just team were in disgrace. Gilbert Silver-Darling was a broken man, and his brother Sullivan was severely bent. P. C. Clam had to carry out an inquiry into himself, though he cleared himself of all charges in the end, and awarded himself a commendation for coming up with the right answer. Albert made his underwear legitimate by marrying the barmaid and living off her immodest earnings, and the others all went back to their normal routines. But every one of them gave up cricket after that. To make the point they were drummed out of all the local competitions by the West Runton Drum Majorettes, and they were forced to disband the club and sell the ground.

Now you might think that the hardest hit person would be the captain, the Left Honourable West-Runton. You might think that, but if you did, you'd be wrong. You see, all this publicity brought orders for his Bodyline underwear flooding in. So much so that they had to find a site for a bigger factory to deal with all the business. So he bought the cricket ground off himself and built it there. Mind you, he drove a hard bargain. He beat himself down and got it for a song.

And that's the end of the story of the Burningham Bodyline. Now, with the ground gone, and all the players gone to that great communal bath up in the sky, it might almost be as if it had never happened at all. Except, a little while back, I was going through some old papers at home, looking for the receipt for mother's mangle which had gone on the blink, when I found a copy of the score-card from the Bodyline match. So it must be true.

JUST NOT CROQUET

Reports have been deceived of a cricket tame in Suffolk who achieved viceroy by the weaning of women's corsetry. This paper washes to stoat that it finds such a thong unsproting and downright underhind. In shot, the men are cods. We truss they will be striped of their victory, as well as the offending garments. Otherwise what is the pant of any sporting contest?

(from *The Manchester Gordian*)

BURNINGHAM INNINGS

1	A. Pratt (Brigadier)	ret. hurt feelings	9
2	F. Gibbon	bowled Haddock	74
3	D. Sardyne*	swaggered out	0
4	F. V. Marsden	bowled Haddock	60
5	S. S. Smith (RN ret.)	bowled Haddock	1
6	Q. Newton-Flotman	bowled Haddock	2
7	N. Newton-Flotman†	bowled Haddock	1
8	'R' Ruddock	bowled Haddock	2
9	'W' J. Smith	bowled Haddock	1
10	'C' Nobbs	bowled Haddock	2
11	H. Larboard (Rev.)	not out	1

No balls	3
Leg-byes	0
Wides	7
Byes	8

Total (all out)	171

Fall of wickets: 1/17, 2/17, 3/159, 4/161, 5/161, 6/165, 7/166, 8/171, 9/171

Bowler	overs	maidens	runs	wickets
G. Silver-Darling	7	0	32	0
C. Salmon	8	0	44	0
A. Gudgeon	5	0	37	0
E. Spratt	7	0	33	0
A. Haddock	4	1	7	8

St JUST-near-TRUNCH INNINGS

1	G. Silver-Darling	stumped b. Smith	18
2	S. Silver-Darling	ret. unhurt	0
3	A. Kipper	bowled Ruddock	0
4	F. West-Runton*	ret. unhurt	0
5	P. C. Clam (P. C.)	run out (Gibbon)	0
6	W. Kipper	handled ball	6
7	E. Spratt	run in (Clam)	0
8	C. Salmon†	sbw Nobbs	0
9	B. Bass	caught mother	0
10	A. Gudgeon	not out	0
11	A. Haddock	not out	0

No balls	1
Leg-byes	140
Wides	6
Byes	1

Total (for 9)   172

Fall of wickets: 1/33, 2/54, 3/54, 4/54, 5/127, 6/134, 7/142, 8/146, 9/152

Bowler	overs	maidens	runs	wickets
H. Larboard (Rev.)	3	–	18	0
D. Sardyne	3	–	0	0
'R' Ruddock	12	11	6	1
'C' Nobbs	11	11	0	1
'W' J. Smith	13	13	0	1

PATHETIC
as told by Sid Kipper

The sinking of the SS Pathetic in 1912 sent shockwaves around the world. The fact that no wreckage was ever found has left the field wide open for all sorts of speculation about what happened to her, and why. A host of theories have been put forward, producing an entire industry of books, films and articles about the event.

If you work in that industry, prepare to find another job. For here is the true story of that incredible Night To Forget.

The *Pathetic* was the oldest cruise ship of the Grey Flannel Line. She was the least luxurious liner ever built. She was the last word in splendour, which is dour. She was the first word in sumptuousness, which is 'sump' (well alright, the first word is 'sum', but it all adds up to the same thing). She was also the middle word in ostentatiousness, which is 'tat'. Thank goodness, then, that nobody tried to describe her as swanky – well, 'swan' would hardly have been appropriate, would it?

Take the ballroom. Well, there was no ball room. Which can be very uncomfortable as any man will tell you who's ever bought his underpants from *Knickers To All* on North Walsham market. You know the one: they have their motto hanging over the stall – 'Hang 'Em High'.

Or take the food. You could eat as much as you wanted. Only, after one taste, nobody wanted to.

As for the crew, well nothing, absolutely nothing, was far too much trouble.

Now the *Pathetic* was making what they call her trollop voyage, which is the exact opposite of a maiden voyage. After that, what hadn't already dropped off would be scrapped. Some people said she was unfloatable, but somehow they managed to get her seaworthy, loaded her up with passengers, and the crowd all cheered as she set sail from Lowestoft. Well, they were glad to see the stern of her.

And as she left port the sailors were singing that favourite old shanty, The Leaving of Lowestoft. You know the one. It goes:

So fare thee well, you silly old fool,
Your loss is surely my gain;

It's not the leaving of Lowestoft that grieves me,
But the fact that I must come back again!
Which was tragic, looking back. Not just because they were rotten singers, but because not a single one of those jolly sailor boys ever saw land again.

But you probably know all that. In fact, you probably think you know everything about the sinking of the *Pathetic*. But I'm here to tell you that you don't, because the true story has never been told before. Only one person ever knew it, and that was my Great Uncle Albert, who was the sole survivor of what happened. And he swore a terrible oath that he would take the secret of who was to blame to his dying bed.

As a matter of fact he went to his grave swearing. Well, he did the first time. I suppose if he'd actually been dead he might not have been so annoyed!

But after that was cleared up and they dug him up again, he still never forgot his terrible oath to take the secret to his dying bed with him.

And that's exactly what he did. But as he was lying there, waiting to get ill, he told the story to me. He swore it was true.

You see, Albert was on the bridge of the *Pathetic* as she set sail. He wasn't a member of the crew or anything. In fact, he'd just retired from the sea, actually. But he'd been given the cruise as a retirement present from a grateful company. They were grateful he'd retired. And as an old hand he had the run of the bridge. So he saw the navigator get out his chart and his ruler and his sexton, and use them to plot a straight line course to get them from Lowestoft to the Baltic. And he heard him telegraph the course back to the Company. And then the *Pathetic* slipped noisily into the dark of the night.

Meanwhile, the passengers were forced to make their own amusement, in their different classes. There were two classes on the *Pathetic*: one was steerage, and the other was ballast. Actually, it was only snobbery that made some people go steerage. The only real difference was that the ballast passengers had to put up with people playing Celtic music all of the time.

Some cruises had people who travelled port out, starboard home, which is where we get the word POSH. As a consequence all the others had to go starboard out, port home, although we haven't got a word for that, but if we had I suppose it would be SOPH. But that doesn't matter, actually, because this wasn't one of those cruises.

And nobody was coming home, anyway.

None of the passengers knew when there was an alarm on the bridge. At 10.47 precisely by Albert's watch (which means it was probably about half past three) the Company came on the wireless. It was a Hamburg warning! Well, that set the cat among the cream, I can tell you. They tried to get the Captain out of bed but they couldn't, because they didn't know who's bed the Captain was in. The First Officer wanted to fire a maroon, but the Purser wouldn't let him because he reckoned it would clash with the Company's livery. There was quite a panic going on, until Albert pointed out that when the Navigator had plotted the course he'd had his dinner plate covering up most of Germany. So now all he had to do was return the plate to the galley, then plot a new course by the more usual route of using the Kiel Canal, instead of what he'd originally planned, which was to sail straight to Hamburg and then go over-land for the rest of the trip.

And it would all have been fine if people had just been content to know their places. Because the rule was that steerage passengers stayed on the upper-lower deck, and ballast passengers stayed on the lower-lower deck, and never the twain shall meet. But there's always one, isn't there? Well, no, there isn't. Not always. And any-how, what I'm going to tell you about takes two.

She was an English steerage passenger, and he was an American in ballast. How they met I don't know, because Albert never told me, but somehow they struck up a flirtation. Actually, that's not giving you the full flavour. How can I put it? Well, they were like two dogs on heat! They were just as desperate to get at each other as all the rules of social class were designed to keep them apart.

So there she was, languishing in her cabin, ripping her bosom and heaving her bodice, thinking of him in ballast just a few feet below her, when she suddenly thought she could see a way. Because she knew that there was hardly a sound piece of timber on the whole ship. So she reckoned it would be easy for her to rip up the floor and get down to him that way. And there and then (although for her, of course, it was here and now) she decided that's what she would do. But first she sent him a telegraph, so he'd be ready to catch her as she fell.

Now she knew he couldn't read so, bearing that in mind, she made the telegraph as short as possible: 'Got plan; Rip up floor; Knickerless.'

She was especially pleased with 'Knickerless'. She reckoned that one word would do three things very cheap. First, it would let him know who the telegraph was from; second, it should get him nicely on the boil for when she dropped in; and third, it would help him to identify her from below as she came.

Now this American was very handsome. And he was also extremely passionate. He even had an irritating bit of hair that kept falling in his eyes all the time. So, you could hardly expect brains as well, could you? So when someone read him her plan – 'Rip up floor; Knickerless' – he thought she wanted him to remove his underpants and tear up what he was standing on. Which was, in fact, the hull. Well alright, he thought, because he was already wishing he'd never shopped at *Knickers To All* on North Walsham market anyway. So he carried out her second instruction first, then he set his feet firmly apart, took hold of a spar in each hand, and with a mighty heave he ripped out a great lump of the hull. Well, he got a hell of a surprise. And so did everyone else on the ship.

But I expect you already know the rest. It was in all the papers. Well, it was certainly in the *Trunch Trumpet*. The next morning the headline on the front page of the *Trumpet* was 'FRED STARFISH ATE MY TURNIP!!!' But at the bottom of page seventeen, after all the details about Fred Starfish, and what other famous people said about him, and an artist's impression of the turnip, it said: 'PATHETIC SUNK; NO ONE FROM TRUNCH HURT.' Which was true. Because Albert was the sole survivor. He was saved by his wooden leg, which kept him afloat until he reached land.

And now you know the true story of the sinking of the *Pathetic*. As a matter of fact I'm hoping to sell it for a film script. I may have to tart it up a bit. Maybe move it into the Atlantic for the American market. It's just a matter of coming up with the right title, really.

As it's a nautical tale I first thought of 'Four Weldings And A Funnel'. Then, given where the ship ended up, I considered 'Wuthering Depths'.

But I think the title should be just a single word, which neatly sums up the whole sorry saga. And now I reckon I've got the word that does exactly that. The word is 'Pathetic'!

SS Pathetic

BOARDING PASS

Passengers are reminded that intercourse between different classes is strongly discouraged. This will avoid any embarrassment when we reach our final destination.

CRACKERS FOR FANNY
by Augustus Swineherd

During the nineteenth century there was a craze for what were termed 'And Ility' books. These included such memorable titles as Lies And Liability, Verse and Versatility, *and* Capes & Capability *(believed to have been written by an illegitimate father of the Prince of Wales). The books deal with the nuances of polite society, discussing at length the niceties of decency, and the decencies of nicety.*

Augustus Swineherd's contribution was Inns and Instability, *from which this is an extract.*

It is a truth, universally acknowledged, that a single woman in possession of a large chest must be in want of a husband.

Fanny Power, however, despite being the possessor of just such a chest, and although she remained singularly single, had no such want. She lived with her family, preferring her own society, and that of her female friends, with whom she loved to talk, laugh and drink copious quantities of laudanum.

So it was with mixed but powerful emotions that Fanny one day received an invitation for Sir Percival West-Runton's Christmas Ball, to be thrown that very evening. As she confided in her maid, Reader: 'When a man such as he holds his ball, it is the duty of one such as I to attend it, even though I know from previous experience that his balls are not at all to my taste. It is his part to carry out his part, and my part to lend a hand to his part.'

Reader could only concur, assuring her mistress that 'If I were in his position I should certainly uphold my part for all to see.'

As a consequence of this invitation the whole house was thrown into turmoil, as preparations were hastily undertaken. There was a veritable flurry of ablutions and dressings, hemmings and stitchings, washings and dryings.

Doctor Billberry was called upon to attend Fanny, to examine her for any infirmity. Not, you must understand, that Fanny was in anything but the best of health. It was but a precautionary measure, for it would not have done for her to be taken ill whilst a guest of the West-Runton's. They would surely consider such a thing to be woefully inconsiderate.

With proper regard to propriety the Doctor, strictly chaperoned, examined Fanny behind a large, ornamental screen. Although this arrangement precluded his examining her either physically or visually, and his failure to bring his ear trumpet made aural contact equally impossible, he nevertheless declared her to be in a state of health which, in less refined society, would undoubtedly be considered rude.

When the Doctor had departed particular attention was paid to the preparation of Fanny's chest, in order to ensure that it would be shown to the very best effect. It first was oiled and powdered, and then the delicate operation of elevating it to just the right angle was undertaken. That having been achieved, though not without doubts and disagreements as to whether it should be just a little higher, or just a fraction lower, Fanny was severely enjoined to do nothing which might disturb the edifice.

Since, despite all the sense of rush and urgency, she was, in fact, quite ready some three hours before she needed to depart, Fanny was forced to spend that time propped up in the gardener's wheelbarrow, ready to be wheeled, in perfect condition, to the carriage. But those hours, as hours will, eventually passed. In due course Fanny's carriage, merrily festooned with Holly and Ivy, her two younger sisters, finally swept down the drive of Beeston Manor, the West-Runton's family seat. As they approached the Manor she was able to take a long look at the house. It pleased her. It stood well. It was four square. At least it was certainly two square, and she felt sure that, could she but observe the reverse of the house, then the other two squares would almost certainly reveal themselves. Once Fanny had descended from the coach, and been helped to the vertical by her sisters, the coach left, with Holly and Ivy once more strapped to the roof, waving goodbye. Soon they would be old enough for balls of their own, but until then they must make do with the innocent pleasures of festooning. Now, thought Fanny, there was nothing for it but for her to make her entrance.

She was dressed for the Christmas season, with bells and candles in her hair. Her chest was neither fully concealed nor wholly revealed. Rather, she carried it before her, high, wide and handsome.

Fanny arrived in the ballroom just behind her chest, which incidentally was not only large, but also artfully sculpted. Every man's head turned at her entrance, but none looked her quite in the eye. None, that is, save the handsome Mr Arsy. He was as dark and smouldering as freshly burnt toast. He was as mean and moody as a bank manager. He was all that a woman could want. Indeed, when the men withdrew, he was often referred to by the ladies as 'the fish's bicycle'.

All of this was set somewhat at odds, however, by two Christmas crackers. These crackers were the very latest thing from town, but no one had, as yet, resolved what they might be for. As it seemed ignorant to enquire, and it would anyway have been impossibly impolite to expose the ignorance of any person of whom one did enquire, people were experimenting with them. Colonel Cod had thrust one down the front of his breeches, leaving just the red, ruffled end protruding. Canon Cuttle, being somewhat short-sighted, had already eaten three or four. Mr Arsy wore a huge ornate pair of them, suspended by wires from his ear lobes.

He approached Fanny indifferently. 'Miss Power,' he snorted, 'I see that you are out of the Christmas fashion, for you have no cracker. Pray, let me fetch one for you from the barrel over there.'

While she awaited his return she reflected just how much she disliked him. He was the epitome of everything she despised – a rich, handsome, witty man. How she longed for something quite, quite different. How she longed for a poor, ugly, stupid woman!

But that, she knew, was not to be her fate. She owed it to her family to marry, and to marry well. Furthermore, she was certain, from Mr Arsy's total and utter indifference to her, from the manner in which he always attempted to put her in the wrong, and by the fact that he referred to her in her absence as 'that overstuffed pigeon';

by all these things she knew that he must be very much in love with her indeed. It was the way of things.

Her thoughts were interrupted by Mr Arsy's return. He carried with him a cracker of a particularly vulgar hue. 'Marry,' he cried, smirking and leering at her chest. 'Why, Fanny, I believe I have the very place for this.' She thought bitterly that he did indeed possess just such a place, and longed to place the cracker there herself, with considerable force, but she said only, 'Marry? I believe you said "marry", Mr Arsy?'

'Fanny!' he ejaculated, but she ignored it.

'If that was a proposal, Mr Arsy, then I accept it,' she said. 'But perhaps that is not what you meant. I will not have it said that I trapped you. You must agree to it yourself – a nod or a shake of the head will suffice, I think.'

And Mr Arsy, still wearing those heavy crackers, and fearful for his earlobes should he shake his head, could only forlornly nod.

Nothing would then suit Fanny, certain now that she would soon be Fanny Arsy, than that the engagement be announced there and then. Soon the air was filled with congratulations and, at the personal insistence of Sir Percival, a shower of champagne corks. Mr Arsy, to his great discredit, then showed his true colours, which were not, after all, dark and smouldering, but rather, in fact, the purest yellow. He hid from the shower of corks under the lee of Fanny's chest. She could only wonder what would have been his reaction had the missiles been exploding from actual bottles of champagne, rather than being merely a collection of old corks tossed gently into the air by a wrinkled retainer.

The thought occurred to her that, once free of his crackers, Mr Arsy might be cad enough to attempt to escape from their contract. Well, she decided, there was but one way to ensure that such an eventuality was avoided. She would have to put Mr Arsy in a position so compromising that he would have no alternative but to fulfil his obligation. To this end she plied him with drink, to which, it must be said, he put up only the feeblest of resistance. And then, when he was scarcely aware of the week of the year, let alone the day of the week, she took him upstairs.

At last they were alone, and Mr Arsy finally got his hands on Fanny's chest. As this was a very private moment we may not know his feelings as he prized it open to discover that it held only an IOU from the recently bankrupted Earl of Earlham, and that its artfully sculpted exterior bore the unmistakable signs of recent woodworm. But we will draw a veil over the way in which Fanny took his honest name away from him. Such matters are best left as a privacy between man and wife, or, when things are not exactly as they should be, as in this case, at least between man and wife to be.

Eventually, Fanny returned home in triumph. There Holly and Ivy waited up to hear every detail of the evening. Who did she see? With whom did she dance? What liaisons had been formed? Their anticipation was not disappointed, as she revealed the news of her own affiancement. At last they had no more questions, and she was able to retire to her bed.

As Reader, the poor, ugly, stupid maid, undressed her mistress, she enquired of Fanny how she could trust the word of a man so notoriously unreliable as Mr Arsy. So Fanny hinted at the way in which she had compromised him.

The maid wondered aloud how it was that, Mr Arsy being almost unconscious at the time, the engagement had apparently been consummated in one of the bedrooms right at the top of the West-Runton's four-square house. How had she managed to get him there?

Fanny smiled, and said simply, 'Reader, I carried him.'

THE SHAMAN OF ST JUST
as told by Sid Kipper and Augustus Swineherd

Many strange things have happened in St Just-near-Trunch, but none was more amazing than the bizarre arrival which shook the village in 1910. Why St Just was singled out for what happened is unclear. Perhaps it was simply a result of the time-honoured meeting of pin and map. But the consequences reverberate to this very day.

I don't know if you know Cyril Cockle. Well, of course I don't. I don't even know if you're reading this. But that doesn't really bother me, because I'm used to it. You see, there's lots of things I don't know. Everybody says so.

For a start, Raquel Whelk says I don't know what's good for me. Then again, Mrs Dace says I don't know which side my bread's buttered (which can be a bit messy at teatime). And Ernie Spratt, at the Old Goat Inn, reckons I definitely don't know when I've had enough.

Then again, according to Mother, I don't even know I'm born, young man, although I suppose I must have been, really. And the Vicar says that I don't know the half of it. Which is all very well, but he won't tell me which half it is I don't know.

But I was talking about whether you knew Cyril or not. And I suppose I'll never find out the answer to that, unless you write and tell me. But then I'd only have to write back, and it could all get very tedious. So I'll save us both the bother, and tell you about him anyway. Cyril is a sort of part-time village idiot. We can't afford a full-time one these days, so Cyril has to make up his hours as lollipop man at Trunch Bored School. But don't be alarmed that any children might be at risk. The school was closed years ago.

And I want to start this story by telling you not to take any notice of anything he says. Because Cyril reckons that none of the story I'm about to tell you ever happened. Which is daft, if only because it did. It's just that the Cockle family don't come out of the story very well. Which is all the more reason for telling it, if you ask me. The only thing the Cockle family ever came out of well was the Old Goat Inn, and then they had to be thrown out feet first.

But to get on with the story. It all started one warm, sunny Sunday in March 1910. People were just going about their usual business, such as starving, and getting nasty diseases, when a cloud of dust was seen approaching the village. It got closer and closer, until it arrived right in the middle, and there it stopped. And then, as the dust settled, they could see what had caused it. There, just opposite the cobblers, was a strange, dusty figure on the back of a horse and cart.

Everyone gathered round to see who it was. And it turned out to be a bloke wearing a gaudy kind of a cloak, plus a peculiar head dress, and holding a sort of a staff. Well, the people all gawped, waiting to see what he'd do. And what he did was to stand up on the cart, wave his staff about, and say 'I have come to bring you the word.'

It was Cyril's great-grandfather, Clive Cockle, who found his voice first. That was mainly because nobody else had been looking for Clive's voice, due to him being the worst singer they'd ever heard. Everyone was hoping it would stay where they'd hidden it.

And Clive said to the bloke, 'What is it?'

So the bloke turned to Clive and said, 'What's what?'

'What is the word that you've come to bring us? Because if it's a short word you can just hand it over now, and we can get back to starving and the like. But if it's a long word you'll have to wait until we find someone who can write, so we can study it later.'

Well, the bloke looked at Clive for a while, and then decided to ignore him, which, if you ask me, shows he wasn't daft. He addressed the crowd, instead. 'Good people, I am a Shaman. I come as a missionary from a far land, to show you the light, and lead you down the true path. I will set up a mission, and preach, and do good works. I bring you gifts, but they are as nothing to the news of the true faith.'

Clive took all this in. 'Well,' he said, after a while, 'I reckon that's the Vicar's department. You'd best go and see him.' And with that he grabbed hold of the horse's bridle, and started to lead it off to the Vicarage, towing the cart and the bloke behind it.

The bloke tried to preach to the crowd, who all followed on, but they hung back. Because they didn't want to get in trouble with Rev. Mullett. They knew that he didn't like people going up to the Vicarage and bothering him unless it was births, marriages, or deaths, due to him getting paid extra for them. So, as nobody wanted to get married, no one looked like giving birth, and it didn't really seem worth killing someone just to find out what happened next, they all stopped at the gate of the Vicarage, leaving Clive, the bloke, and the horse to take their chances.

Now this wasn't the only thing going on in the village at the time. They had recently set up a branch of USBAT – the Union of Swede Bashers and Allied Trades. Of course, this had to be done secretly, because the farmers would have had them all sacked if they'd known they were part of a union. And, as a matter of fact, they were just about to find out.

You see, the next day was the first day of the springtime adjustment of working hours. The custom was that, as from that date, instead of working nine hours a day, six days a week, for bugger all, they would henceforth work ten hours a day, six days a week, for bugger all. And USBAT had decided to oppose the change. This would lead to the famous St Just Lockout, but we haven't got there yet. We've only got to the arrival of the Shaman.

The crowd outside the Vicarage knew something serious was

128

going on when Lord Silver-Darling arrived, and rode straight in without stopping to hit anyone with his riding crop. They knew it was even more serious when he rode straight out again, ten minutes later, with his riding crop snapped in two and a face like thunder.

I bet you're wondering what had happened. Well, I'll tell you now, and collect my winnings later. You see His Lordship had told the Shaman, straight, that there was no way that he would ever be allowed to set up a church in St Just. And the Shaman had told him, just as straight, that he wasn't going to. He said he'd already set it up, just over the border in Trunch, on a piece of land called Great Stone Hill.

Well, His Lordship got very excited, and started to rant and rave, waving his riding crop about in a threatening manner. At which point the Shaman stood up, took the crop from him, broke it in half, and calmly handed the pieces back.

Well, Lord Silver-Darling was amazed. Nobody had ever stood up to him before. Normally, when he went about the village people didn't just doff their hats. They got down on their knees as well. So he was speechless, which was hardly surprising, since he hadn't been expecting to be making a speech. If he had, no doubt he'd have got his speech writers to prepare one. But he hadn't, like I told you. So instead he stormed out and rode off, like I also told you, and the Shaman was left alone with the Vicar.

Well, then it all came out, and he told Rev. Mullett all about it. It seemed the Shaman had been brought up as Brian Bass, in Dersingham, which is near Sandringham, but not quite so royal. After school he'd gone to university to study what I think they call 'the ology'. He came top of his class, and then he went out to the North of Asia to find out about their religion. And he studied it so well that he went native, and got converted to it. Well, that was all very well, but the people there didn't know what to do with him. So they had a whip round, and I dare say a raffle and a tombola and so on, and raised enough funds to send him back to England again, as a missionary. And that's how he came to our village.

'I expect you'll be glad of the competition,' he told the Vicar, but the Vicar wasn't so sure. He was worried about Lord Silver-Darling: His Lordship was all in favour of competition, but only as long as it was rigged in his favour.

'So, what is your god called?' asked the Vicar, by way of conversation, but it turned out there were seven of them. Some of them were even female. And there were other things about the Shaman's religion which Rev. Mullett wasn't too happy about. For instance, a man could have several wives, and a woman could have several husbands. And they had sacrifices (but only on special occasions). When the tea and biscuits were finished, and the sherry was all gone, the Shaman got up to leave. 'Very nice to meet you,' he said. 'And I trust you'll come and see me in my yurt before too long. We could sacrifice a virgin.'

Of course, the Vicar didn't know that the Shaman had a wicked sense of humour. He didn't mean that they would kill a young woman. He meant they would find a willing virgin and – well, suffice it to say that she wouldn't be a virgin afterwards. But the Vicar didn't know that. And, even if he had, I doubt he'd have been interested, since he specialised in women who had fallen, rather than ones who hadn't jumped yet.

And then the Shaman emerged from the Vicarage, and Clive Cockle led the horse and cart and passenger back down the drive-way, and the Shaman got ready to preach to the crowd. But the crowd had all gone, due to the pub having opened. So he took Clive back to his yurt, and converted him, there and then. There never was such a quick conversion until North Sea gas came in. Clive came away with a handful of beads and a new name, which I can't remember, but it wasn't English. Apparently it meant 'Him Without Enough Sense To Go To The Pub When It Opens'.

And that was the end of that day, and soon it was the next day, when the hours of work were due to go up, as I've already explained. All the men went to work at the crack of dawn as usual. But they had decided not to do any work until they had a new agreement. They were determined that they wouldn't do the extra hour unless they got paid their usual wage, which was bugger all, plus an extra bugger all else, on top. That meant they had to wait till the farmers got up, so there was a lot of hanging around. And when the farmers did eventually get up, and heard what the men demanded, they said they must be joking. And, to teach them a lesson, all the men were locked out until such time as they came to their senses.

Well, they all met up in the middle of the village, to decide what to do next. And along came the Shaman on his cart, with the horse led by Cecil. When he saw the crowd he immediately went into action.

'Good people of St Just,' he preached. 'Give up your old worship and follow me. I have beads and bangles to give you. You will have many wives, and hunt much game. Please come for afternoon coffee, 2.30 for 3.00.'

Well, that all sounded pretty exotic to people back then. Especially the coffee. So a lot of them decided that they'd go along and give it a look. After all, they were locked out anyway, so they'd got nothing else to do. And, to cut a long story short, a lot of them decided to give it a go.

And the new religion did really well for a while. The weather was good, and there was dancing in the fields, and chanting, and bonfires, and so on. A bit like a folk festival, really. Of course, the farmers were put out, because they expected the men to be begging them to come back to work, rather than having a good time with the Shaman. USBAT made him an honorary member. And the Cockle family got all the top jobs, such as Yurt Warden, and so on, and started asking about for spare wives.

So, for about a week, the whole village was like the world turned upside-down. Nobody went to work. Nothing got done. They reckon Lord Silver-Darling even had to open his own bottles of claret, which was the hardest work he'd ever done. He had to have a lie down afterwards to recover.

But, when he had recovered, His Lordship decided that enough was enough, and all this nonsense had to stop. So he went straight to the Vicarage, and demanded to know what the Rev. Mullett was going to do about it. Now, as a matter of fact, the Vicar hadn't been too bothered. He'd been enjoying catching up with his darning, and so on. But His Lordship made it clear that he wouldn't have a job much longer if he didn't come up with something. 'You'll have to challenge him,' said His Lordship.

'Well,' said the Vicar, 'that's all very well, but there aren't many things I could challenge him at. I can't do all that dancing round the fire and yodelling, like he does. I have had a lot of practice at lighting candles. Perhaps I could challenge him to a candle lighting contest.'

And now we see how the Aristocracy got where they are (apart from the cheating, murdering, and in-breeding, that is). Lord Silver-Darling told Rev. Mullett to jolly well pull himself together and act like a man, even if it was only acting. He dictated a note of challenge, which he made the Vicar write out, and His Lordship had it delivered straightaway to the Shaman.

I can't tell you what a ruction that led to. Well, I can tell you, actually, but, to be fair, I wasn't actually there, due to not being born for another 36 years. But then, that's hardly my fault, is it? But Augustus Swineherd was there. And he wrote about it in his book *Saprise To Cringleford.* So I reckon I'll let him finish off the story.

It was twelve noon. The unseasonable weather had reverted to type, and a cold wind blew up the village street, from the Vicar, standing alone at one end, to the Shaman and his followers, grouped at the other.

At the agreed signal, the striking of 6.45 by the church clock, the two protagonists advanced slowly upon each other. The Vicar held a twelve-bore shotgun, while the Shaman carried his ornately carved staff of office. Nearer and nearer together they came, until Vicar faced Shaman, nose to chest.

'Begone from my parish,' called Reverend Mullett, 'or you will feel the wrath of my thunder stick.'

The Shaman responded by reaching into his robe, and pulling out a notebook and pen.

'Yes!' said the Vicar. 'Write your last will and testament, or whatever you fellows have in place of it.'

'Oh, no,' replied his adversary. 'The first task of a missionary is to gain a command of local terms, so I am keeping notes, you see. Now, have I got this right? You call a shotgun a "thunderstick" in these parts?'

This was not what the Christian had expected. Checking to see that they were not overheard he spoke conspiratorially to the other.

'Look, I expect you're a decent enough sort of chap, despite the outlandish dress, and your somewhat unconventional views on marriage and so on. Can't we work together in some way? Pool our efforts, so to speak?'

The Shaman looked puzzled. 'I'm not quite sure what you're suggesting,' he said.

'Well, you know,' said the Vicar. 'We could share the church on alternate Sundays, hold ecumenical jumble sales. That sort of thing. What do you say?'

The Shaman looked shocked. He drew himself up to his full height. 'Mine is the one true faith,' he intoned. 'It cannot be polluted by false religions.'

The Vicar's face fell. 'In that case,' he said, 'this means war.' Raising his voice again, for all to hear, he announced: 'I will call on my God to perform a miracle, to show His people that He is the One. Please stand back.'

And so the Vicar of St Just-near-Trunch stood in the middle of the main street, just outside the New Goat Inn, and prayed for a miracle. He prayed long. He prayed hard. He prayed until he was blue in the face. His opponent looked on, himself turning blue as his goose pimples began to join together into one huge pimp.

After half an hour, with no miracle apparent, the Shaman stepped forward. 'You have had your chance, man of Christ. Now it is my turn.'

With that he began to dance, jumping and jiggling, and gyrating vigorously. After some minutes of this he gasped to a halt.

'So much for that,' said the Vicar.

'Oh, no,' puffed the Shaman, 'I was simply warming myself up. Now, I need something to sacrifice for the miracle ceremony. Perhaps that old lady's dog over there?' The old lady in question disappeared rapidly round a corner, dog in tow.

'Ah, well, it's not essential, although it does make for a better show. I must just do without it.' And he drew from his robe two sticks, which he proceeded to rub vigorously together. After ten minutes or so they began to smoke, and five minutes later he actually had a small fire going in the middle of the road. 'There!' he cried triumphantly. 'Behold, the miracle of fire!'

But, even as he spoke, the flame began to splutter, and went out. Several of the crowd, who had been grateful for the warmth, stepped forward with matches to rekindle it. 'Oh,' said the Shaman, obviously disappointed. 'You've seen it before then.'

After this the crowd slowly dispersed, though the two would-be miracle workers continued to look for a sign from the heavens. Eventually it came, in the form of heavy, driving sleet, forcing them both to seek shelter.

Over a pint of firewater in the Goat Inn, as they dried themselves in front of a roaring grate, the two finally agreed to differ, and tend whatever flock each could herd together.

But hang on. That's no ending. They can't all live happily ever after, can they? Because if they did then there'd still be a yurt and a mission hall, and beads would be legal tender. So I'll just have to finish the story myself, after all.

You see, it's true that the two of them did have an agreement of sorts for a while, but it didn't last even as long as it took them to finish off what Swineherd called the 'firewater', which I reckon must have been a pint of Old Nasty. Because word soon got to Lord Silver-Darling about what had gone on, and he arrived post haste, which was a lot quicker in those days due to there being a second delivery. He came roaring into the Goat, waving his second-best riding crop, shouting and demanding that he wanted the Shaman out, the men back to work, and everything back to normal. Or Else.

Because Else, whose full name was Elsie Eft, was the only one who could ever take his Lordship's mind off things. She plied her trade in a little cottage in Back Lane, where she entertained gentlemen, as they say. And very entertaining she was, by all accounts. They reckon she could do magic. And she always went out on a song. But on the day I'm talking about Else was unavailable, due to visiting her aunt in Whissonsett, so, as far as his Lordship was concerned, he would just have to have all those other things he'd demanded instead.

Now, you're probably expecting the Shaman to stand up to him again. But His Lordship had worked that one out. As a consequence he did his shouting and demanding while sitting on the Shaman's lap, so he couldn't stand up, even if he'd wanted to. Which you would, I can tell you, if Lord Silver-Darling was sitting on your lap. And so, as usual, His Lordship got his own way. And, what with the weather no longer being suitable for outdoor dancing, and everyone already having more beads than they knew what to do with, and with people frankly getting bored with having no work to do, somehow everything just returned to what passed for normal in those days. They all went back to working, and starving, and going to church, just as if nothing had ever happened. The men even stayed on for the extra hour at work, for no pay increase. Mind you, as a compromise they turned up for work an hour later in the morning, but the farmers never noticed, because they were still in bed.

And as for the Shaman – well, that was a bit of a mystery, really. He did hang about for a while, although his lap was never the same again. But now the Cockle family were his only followers. Then his mission hall blew down in a stiff wind, and his yurt was attacked by some kind of fungus apparently not found in Northern Asia. Finally, his bead supply ran out, and one day the Cockles turned up for worship, only to find him gone. They waited for him to return, thinking perhaps he'd just nipped out for some more bangles, but they waited in vain.

The Cockles kept things going for a while without him, but it wasn't the same. People laughed at them, which was nothing new, but that didn't make it any more pleasant. Eventually even they gave the whole thing up, and went back to being C. of E. Or, at least, they always said they did.

Even now they attend church as regularly as everyone else in St Just, which is to say, hardly at all. But there are rumours. And sometimes, on the night of a full moon, you might notice that the Cockle family are not in the pub. And, if the wind is in the right direction, you might just hear the sound of chanting coming from the direction of Great Stone Hill.

Now, I don't know that they're still carrying on the old religion. But then, that means that particular piece of information is in very good company, doesn't it?

DEREK'S *FIFTH* LETTER
TO THE TRUNCHEONS

Life's like that, isn't it? Only the other day I was driving through Dunston, when I saw a cricket match being played. I do so love to watch the flannelled fools, so I immediately got out of my little VW Beetle, 'Betsy', to watch. Of course, if I had the chance to do it all over again, I would stop the car first. But not to worry. As it turned out, that barn was just as effective in stopping Betsy as her brakes. If not more so.

And after the cricketers had pulled Betsy out of the barn, and re-housed the pigs, they carried on with their jolly game. And then it struck me. No, not a lusty six, hit out of the middle of the bat, straight back over the bowler's head. Although it might as well have been that, because I was too deep in revelation to have noticed such a petty distraction.

What I realised there is that life is like a game of cricket, isn't it? Sometimes it's all bats, and sometimes it's all balls, but we each have our place in the field of life, and we're all hoping to score. But when the great umpire in the sky raises His finger, we'll know then that our innings is at an end. And, when the game has been played out, what will it say about us in the scorebook of life? Will it be full of fours, and sixes, and quickly scampered singles? Or will it simply say 'stumped, nought'?

You see what I'm saying, don't you? Well, if you do, I wish you'd write in and tell me. Because I fear I've rather lost my thread. But, in the meantime, just remember this. If The Good Lord had meant me to see what I was saying, He'd have put me on the telly, not the radio.

DOT KIPPER'S HANDY HOUSEHOLD HINTS

ANTIMACASEROLE – This here is what you might call slow food, due to it taking a long time to cook.

METHOD – Take two or three antimacassers and put them in a pot with some fresh water and seasonal veg. Pop it in the bottom of the oven, and cook it really slow until the antimacassers are soft, which should take about 3 months or so. Then pop it out of the oven again and serve with seasonal veg, which by now will be different to the ones you used when you first started.

TIP – For a fuller flavour you want to make sure the antimacassers have been well used. My Sid could probably help you there.

THE SIRENS OF SCROBY SANDS
as told by Sid Kipper

Scroby Sands lie about four miles off the east coast of Norfolk, and have very little use except as a danger to shipping. Since wrecking has, in recent years, been seen as a somewhat antisocial activity, even that use has been put into abeyance. But the Sands did inspire this marvellous example of the storyteller's art, even if nothing ever happens there now.

Actually, there is one thing that still happens on Scroby Sands. It's in the paper every year. Because on Boxing Day some blokes row out there and play a game of cricket. People often wonder why they do that, but I don't, because I know already. It's like all the other outdoor events that happen on Boxing Day. It's an excuse to get away from the in-laws.

In our village the two big getting-away-from-the-in-laws events on Boxing Day used to be fox-hunting and morris-dancing. Of course, these days fox-hunting is a bit dodgy. And morris-dancing has always been a bit dodgy. So what they've done now is to amalgamate the two. Hunting the morris dancer keeps everyone happy except for one, and he doesn't hang around to moan about it, I can tell you. But never mind all that. I set out to tell you the story of the Sirens Of Scroby Sands, so hold on to your sea-horses, and here goes.

Long before I was born (although I don't suppose he knew that at the time) Samuel Kipper put out from the port of Happisburgh in the good ship *Defeat*. Now he favoured Happisburgh because of Happisburgh Light, which was his favourite beer. It was a sort of export beer which was mostly sent to America. What they called an RIPA – that's a Red Indian Pale Ale (although some people say it was more of an RIP and never mind the A).

On board the *Defeat* were Samuel, as I said, Cedric Cockle, and Donald Dack. And they set a course for the fishing grounds, to search for red herrings. Now those are very elusive fish. Some people say that if you want to find them you have to chase wild geese. Some say you should take a shaggy dog along to sniff them out. But never mind what they say, because this is my story, so they can say what they like, and probably will, only I won't be listening, so much good may it do them.

Now the *Defeat* was an old sailing lugger. Years ago there were two sorts of luggers: there were sailing luggers, and there were non-sailing luggers. On the whole, the first sort was the best. Especially if you wanted to go sailing. Which the crew of the *Defeat* did, on account of that was the only way they knew to catch fish. So off they went. They sailed north, they sailed south, and they sailed east, though not at the same time, obviously. They would have sailed west, but if you sail west from Happisburgh you end up in North Walsham town centre wondering where the sea went to, so it's not advisable.

Having tried all those directions they sailed nor-nor-east and sou-sou-wester, but no matter which way they went, no red herring could they find. Well, they began to get a bit worried, because it wouldn't look good if they went home empty-handed. Or, more to the point, empty-holded.

They hove to have a think about what to do next, and that was when they heard it. It was a sort of strange, horrible, unworldly singing, such as nowadays we might call World Music. It sounded like this (only being in a book it looked like this instead, even though they couldn't see it themselves):

'As we were a sailing past East Runton Gap,
Up jumped a swimmer in goggles and cap.
He cried, 'I am trying the channel to cross.'
We didn't know what to say, 'cause he'd already got lost!'

Of course, they knew at once what it was. It could only be the Sirens of Scroby Sands. 'Quick,' said Samuel, 'lash me to the mast and stuff up all my orifices.'

'Why?' asked Cedric. 'Are you thinking of becoming an MP?'

'No,' said Samuel, 'but they reckon if you hear the singing of those sirens it can drive you stark, swearing mad, and you'll dive overboard to get away from it, and be drownded, due to the water.'

So Cedric and Donald tied him up with his tie. And then they trussed him up with his truss. And then, since he couldn't stop them, they belted him up with his belt as well. But, of course, as they did that, they could still hear that terrible singing:

'As we were a sailing past Wells-nest-the Sea,
Up jumped a merman, crying, 'Oh, woe is me;
You'd think topless mermaids would keep me amused,
But they're always legless, so nothing ensues.'

And they thought, 'Hang on a minute. What about us? We can still

hear the singing. We can still go stark, swearing mad and dive overboard and be drownded due to the water, can't we?' So they asked
Samuel about it. But, of course, he couldn't hear a thing, due to him
having had all his orifices stuffed up. So they untied him again, and
asked him, and he said alright, he'd tie them up first, if they liked,
and then they could tie him up again after. And they said that
wouldn't really work, would it? And he said that was the trouble
with them, whenever he came up with a good idea they were always so negative. And they said, 'Oh yeah!' and he said, 'Oh yeah!'
back, and as it developed there may even have been a bit of argy-
bargy and some pushing and shoving going on. But that all stopped
immediately when there was a bump, and a grind, and a judder
went through the boat, and they realised with horror that they'd
run aground on Scroby Sands. And that terrible singing filled their
heads:
'As we were a sailing past Winterton Ness,
Up jumped a mermaid, crying, 'I'm in distress:
I'm cursed with vast bosoms (as I see you note),
So when I try to dive they just keep me afloat.'
They could stand it no more, and all three of them ran and dived
head-first overboard. But they weren't drownded, because they'd
run aground, as you'd know if you'd been paying attention. So after a while they regained consciousness, spat out the sand, and shook
their aching heads. And then, then they heard it.
Nothing!
The singing was all gone. And there, large as life and twice as
naked, were three beautiful Sirens. 'Hello, sailors,' they said. 'Anything you fancy?'
Now some people say that Donald Dack asked for 'White Christmas', but that's just a nasty rumour. In fact, they looked those three
beautiful naked Sirens up and down, and they said, well, yes, there
was something that came to mind, now that they mentioned it. As
long as they promised not to sing.
'Oh, that,' said the Sirens. 'Why, we only do that when we're
lonely.'
Well, by the time the tide lifted the good ship *Defeat* off the Sands
again those Sirens were no longer lonely, and those three jolly tars
were even jollier, so they set sail for home in high spirits. And when
they got there everyone wondered why they were in such a good
mood, even though they'd come home empty-holded.

But, do you know, everyone just had to go on wondering, because Old Samuel and Young Cedric and Middle-aged Donald never told anyone the true story of their trip. They refused to talk about it. Oh, they hinted at a few things, and they always maintained that as a consequence no one should ever go anywhere near Scroby Sands. Except, that is, for them. And from then on their lips were totally sealed.

And now, of course, they're sealed even more. Well, it's hard to argue with six foot of earth in Happisburgh churchyard.

So you may be wondering how I came to know the story myself, if I didn't hear it from them. Well, I'll tell you. One day, not so long ago, I put out from Happisburgh in an old sailing lugger. And I heard the story from some old friends of theirs, who weren't singing when I left, if you take my meaning. But I'll say no more about that. Because they only sing when they're lonely, and it wouldn't do to discourage singing, would it? So take my tip, and never go anywhere near Scroby Sands. Or, if you do, you might hear something terrible, that looks like this:

'As I went a-sailing by old Scroby Sands,
I came on three sirens – it was jump up all hands;
They made me to sigh and they made me to smile,
But when those sirens went off you could hear them for miles!'

BIGOTS AGAINST TOLERANCE
– A MANIFESTO

Bigots Against Tolerance is just the most recent example of a long standing right-wing tradition in Norfolk politics. It is run by Farmer Trout, who wrote the following in the barn which he has recently had converted into a sweatshop, in anticipation of election victory.

Bigots Against Tolerance represents all Right-Minded People. We listen to the Silent Majority, and we hear what they say Loud and Clear.

FOREIGN POLICY

- **Europe** We are Great Britain because we are Great, and English. They're not because they aren't. Our policy is to Say No to

140

Europe, ban garlic, and stop all French lessons (except the sort given by Madam Whiplash in Aylsham).

- **The Pound** Saving The Pound is only a start. We will save the Ounce and the Stone as well. We will also bring back Shillings and Pence, because foreigners would never be able to work them out.

- **Immigration** People only want to come here because this is a Fine Country, even though it has been Completely and Utterly Wrecked. We will immediately throw out all Bogus Asylum Seekers. Then we'll throw out all genuine asylum seekers.

ECONOMIC POLICY

- **Tax** There must be Low Taxes for Wealth Creators. Therefore, we will Tax The Poor, because if they had any backbone they would have become rich by now. Let them pull themselves up by their own bootstraps. And, if they can't afford bootstraps, let them use cake.

- **Privatisation** We will Privatise Everything. That way the Private Sector can run things efficiently. Then the Trains Will Run On Time.

- **Enterprise** We will get rid of red tape and subsidy, and Let The Market Decide (obviously there will have to be financial assistance for the red-tape industry).

SOCIAL POLICY

- **Freedom Of Choice** People have rights, not foxes. The Eco-Fascists should be glad that we don't hunt them instead, although they wouldn't give us much sport, because they are all Vegetarians.

- **Unemployment** We will make Unemployment Illegal. That way there won't be any.

- **Multi-culturalism** We Say that this country shouldn't be cultural at all. Because most culture is just people poncing about in tights and tutus at Public Expense, or singing foreign operas while being paid for by Taxpayer's Money.

- **Homosexuals** We Say that it's not natural, it's not clever, and it's not nice. We will make 'gay' mean 'jolly' by law. We will make this Country fit for Men's Men. This is not a local problem anyway, because we are all Decent People around here, and it is all the fault of the Chattering Classes.

- **Youth** We will Bring Back National Service, which will teach all the Young Yobs proper Respect For Authority – that is, us.
- **Family Values** Children should be seen and not heard, and women should get back into the kitchen, and stop complaining about the heat. We Say that the only good social worker is a bee.

PUBLIC SERVICES

- **Law And Order** We will bring back the birch, the cat, and the death penalty. We will return to the Smack Of Firm Leadership, with the emphasis on the Smack. Life Should Mean Life – except when it means Death, of course. Our first act will be to stop all do-gooders from doing good.
- **Health** We Say that free health care only encourages people to be ill. Half of them are malingerers, and the other half are just namby-pamby moaning minnies. We Say Save Cromer Cottage Hospital.
- **Education** We will stop educating people above their station, which only leads to discontent. Our official policy is We Blame The Teachers.
- **Transport** Public transport is used by the public, and therefore no Decent Person would have anything to do with it. We Say Full Speed Ahead for the car economy, and No Turning Back. We will reverse the one-way system in North Walsham, which is simply a typical example of the Nanny State.

BAT are ON the right and IN the right. Vote for us, because we know what's good for you.

B
A
T
vote
TROUT
BATty for Britain

Good King Whence The Last

Good King Whence The Last looked out, on the feast of Steven.
As the snow lay all about, deep, and crisp, and even.
King Whence he was feeling bright, watching snowflakes glister,
Till a poor man came in sight, completely spoiled the vista.

'Hither page, be by me stood. What's that peasant doing?
He's nicked all my firewood, and ruined all my viewing.'
'Sire he keeps some goodly hens, and some lovely turkeys;
Perhaps he needs to build a fence; he is rather quirky.'

'Right' said Whence, 'well, now we must teach the wretch a lesson.
It just shows that you can't trust a rotten thieving peasant.
Bring me flesh, and bring me wine, bring me best Havanas;
And then after I have dined I'll teach the scum some manners.'

When the monarch forth he went, his page could not ignore him,
For through the wild wind's rude lament, on his back he bore him!
Through the snow the page did plod, as the wind blew wildly,
Thought the King a very sod, and that puts it mildly.

Thus the page trod on and on, carrying the monarch.
Till he thought, 'He weighs a ton; this is something chronic.'
Then, at last, he'd had enough, halfway up a mountain;
'Sire, methinks thou should'st get stuffed',
                            and dumped him in the fountain.

Now the peasant, and the page, sit before a log fire,
Leaving Whence outside to rage, in that wintry quagmire.
Therefore nobles all look out, or lessons you'll be learning;
Once they find what you're about your pages will be turning.

SLEEPING BEAUTY AND THE BEAST
A Fairy Tale for Childish Adults
and the Children of Adultery
as told by Sid Kipper

Many people know the stories 'Sleeping Beauty' and 'Beauty and the Beast',
but most are not aware that they were originally one. At some point someone
seems to have realised that they could split it into two, double their money,
and make two weak stories from one strong one. Rather like railway
privatisation, some might say.

This is a proper fairy story. That is to say, it's actually got a fairy in
it. Too many so-called fairy tales are all about clever foxes with sour
grapes and the like, and you reach the end thinking 'That was all
very well, but where was the fairy?' But not this one, though. So
here goes.

Once upon a time a Princess was born, which is something that
doesn't happen every day. As a matter of fact it happens precisely,
and exactly, once upon a time.

Well, the King and the Queen were very happy, and after some
discussion, and even a bit of healthy debate, which is to say a stand-
up row, they decided that the Queen had been right all along and
they would call her 'Sleeping'.

They planned a grand christening party, with jelly and balloons,
and everything. They invited all their friends. And they invited all
their relations, which is quite a different matter. But in all the
excitement, and the invitations, and the blowing up of the balloons
they forgot to invite someone. They forgot to invite the local fairy.
Well, I mean! Of course, it's easy to forget someone like Uncle Bert,
because he'll probably just get drunk and fall out with everyone.
But forgetting to invite a fairy can only lead to bed before tea-time!

So, as the party was going on, and everyone was having a lovely
time (except for Uncle Bert, who, what with all the jollity and good
will, couldn't find anyone to have a row with); while all that was
going on the fairy suddenly appeared, uninvited. Well, everyone
was shocked. I mean, fancy arriving without an invitation! It just
wasn't done. Which was why nobody did it.

But the fairy did.

And the fairy said, 'So, ho! You thought you could get away

without inviting me, did you? You thought I didn't like jelly, perhaps? You thought because I'm a fairy I'd be nice and sweet about it and say, "Never mind, I expect they meant to invite me and it just slipped their minds because they're such busy people?" Well, think again, suckers. And just to serve you right I'm going to put a spell on the princess.'

But no one seemed bothered. In fact, they said alright, go on then. Because everybody knew that the fairy was a rotten speller. They knew that she couldn't spell Photoffi (which is a small village in Wales that hardly anyone can spell, including half the people who live there).

And the fairy said, 'Alright, then, I will.' And she got out her wand, and she waved it about, and she chanted the magic words: 'Hugh, Pugh, Barney McGrew, Cuthbert, Dibble and Thingy.' And, as if by magic, absolutely nothing happened!

Well, all the people laughed and mocked. 'Call yourself a fairy,' said the Queen's dressmaker, and he should know.

'Just you wait,' said the fairy. 'Just you wait. It's a time-spell. It won't go off until her eighteenth birthday, and then you'll wish you'd invited me. And, anyhow, I never wanted to come to your rotten Christening in the first place, so there.' And with that she disappeared in a huff of smoke. And everyone carried on with the party, got drunk on the sherry trifle, fell out with Uncle Bert, and forgot all about it.

Until, that is, the approach of the Princess's eighteenth birthday.

Well, by now the Princess had grown up. She'd grown out, as well. In fact, she was absolutely beautiful, and she stole the hearts of everyone and wouldn't give them back. And all the handsome Princes for miles around paid her court. (Although you'd think a Princess might be able to pay her own court, wouldn't you?)

And then someone remembered what the fairy had said. Something about a time-spell. Was it like time-share, they wondered?

Well, the King and the Queen had a bit of a discussion, and the King immediately decided that the Queen had been right all along (he'd grown wiser over the years) and they decided to send her to her aunty's in Suffolk. They thought she'd be safe there. Because they knew that nothing interesting ever happens in Suffolk, as anyone from Norfolk will tell you. Anyway, it would get her away from all those drooling Princes.

Now her aunty lived in a rusty cottage in the middle of the

woods. She did that because she'd built a better mousetrap, and she wanted to see if the old saying was true. And the Princess stayed with her happily enough until one day her aunty had to go out and attend to the woodcutter's ball. She left Sleeping behind in charge of the cottage. 'You just watch the pot,' she said, 'to make sure it never boils. And whatever you do, don't open the door to any strange men.'

So the Princess got on with her spinning, until after a while she heard a knocker at the door. Now it was one of those doors with a top half and a bottom half, so she opened the bottom half, thinking it might be the pig wanting to come in.

But what she saw was not the pig. It was a handsome manly ankle. And next to it was another one, just as handsome. And above those were a couple of elegant calves. And above those, separated by a pair of rather fetching knees, stood a brace of comely thighs. And over those hung – well, from where the Princess stood, over those hung the top half of the door.

But then she remembered what her aunty had said, so she called out to the legs, 'Are you strange?'

'Not to me, I'm not,' came the reply.

So that's alright, she thought, and she opened the top half of the door, and there was the rest of a handsome man.

'Don't tell me,' she said. 'I know you. You're Prince Roger.'

'No,' he said, 'not now I'm not. Oh, I was formerly known as Prince, but now I am King Roger. King Roger the Sheep.'

'Oh, so why are you called "the Sheep"?'

He looked a bit embarrassed. 'Well, strictly speaking I'm not. Strictly speaking I'm called "Roger the Sheep". But it was only the once, honest.'

'Well, that's all very interesting,' she said, 'but what brings you here?'

'Oh, you know, I was just passing.'

'Well, where are my manners?' she said. 'Won't you come in? You can keep me company while I do my spinning.'

So he went in and he sat down at one end of the sofa while she sat down at the other end, and did her spinning. And after a bit he said, 'Would you mind if I moved a bit closer?'

And she said, 'Certainly, if that's how you feel.' So he did.

Then he said, 'Would you mind if I put my arm around your shoulder?'

And she said, 'Certainly, if that's how you feel.' So he did.

Then he said, 'Would you mind if I put my hand under your blouse?'

And she said, 'Certainly, if that's how you feel.' So he did.

And he felt very well. And the Princess was so surprised that she pricked a finger on her spinning, and immediately fell into a deep slumber.

But the King had been about a bit. He knew his fairy stories. 'Just as well I'm here,' he thought, 'because unless I'm very much mistaken what she needs to revive her is a royal kiss.' So, he arranged himself next to her on the sofa, took her in his arms, and gave her a long, slow, lingering, passionate kiss. But nothing happened. Well, not to the Princess it didn't.

'Oh,' thought the King, who wasn't quite so confident now, 'perhaps I ought to loosen her clothing,' he thought, although, to tell the truth, if anybody's clothing needed loosening it was his. Anyhow, he loosened her collar, but nothing happened. So then he loosened her belt. Same result. And he was just wondering what to loosen next when the Princess's aunty returned.

Well, she was stunned. She took one look at the Princess, lying unconscious on the sofa with her things all loosened and she was shocked. She threw up her hands in horror. They fell on the floor of course, because she'd got nothing left to catch them with. So the King picked them up for her, and stuck them back on the ends of her arms, and he quickly told her what had happened.

'I see,' said the aunty, although I think she still had her doubts. 'It must be the fairy's spell. We must go for help immediately. Do you have a horse?'

'Do I have a horse?' said King Roger. 'Do I have a horse! I've only got a top-of-the-range grey, soft-top Hillman hunter, with streamlined ears, colt-skin upholstery and four hoof drive, that's all!'

'Well, that'll have to do I suppose,' said the Princess's aunty, and the two of them jumped on the horse and set off to look for help in a cloud of dust. Though what help they expected to find in a cloud of dust I have no idea.

And they left the Princess sleeping beautifully, looked after by the birds and the beasts of the forest, who all crawled and flew and slithered round to see her. And the wise old owl, who was the top bird and beast due to his extreme wisdom and very sharp talons said, 'Well, will you just look at that. That's typical of today's youth that is. Typical. I mean, all they ever think about is looking beautiful and sleeping.'

And all the other birds and beasts of the forest agreed with him immediately, because they knew he was extremely wise, and had very sharp talons. And the robins flew off and fetched leaves to cover her with (especially the bits where the King had been doing his loosening), and the field mice scuttled off and brought nuts and berries in case she woke up and was hungry, and the snake slithered off and came back empty-handed, but with a lump in the middle, and a smirk on his face. And the magpie, who had counted the field mice out and then counted one less in, was just going to say something about it when a hair-curdling cry rang out through the woods, and all the animals scattered. And, as the echo of that terrible cry died away, up to the cottage limped the ugliest man you ever didn't see. It was The Beast.

And The Beast went up to the cottage, and he opened the door and went in, and there he saw the Princess, sleeping. And he was instantly won over by her beauty. And something good stirred within him. And gently he went over to her, and he knelt by her side, and he gave her just the teeniest, weeniest kiss.

And straight away the Princess began to wake. Because it wasn't a royal kiss she needed. No, she needed love to be in it. Slowly she gave a beautiful little sigh. Then she opened her beautiful eyes. And with them she saw The Beast. And she let out a beautiful scream and instantly died of shock at the sheer horror of him.

Well, just then King Roger burst in, and seeing The Beast and the expired Princess he put two and two together, and lost count. So he shot The Beast dead. He rushed to the Princess's side, but he tripped over The Beast and fell and broke his neck. Seeing all that, the Princess's aunty ran to help, but she caught her arm on a rusty nail, and slowly bled to death on the cottage floor. And after a while not a thing stirred in that cottage but for the rats.

And that's the old traditional ending of the story. But nowadays, of course, that sort of ending just won't do. So now there's been a bit added on: –

The Princess woke up in the shower to find it had all been a dream. Here she was in her own rooms, getting ready for her eighteenth birthday party. And what a party it was. She danced the night away.

And much later, after the party was over, the Princess finally got Prince Roger up to her room. Because she'd promised herself that tonight was the night when she would discover what it was to be a woman. Now he came to her, as she lay waiting, all a-tremble, in her four-poster bed. He got in beside her, both of them naked as the day they were born. Well, even more naked, actually, as they didn't have silver spoons in their mouths.

But, as it happened, Prince Roger was quite unable to teach her what it was to be a woman, because he hadn't got the first idea about it. He knew all about what it was to be a man, though. So he climbed into the bed, rolled over with his back to her, and fell fast asleep, snoring loudly. And the Princess was left wide awake, and quite unfulfilled.

So perhaps Roger had taught better than he knew. Because that, as the Princess was to discover as she got older, was exactly what it was to be a woman.

TOMMY KIPPER
by Rudyard Kipper

It is clear, from poems such as this, that Rudyard Kipper enjoyed capturing the sound of real people in his poetry. Either that or the 'h' on his typewriter was continually sticking.

I went into a public 'ouse, to get a pint o' beer,
The publican 'e up and sez, 'Well, Tom, yer welcome 'ere';
The girls be'ind the bar all smiled, as I drank an 'onest drop,
But when I got me fiddle out the buggers shouted 'Stop!'
For it's 'Tommy Aye', 'Tommy Oh', and 'Tommy won't you stay?'
But it's 'No, thanks, Mister Kipper', when I begins to play.
When I begins to play, me boys, when I begin to play,
Oh it's 'No, thanks, Mister Kipper', when I begins to play.

So I went up to the bandstand, the band leader was new,
I says, 'I'm a musician', says 'e 'I've work for you;
We need you on the drums, me boy', his lips a-smile an' all,
But it's a thin red line of lips, boys, when the drums begin to roll.

Then it's 'Tommy Ow!' 'Tommy Ouch!' and 'Tommy, stop it do',
And it's 'Thank you, Mister Kipper, don't call us, we won't call you;
Don't call us, we won't call you, me boy, be sure we won't call you',
It's 'Thank you, Mister Kipper, don't call us, we won't call you.'

Now when I joined the orchestrer, to play the bass trombone,
The conductor 'e was spiteful – 'e would not leave me alone.
And if 'e 'eard a discord 'e would look to me straightway,
And say 'Look 'ere young Kipper, why don't you learn to play?'
For it's 'Never mind', when trouble starts in percussion or the strings,
But it's 'Special coach for Kipper', when there's trouble in the wind.
When there's trouble in the wind, me boys, trouble in the wind,
It's 'Special coach for Kipper', when there's trouble in the wind.

Well just 'cos I'm a Tommy I am not deaf, dumb and blind,
And I 'ears the things you says, and I sees yer fingers fine;
I see yer jeerin' faces and the gnashin' teeth and all;
Don't think that you're the only ones – it 'appens national.
Well it's Tommy rot, and Tommy gun, and Tommy's 'ad enough,
And before I play for you lot you can all go and get stuffed;
You can all go and get stuffed, me boys, and me girls as well;
And while yer doin' that, then I shall bid you all farewell.

DEREK'S *SIXTH* LETTER
TO THE TRUNCHEONS

Life's like that, isn't it? Only the other day I was edging through
Elsing, when I saw a man, sowing potatoes. And do you know, that
set me to thinking. As he stood there, with his dibbler held proudly
in his hand, I thought we all like a bit of a dibble, don't we?

And if we're not dibbling then we're probably dabbling. Or perhaps doubling. And, really, that sums up our lives, doesn't it? We
are all just a mixture of dibbling, dabbling and doubling. 'Do you
do any painting?' they ask, and we answer, 'Well, I have a dabble.'
'Were you in the wolf cubs?' they pry, and we say, 'I admit I had a
dib-dib-dibble.' 'Would you care for a drink?' I enquire, and they
all immediately reply, 'I'll have a double.'

And as I watched the man with the dibbler work his way up and down the rows, proudly planting his King Edwards, I thought 'Derek, as you sow, therefore shall you reap.' And I knew then that when the day came that he returned to that field, with his sythe over his shoulder, ready to reap his potatoes, he wouldn't expect them to be tomatoes, would he? And as he thrashed them, back in his barn, he wouldn't expect them to be radishes, would he? Of course he wouldn't. He'd simply expect them to be good, honest spuds.

Are you a good, honest spud? I know I try to be one. But you see what I'm saying, don't you? Whether, in life, we're bakers, or mashers, or boilers, when the great potato peeler in the sky tips us into the great bowl above, we don't want Him to have to cut out lots of bad bits, do we?

So just remember this. If The Good Lord had wanted us to be all eyes, He wouldn't have given us ears.

SHIP FASHION AND BRISTOL SHAPED
Number Three – A Yule Log

Some of us sailor boys has a saying. We say that a ship is like a woman. Some of them are trim little craft that go like the very wind. Some are slow, comfortable and dependable. Some are more sort of top-heavy, with patched-up canvas and a bottom covered in barnacles. That last one's my type. So heave to a minute me hearties, and let me spin you a yarn or two about how we mariners celebrated Christmas.

Now you might think that Christmas at sea would be no fun. And sometimes you'd be right. Oftentimes it was worse than having seaweed on your scuppers. More terrible than getting your tackle caught in the capstan. But it weren't always like that, me bullies. We often had jolly skylarks. Us sailor boys had many ways of abusing ourselves, so we did.

Now, on some ships there was no expense spared. There'd be lashings of extra lashings, and as much rope as you could climb. And more duff than a simple sailor could dream of. I tell you, a sailor at Christmas, on a boat like that, really gets duffed.

Some of us sailor boys has a saying. We say that duff is like a woman of easy virtue. They're both cheap and cheerful. You're keen enough to have them. But when you finally get them you wish there was more fruit and a lot less stodge.

First thing we did on a Christmas morning was to tricolate up the rigging. Davy Jones, he kept all the trimmings in his locker. And all us salty dogs would swarm up the painters, and festoon the rat lines with signal flags. That looked a rare treat, I can tell you. One year, when we were docked in Shanghai, we spelled out a message in Chinese by accident. They took against it, they did, and we had to fight off thirty-three marauding junks. After that we always took care to spell out proper seasonal messages. Such as 'England Expects A Happy Christmas', or 'A Prosperous New Year To All Our Readers'.

Come eight-bells we messed on the poop deck, and set to singing the old festive sea-shanties like 'O Come, Get A Face Full', and 'Parts of Oak Have Our Men'. And we exchanged simple sailors' gifts.

Some of us sailor boys has a saying. We say that a sailor is like a Christmas present. They both come done up all lovely. You can get all excited in anticipation. But, when you get the wrapping off, they're exactly the same as you got last year.

Then, bless me bellbottoms, if Mister Mate didn't get out his squeeze-box, and the handsome cabin boy showed us all his horn-pipe. Ah, Jim lad, what a show. And then Mister Mate hollers out 'Show us yer party piece, Albert.' And so I does. Oh, I've wined and dined in every port on the seven seas thanks to the popularity of my piece. Until I lost it to pirates, one cruel day, off the coast of Zanzibar. I wouldn't have minded so much, but I was one of the pirates. It just shows, you can't trust anybody when you're out on the deep drink.

But that was all a long time ago. I've retired from the sea now, so I suppose I'm just another land lubber. Nowadays I have to mix with all manner and classes of people.

Some of us sailor boys has a saying. We say that some people are like a woman. Well, now I know why. It's because half of them really are women.

But that's enough tarry tattle to be sure. The glass is falling, the tide is on the turn, and the bum boat is a-coming. So I'll grab me rollocks and pull off.

Haul The Deck

Haul the deck and bows with holly, fa-la-la-la-la-la-la-la-la;
There's no reason to be jolly, ha-ha-ha-ha-ha-ha-blooming-ha.
Times are hard and rations scanty, bah-bah-bah-bah, humbug, bah;
Troll an ancient Christmas shanty, rah-rah-rah, hoo-flipping-rah.

It came upon the midnight clear, and wasn't that a shock?
An infant born on Christmas Day, at sea, and far from dock.
Now questions they are being asked, and accusations hurled,
For someone must have known, since March,
                                that the cabin boy was a girl.

Seeking we for Lowestoft are,
Lost in fog, don't know where we are,
There's a sailor in front, rowing a punt,
And we're following yonder tar;
Oh tar of blunder, tar of blight, tar of Royal Navy tight.
Off he hurtles, round in circles; I don't think he's very bright.

Windy night, stormy night, twelve-foot waves o'er us smite.
Round the capstan we must go, while the skipper down below,
Sleeps with a heavenly piece; she's the first officer's niece.

See the swelling tide before us, na-na-na-na-na, hay-hay, na-na;
'Bloomin' hell' we bleat in chorus, baa-baa-baa, baa-baa, baa-baa.
Swing the cat and think of pay-day, rah-rah-rah, cha-cha-cha;
Bugger Christmas, roll on Mayday, fa-la-la-la-la, fa-la, ta-ta.

Cut out and colour your own
Trunch Wireless sticker

PICK OF THE WEAK
Highlights from Trunch Wireless

Trunch Wireless broadcasts on CB Channel 33, and is easily recognised by its cheery call-sign – 'Tune In & Turn Off'. Every Sunday a guest presenter has to find 45 minutes of material worth repeating in the tea-time slot, while the regular presenter takes a break. Sid has taken on this task a number of times, most recently in January this year, and a sample of his choices on that occasion is as good a way as any to give you a flavour of this lively, community based service.

How d'you do? This here is Sid Kipper with the pick of this week's Trunch Wireless programmes. So, without further adieu, let's get on with it.

Now, if you were listening last Tuesday, which I wasn't because I was washing my ferrets, you'll have heard our series 'File On 33' in which our YTS boy from the BBC, Tony Turbot, did a probe into the subject all the village has been talking about – how come the school bus was late last Monday? He started by going down to the bus-stop to talk to some of the children:

'Hello, I'm Tony Turbot from File On 33. I believe you were one of the ones who missed the bus on Monday.'

'Well, we didn't really miss it. I mean, it wasn't actually here to be hit, was it?'

'And tell us how you suffered.'

'Well, I didn't really suffer, as such. Of course, I did miss double maths, but I wouldn't hardly call that suffering.'

'But you must have been worried.'

'Well, I was a bit, because when he did get here he drove ever so fast.'

'And you feared for your life?'

'Well, no. I feared that he'd get us to school before maths had finished.'

I decided it was time to talk to the bus driver, Mike Moray. So I laid in wait where he would be most likely to show up, at the bus-shelter.

'Well, here I am, back at the bus-shelter. I'm just taking a look around to get a bit of ambience.'

'Oy! what's your game? Sharon, pull 'em back on, quick. There's some sort of a peeping Tom out there. I think I'll give him a thwack round the ear.'

'I'm terribly sorry – I was just waiting for the bus, honestly. Ah, here it comes now. It's pulled up, and I'm just getting on to talk to Mike Moray.'

'Fares, please. Where to, mate?'

'Er – nowhere, thanks.'

'Well, what are you doing on my bus, then?'

'Oh, yes – my name is Tony Turbot, and I'm here to interview you, now, about the late running of the bus last Monday. Tell me, Mister Moray, do you enjoy seeing people suffer?'

'Well, that all depends on the people, I suppose. For instance, I shouldn't mind seeing you suffer, for always poking your nose into other people's affairs.'

'What about innocent children, Mister Moray?'

'No, thanks. Anyhow, they wouldn't last five minutes on my bus. The hooligans I have to carry would have them for breakfast. I mean, just last Monday they threw tacks in the road and gave me a puncture so I was late getting them to school. Little horrors the lot of them. Anyhow, you'd better get off or I'll be late.'

'That's right, Mister Moray. Just drive away from all the despair and misery you've caused.'

'Well, I don't know about that, but if I'm not careful I'll be late in Knapton, and I've already been probed by their wireless twice this week. You lot really ought to find something better to do.'

'Well, that's it from me for this week. I'll be back next week, when I'll be investigating the peeping Tom who has been reported hanging round the bus-shelter recently!'

Great. Now, the other day Trunch Wireless had their regular programme which tells you all about foreign parts – 'Don't Drink The Water'. Of course, being an international mego-star I already know about that, so I never listen. But, this week our trepid reporters, Mike and Muriel Marlin, had been out and about once more:

'Wotcha.'

'This week me and Muriel is doing Yorkshire.'

'And if you've never been to Yorkshire don't worry, 'cause nor have we.'

155

'Well, not deliberate we haven't. What happened was we were going to see her Uncle Jimmy in a place called Gateshead, which is very hard to get to from here without going through Yorkshire, due to it being in the way.'

'We only meant to pass through the place, but we had a breakdown, so we had to stay the night. And now we know all about it.'

'The first thing to tell you is they have a terrible problem there with hills. Great big things they are, so you have to spend all your time going round them.'

'You'd think they'd want to get rid of them, but no! In fact, for a long time they had all these mines, where they dug stuff out of the ground and then piled it up into even more hills.'

'They've stopped doing that now, so I suppose that's some progress. Now I reckon they ought to get rid of some of the hills by stuffing the stuff back down the holes they dug. Always assuming they can find enough local people with the spare time to do it.'

'I agree. Now the word that always goes with 'Yorkshire' is, of course, "bitter". But when we were there something was wrong with the beer pump, so it came out all aireated, with loads of froth on the top. Just like something for kiddies, it was.'

'I offered to give them a hand fixing the pump, but they weren't at all grateful. Anyhow, the upshoot is that we can't tell you what the bitter is like, because we couldn't taste it properly for all that froth!'

'One thing you notice in Yorkshire is how they talk funny. They don't talk proper like what we do. For instance, up there "grass" rhymes with "gas".'

'Yes, and they can get a bit touchy if you put them right, as we discovered.'

'So take a tip from us and don't mention it.'

'Not if you don't want to get your donkey kicked.'

'Now, here's some more things about Yorkshire in briefs.'

'The capital of Yorkshire is Y, which seems a bit inconvenient, because it sounds like a river in Herefordshire.'

'They have loads of puddings, but no dumplings.'

'They also have Yorkshire Terrors, which are little dogs that chew your ankles.'

'Yorkshire people are especially famous for arguing about cricket. In fact, they're the cricket-arguing champions of All England. I don't know if they actually play cricket in Yorkshire, because it wasn't the cricket season when we were there.'

'Anyhow, it wouldn't be easy, what with all them hills we mentioned. I mean, they can't even find a flat bit big enough to play proper bowls on.'

'Years ago Yorkshire used to have ridings, but they don't have them no more, on account of building loads of motorways, which are too dangerous for the horses.'

'And, finally, they have Yorkshire grit. I tried some, out of curiosity, and to tell the truth it tasted just like any other sort of grit to me. I don't see what all the fuss is about.'

'I agree. Anyhow, that's all there is to know about Yorkshire, so now you don't need to go there, do you?'

'So, until me and Muriel get round to visiting my Aunt Ethel in Gloucestershire, mind how you go.'

'And mind where you go, too. Because there's a lot of funny foreigners out there.'

Super. Now, on Thursday night there was the one Trunch Wireless programme that I never miss. Only this week I did miss it, because I was out at the time. That was because I was actually appearing live on the programme myself. I was the special guest star on P.C. Chubb's quiz show – 'Helping With My Enquiries'.

"Ello, 'ello, 'ello. Evening all, and welcome to the Interview Room. Well, the tape-recorder is running, my guest has been cautioned, so let's get straight on with it. Welcome, Sid Kipper.'

'Evening all.'

'Now, now, that's my line. So, here's your starter for ten days. Where were you and your great-nephew Kevin on Tuesday night at about 11.45 p.m.?'

'That's an easy one. We were in the Old Goat Inn.'

'I'm sorry, Sid. "In the Old Goat Inn" only gets you a small fine for drinking after hours. For the big prize the correct answer was "In Demon's Wood with an unlicensed shot-gun".'

'Oh yes, I remember now. It was on the tip of my toes.'

'Never mind, just relax. You've still got a chance to go for tonight's star prize, which is six months for two at Her Majesty's Pleasure. Are you ready?'

'Well, I'm quietly confined.'

'Here we go then, and remember that, if your first answer is not correct, I may have to change it later to one that is. When you were in Demon's Wood, who did you hit over the head with a blunt pheasant?'

'Ah, now I know this one. It was a big bloke in a helmet.'

'I shall have to insist on a name.'

'Let me see … a big bloke in a helmet. Was it Edward the Confessor?'

'That is so close. Can I give him the six months? No? I'm sorry, Sid, but we do have to be strict with so much at stake. The correct answer was me, "P.C. Chubb".'

'Of course. Fancy my forgetting that.'

'Well, it's too late now, I'm afraid. But you don't go home scot free, Sid, because there's still the little matter of a small fine for drinking after hours. Look, I tell you what I'll do. You've been a great contestant, so I'm going to double the fine for you.'

'Well, thank you very much.'

'Don't mention it. But before you go, tell us more about this Edward the Confessor bloke. I'd love to get him on the show some time. I've got loads of unsolved crimes he might like to own up to.'

Fantastic. Now, if you're the regular listener you'll know that every morning Trunch Wireless has a phone in. On Monday this week the hot topic was the dogs' mess on the playing field. On Tuesday they talked about litter, in particular the litter Farmer Trout's old sow had last week. And on Wednesday it was all about why Trunch United are doing so badly just now. I only wish I'd heard it.

'Hi, this is me, Nicky Barbel, and I'm all ready to take your calls and put the agenda in the blender. And our first call is from Jim, on line one. Jim, you're calling from Swafield.'

'Am I? Well thanks a lot, Nicky. That's what I rang to ask about. Cheerio.'

'That was Jim there, from Swafield. And you can join him here on Trunch Wireless. Ring now, to get microscopic on the topic of Trun U. If you'd rather send an e-mail then you'll just have to send it to someone else, because we haven't got a computer. And on line one we've got Rachel. What's your point, Rachel?'

'Hi Nicky. Well, my point is, what's the point? I mean, why don't they just give up? Or take up something else they might actually be good at?'

'Are you a Trun U supporter, Rachel?'

'Oh, is it about Trun U? I thought it was about the dogs' mess on the playing field. Sorry.'

'Rachel there, a little bit off the subject, but, hey, who am I to say what you have to talk about? Let's go to Martin on line one.'

'Hello – am I on?'

'You're on something by the sound of it, Martin! Just my little joke. Go ahead, but I'm going to have to ask you to keep it brief.'

'When?'

'When what, Martin?'

'When are you going to have to ask me to keep it brief?'

'Well, I'm going to have to cut you off there Martin, but you've made some very interesting points. Don't forget, you out there, that this is the place to make your case. Phone now, or hold your row. That's what Keith did, and he's on line one now. Hi, Keith.'

'Hello, Nicky. Great show. I think you're absolutely wonderful.'

'Well thanks, Keith, but actually that's the topic for tomorrow's show. What would you like to say about Trun U?'

'Well, as I told your researcher, I think they should play with a flat back four and a wiggly front six. That way they'd keep their shape better.'

'That's very interesting Keith, but it's a load of rubbish, so I'm going to take another call. I've got Neil on line one. Hi, Neil!'

'Hello Nicky. Hate the show.'

'Ha, ha. So, why are you calling, then?'

'That is why I'm calling. I'm calling to say that I hate the show, and that I find you patronising, rude, egotistical and superficial.'

'Well, you're entitled to your opinion, Neil, but I think you'll find you're the only one who holds it. Nobody's ever called me any of those things before.'

'Well, that just shows that you don't get out much, doesn't it? Everyone I know says the same thing.'

'Tell me, Neil, where do you live?'

'47 Low Street, Trunch. Why?'

'Because I'm on my way round there to sort you out. You've been listening to "Call Nicky Barbel", and that's what Neil's just done, so now I'm going to carry on the discussion with him, in person. I'll be back at the same time tomorrow, just as long as I'm right in thinking that he's that little weedy bloke on crutches. And, Neil, don't go away.'

159

Tremendous. Well, that's it for this week. Listen again next week, if you must, when the person in this chair will be me, because it's my own chair that I brought with me from home. In the meantime keep listening to Trunch Wireless live, happily ever after.

SIR WAYNE AND THE GIANT, PEACH
as told by Sid Kipper

Any successful story naturally attracts sequels, and Sir Wayne, The Green Knight *was no exception. Many were pale imitations, such as* Sir Wayne Goes On Holiday To Mundesley *and* What Sir Wayne Did Next. *Later efforts were simply blatant attempts to cash in on the name, like* Tarzan and Wayne. *But whatever these may have achieved in popularity, they singularly failed to deliver in quality. This story, alone, truly matches the stature of the original.*

Long ago, when our forefathers four fathers were alive, the world was full of green men, and everything was organic. And the greenest of all the men was Sir Wayne, who is proclaimed by the seers to be the greatest hero of the Iceni, and the true ancestor of Arthur, whose Seat may still be sat on near Edingthorpe.

When Wayne brought Lebam, his new bride, back to Norfolk, they were met with terrible news. The people were sore afflicted, for they were beset by a giantess. But this was not just any giantess. This was a miserable giantess. So, not only did they have to give her whatsoever she demanded, they also had to endure her terrible moaning.

And no sooner had Wayne unpacked his sponge bag than the people beseeched him to save them from their affliction, for Wayne was a fine figure of a man. He stood over six feet tall and had a large, muscled chest, legs like tree trunks, and sinews of iron. As a consequence he had to beware of wet weather, lest rust set in. He wore much leather, and weighty jewellery.

So Wayne left Lebam with the next door neighbours, girded up his mighty loins, and straightway set forth. And after very little searching he soon came upon the giantess. Which was a disappointment to Wayne, for he always considered that the searching, and

160

the questing, and so on, was the best part of the job. But finding a giantess, in fact, is not actually all that difficult.

The giantess was far from ugly. She had, in fact, a most comely figure, which the Iceni sages had estimated as measuring 36–22–36. But that, of course, was in cubits. She wore the usual garb of her kind, with tunic, thongs, amulets, and a very short skirt. As Wayne approached her she was standing, contemplating the horizon, with her arms folded across her chest, and her feet set firmly apart.

She had not noticed Wayne's approach, so crept up to her, as close as he could. But as he neared the lower slopes of her left foot, he heard her cry out:

'Fo, Fum, Fi, Fee, I smell the blood of an Iceni.

Be he alive or be he dead, I'll spin his skin to make my thread.' But that put no fear into Wayne. For he was brave, and he was strong, and, to put it kindly, it wasn't just his arms that were thick. Besides, it was a fairly standard threat in those days. So Wayne stepped boldly out into the open, and called up to the giantess. Well, he set out to call up to the giantess, but when he lifted his head he found that he was looking straight up her skirt. And he was far too gallant to look up a woman's skirt like that. Even if it was 35 feet above him.

So Wayne blushed, and looked at the ground. 'Giantess,' he called, 'why do you plague my people?'

Well, the giantess peered down, and looked around, and tried to see from whence the voice had come. And after a while she spied him, standing beside her foot. She reached down a giant hand, and with a giant finger she beckoned Wayne to step onto it. And Wayne, being a hero, did so. Now the giantess lifted him up. Past her giant hips he went, on past her giant waist, up and round her – well, there is no need for indelicacy. Suffice it to say that Wayne concluded that it might be possible, after all, to have too much of a good thing. And the giantess continued to lift Wayne skyward until his eyes were level with hers. And then she spoke: 'Hello, big boy,' she said.

Now, when Wayne heard those very same words from his belovéd Lebam, when they were alone in their tee-pee, they always made him feel good, and proud, and manly. But, when the giantess said them, they somehow made him feel rather inadequate. And he knew not how to reply.

'Well?' said the giantess. 'Was there something you wanted?'

Wayne was staring deep into her big, blue eyes, and he had to gather his thoughts a while to recall his purpose.

'Giantess,' he said eventually, 'why do you plague my people?'

'Plague?' she answered. 'You cannot call that plaguing. Given all my troubles, and all my problems, I consider that I let them off lightly. It is not easy, you know, to be a giantess. You must eat vast amounts of provender simply to sustain yourself, yet still try to keep trim. And then they make nothing attractive in your size.'

'I suppose you have a point,' Wayne began, but the giantess had not finished.

'Consider another thing. It takes me a week simply to wash and dry my hair. Then there is all the work to be done on my nails and cuticles. And the ironing takes forever.'

Wayne began to see just why his people were so discontented.

'And as for shaving my armpits,' she continued, but Wayne was not accustomed to discussing such topics.

'Giantess,' he said, 'you are clearly suffering from melancholy. What you require is something that will lift your spirits. You need to jape and jest. In short, to have a good laugh.'

'Have a good laugh!' she exclaimed. 'And what have I to laugh about?'

'Surely there must be something,' said Wayne.

'Such as?'

'Well, there might, perchance, be some pun, or epigram, that amuses you.'

'I know nothing of such things. I have no time for such flummery. But wait, I will give you a challenge. If you can make me laugh, then I will give you what you want. I will go away and oppress some other people.'

'And if I cannot?' asked Wayne, who knew that in his occupation it was always wise to hear the small print before accepting a challenge.

The giantess thought a moment, and then declared, 'If you cannot make me laugh then I will remain where I am, and you shall become my slave.'

It was the standard contract of the time.

'Very well,' said Wayne. 'I accept your terms. I shall now endeavour to make you laugh. But first we should be introduced. I am Sir Wayne, the green knight. And you are?'

'They call me Peach,' said the giantess.

162

'Very well then, Peach. I shall proceed. Tell me, why did the chicken cross the road?'

Peach's face betrayed puzzlement. 'I was not even aware that the chicken had crossed the road. But then, that is not surprising. Nobody ever tells me anything.'

'You misapprehend,' said Wayne. 'You are supposed to ask me the question in return.'

'Why ever should I?' asked Peach. 'I have no interest in poultry, and even less in their perambulatory motivations. I see nothing amusing in that at all.'

'Very well,' said Wayne, 'let us try again. How many churls does it take to change a light bulb?'

'Well now,' mused Peach, 'would that be a crocus? Or a snow-drop, perhaps. Verily, I think you have asked me an unfair question, for all bulbs are light to me.'

Wayne decided that the joke must go the way of the first. After all, a joke is never funny once it has been explained. He began again.

'Knock, knock,' he said.

'Is that funny?'

'Not as such. It is but part of a joke. I say 'Knock, knock,' and then you reply 'Who is there?' I tell you that it is Wayne, and you enquire "Wayne who?" which I cap by exclaiming "Wainscoting". Do you see?'

Peach was beginning to be rendered cross-eyed, trying to focus on Wayne. 'Are you a noted humourist amongst your people?' she asked.

It was becoming apparent to Wayne that he might not to be able to make Peach laugh, after all. But then he remembered a truly mirth-ful joke, which he had heard from the knight soil man. Surely, he thought, this would make her laugh. He tried to remember all that he had seen of the Icenic fools.

'Alright, settle down, settle down. It's the way I tell them. Here's one, here's one. You're going to like this – not a lot, but you're going to like it.'

'Is that funny?' interrupted Peach.

'No, that is but the preamble. Now I shall have to begin again.'

He took a deep breath, and then proceeded. 'Nice to see you, to see you, nice. Stop me if you've heard it. You see, there's this wood-cutter, and he's got an enormous great ...'

But Peach interrupted him. 'I have heard it,' she said.

Wayne was downcast. 'You have heard the joke before?'

'No,' she replied, 'but I have heard about the woodcutter. I investigated, as a matter of fact, and it really is more than ample. Nothing by giant standards, but quite striking for your sort.'

And Wayne, in the face of this deflating reply, had to admit defeat. Making giantesses laugh really was alien to his calling. He felt, indeed, that it was rather demeaning for him to be required to try. He would simply have to live out the rest of his life as her slave.

'But first,' he pleaded, 'Grant me one boon. Allow me to go and say a last farewell to Lebam.'

'Very well,' said Peach. 'But remember that as my slave you must never turn your back on me. And be quick about it, or I shall come to the village after you, and discuss my underwear.'

With that she returned Wayne to the ground, and he quickly began to back away. He held his head high, trying to retain his dignity, but kept his eyes fixed on the ground, due to his gallantry.

So it was that he saw nothing of the low-hanging tree branch, which consequently caught him a solid blow across the back of the head. It stopped him, with a jerk. The ground being damp, that caused his feet to slip from under him, and he flew up in the air, with a graceless somersault, and landed face first in the mud.

And then, as Wayne tried to regain his feet, all dignity flown, he was dashed to the ground once more by a gale of wind, accompanied by a huge clap of thunder. The sound grew and grew, until it was so prodigious that Wayne had to clasp his mud bespattered hands over his ears. The ground trembled and trees shook off their leaves. And, when Wayne cautiously looked up from his prone position, he saw the cause of all this tumult. It was Peach. She was laughing. Somehow she gasped a few words, between the guffaws.

'The look on his face!' she exclaimed. 'First the tree, then the fall!' she sobbed. 'And finally the landing!' she whimpered. 'Nobody ever made me laugh like this before!' And with that she turned upon her heels and, with a final salute to Wayne, she fulfilled her promise, and marched away. Her retreating laughter could be heard for a full hour.

And, when all was finally still, Wayne picked himself up, brushed himself down, and started all over again. He went back home, where he collected Lebam from the neighbours, and told them all his story.

Over the coming weeks and months he told it over and over again. And each time his role in the tale became more and more auspicious. He had decided from the start to say nothing about the jokes, or the laughter, or any such thing. Which left a paucity of detail, which Wayne was forced to alleviate – after all, a hero is expected to have a tale to tell. So he told how he had fought the giantess with his bare hands and defeated her. How he had outwitted her with his stealth and cunning. I believe a magic bean may have come into it somewhere.

But that, by its very nature, is another story.

DEREK'S *SEVENTH* LETTER
TO THE TRUNCHEONS

Life's like that, isn't it? Only the other day I was freewheeling through Feltwell, when an old woman called out to me from her washing line. 'Be off,' she called. So, thinking that she wanted me to dismount from my bicycle – 'Beryl' – I did just that, only to find that I had stepped in something I would rather have avoided.

And that set me to thinking. We all, from time to time, step in something we would rather avoid, don't we? We can be sailing along, without a care in the world or a thought in our heads, when suddenly we feel an unpleasant oozing over the top of our sandals. And then we have to appeal to our fellow man or woman, to help us to clean it off.

Which is exactly what I did with the old woman in Feltwell. But I have to report that she only repeated her request that I 'Be off'. I assured her that I was off, and that, indeed, it was in the getting off that I had reached the unfortunate state I was in. She thought about that for a while, and then she changed her tune, I can tell you.

'Eff off, then,' she said, with some vehemence, and that being her final utterance before returning to her washing line, I was forced to remount Beryl, and bicycle off with a rather nasty squishing in my left sock.

I have thought about her words long and hard since then, but I am still unable to draw any meaning, however profound, from her pithy rejoinder. And so now I am throwing the puzzle open to my audience, your good selves. Is 'Eff' an old Norfolk word, perhaps? What should I have done in response to her request? Should I have questioned her further? I do hope you will be able to enlighten me.

And, until you do, let me leave you with this thought. We shouldn't be afraid to not understand. After all, if The Good Lord had meant us to understand everything that was said, He would never have given us Janet Street-Porter.

MUTINY ON THE *BOUNCY*
as told by Sid Kipper

Sid got into trouble with an older version of this story when he told it at the Lancaster Maritime Festival in 1999. Being a council-run event it was checked out by the Trading Standards Department, who took exception to Sid's use of Imperial measurements throughout. They insisted, on threat of prosecution, that he convert the story to metric terms, and so he was forced to make some alterations.

The necessary calculations were carried out by Sid's second cousin Kenneth, who is known as the brains of the family. Kenneth insists that the letters BF after his name indicate a degree in French. The changes he made have now become so much part of the story that it would be imposs-ible to reverse them. So here is the story in its modern form.

The year was seventeen hundred and eighty nine, and the temperature was 30 degrees in the shade, which doesn't sound a lot, but this story has been metriculated, so it was at least twice that in real therms. The longitude was 1.25 degrees East. As for the latitude – well, there was no room for any latitude. Because Captain Blight didn't hold with latitude. He thought there was far too much latitude about in those days. He reckoned if you gave them 2.54 centimetres they'd take 1.609 kilometres!

Captain Blight was the master of *HMS Bouncy*, so-called because she was an experimental vessel with a sprung deck. The experi-ment failed, as a matter of fact, because they were always losing sailors shot overboard as a consequence. But you don't know till you try, do you?

Like I told you, the temperature was 30 degrees in the shade. Now, you'd think they'd all get out of the shade to cool down, wouldn't you? But Captain Blight wouldn't let them. He thought the heat would toughen them up, although if you ask me it was more likely to tenderise them.

Along with Captain Blight was his first officer, Mister Christian. He was known to all as Fetcher Christian, because of his main duties on board ship.

The story goes that on that fateful day Captain Blight threw the stick overboard into the water just once too often, and Fetcher Christian refused to dive over the side and retrieve it. And some people say that was what led to the mutiny on the *Bouncy*.

But it wasn't.

Ever since the *Bouncy* put out from Wells-on-Sea all had not been well. For a start, most of the crew had been pressed. Well, that was fine and dandy when they were standing up, but when they lay down they hung over the sides of their hammocks and made the place look untidy.

The ship's fiddler, Dransfield, was blind. Well, no, he wasn't actually blind, but he wore a blindfold at all times. This was because Captain Blight insisted on having a blind fiddler, and, given the choice between having his eyes poked out with a sharp stick and the blindfold, Dransfield had decided to go for the latter of two evils. But it did mean that he kept bumping into things. He couldn't see to play the fiddle very well, either.

The men were low and scurvy, and the officers were high and mighty, which left the middle ranks rather unsure of their position.

Then there was the Captain. Blight was a sticker for discipline. He once flogged a man for £5.25p to a passing brigadoon. He had the sails starched and ironed every morning without fail. And if they did it with fail they had to do it all over again, without. He even insisted on table manners.

The *Bouncy* was carrying a cargo of 10.161 metric tonnes of fruit-bread from Scratby in Norfolk to Boston Links, which was a golf course not far from Skegness. They would have carried more, but like the old saying goes, you can't get 1.13 litres in a 56 centilitre pot.

This bread was made with the very best yeast, the finest flour, and the fruitiest fruit available. But the crew weren't allowed to eat any of it. They weren't even allowed to look at it, in case they drooled all over it. Because rations were low. In fact, they were reduced to eating ships biscuits, full of weasels, plus the odd limb cut off unwary crew mates – which is why so many sailors in those days had wooden legs or hooks.

Even the rum ration had been cut. What it had been cut with nobody was sure, but it may have been anti-freeze, which was the last thing they needed. Because the temperature was still 30 degrees in the shade, and the Captain still wouldn't let them get out of it.

'I'll make men of the lot of you, yet,' he cried, striking Dransfield a low blow with his sword which nearly had exactly the opposite effect.

'But Sir,' said Fetcher Christian, 'if you make a man of the cabin boy he'll be a cabin man, and want more wages.'

Blight's face went black as thunder. 'I'll thank you to speak when you're spoken to, Mister Christian.'

'Very well, Sir,' came the reply. 'Say no more'.

Blight's face went grey as drizzle. 'I said when you're spoken to, Mister Christian.'

'Well you did speak to me,' said Christian. 'If you want me not to speak you'll have to stop spoking to me first.'

The Captain said nothing for a while. The look of concentration on his face and the steam coming out of his ears bespoke the fact that he was thinking. He went white as a sheet, which is a sort of a rope so it probably wasn't all that white. Then a look in his eyes suggested he was coming to a conclusion.

Finally, he said – although when I say 'finally' I don't mean they were his famous last words. He didn't say them till 1817, and they were: 'I tell you, nurse, I'm quite sure I'm not actually supposed to swallow the leeches.'

Finally – in the other sense – he said, 'All of you, except for Mister Christian, who I'm not speaking to, will do double duties on half rations. The first officer will give you the details.'

So the men all looked at the first officer – Fetcher Christian. He said nothing.

'Well, Mister Christian,' said Captain Blight. 'What are your orders?'

'Sorry,' said Mister Christian, 'I wasn't listening.'

And it might have gone on like this for ever, with listening and speaking, and not listening and not speaking unless spoken to, if it hadn't been for a cry from the look-out, who was sitting astride the 0.914 metre-arm.

'Stan-hoe!' he cried, 'Stan-hoe,' which immediately caused constipation amongst the crew, because the village of Stanhoe, as you

168

probably know, lies ten kilometres inland and 61 metres above sea level as the crow flies. And the *Bouncy* was drifting towards it.

'What shall we do, Sir?' asked Mister Christian.

'Do?' cried the Captain. 'What shall we do?'

'I asked first,' said Christian, but Captain Blight had made a decision. He'd decided to not hear unless listened to.

So, as the ship was liable to run aground, Fetcher Christian decided it was his duty to take control. 'In for a penny, in for 1.58 Euros and rising,' he thought. 'We'd better tow the *Bouncy* out of danger.'

So he cupped his hands together and cried, 'Launch two boats and row for your very lives away from land,' which the sailors immediately did. But as Fetcher Christian hadn't specifically said that they should first attach ropes to the *Bouncy*, the two boats quickly vanished over the horizon, leaving the rest of them no better off.

This caused Captain Blight to go into a fury, and he began flogging people left, right and centre with the cat-o-ten tails (which had been rounded up under the metrical system).

And at that moment, something about Fetcher Christian snapped. As a matter of fact it was his braces. So, just as he was stepping forward to stay the Captain's hand, his breeches fell down, and he stumbled and fell headlong into Captain Blight.

'This is mutiny,' cried the Captain. 'Take Mister Christian below and clap him in irons.' But the men refused. Oh, they clapped Fetcher Christian alright. They clapped him, and they cheered him, and they carried him head-high around the deck.

'What's going on?' asked the blind fiddler.

The Captain was furious. 'Did I speak to you, Dransfield?' he demanded.

'Who said that?' came the reply, but then their conversation was totally overwhelmed by the uprising of the crew. And, almost before he knew it, Fetcher Christian found himself in command of the *Bouncy*.

Captain Blight was cast adrift with eighteen men, a map and a few provisions. The map was a map of the Lake District, so when the provisions ran out they ate that. With the provisions gone, and the map gone, they drifted for day after day with nothing to eat, and Blight began to see the men in a different light – that is, the glow you get from a good, hot cooking fire. But they were spared at the very last minute when they reached land at Hartlepool, where they were mistaken for monkeys and put in the zoo.

One sailor had been captured by the mutineers, and then escaped. He was picked up and taken to Neatishead, to see if he ought to be tried. Being tried was a punishment usually reserved for whalermen, where they were rendered down for their fat. But in the end he got pardoned and let off with a loud report.

The mutineers sailed the *Bouncy* to a Norfolk island. Well, there's only one Norfolk island, actually, which is Scolt Head Island. There they founded a naturist colony with some exotic women from Lincolnshire, about whom it was often said: 'You don't get many of them to the .454 kilo.' It was fine during the summer, but they eventually discovered that going topless in grass skirts was no fun in a Norfolk winter. The women soon found that out, too, which is what led to the invention of the duffel coat.

Dransfield had a miracle cure when he took the blindfold off, and he was able to see the Lincolnshire women in their grass skirts and nothing else, who were a sight for sore eyes, which was exactly what he had, due to the blindfold being too tight.

And, most importantly for nautical history, Boston Links never got their fruit-bread. And that led to the catering manager of the golf course being fired. Now he was a Norfolk man, from Burnham Thorpe, and his name was Horatio Nelson. He was forced to give up a promising career in catering and run away to sea in disgrace.

And we all know what happened after that.

So, if it hadn't been for the mutiny on the *Bouncy*, and then the sacking of the catering manager, and 'England expects', and all that, I might very well have had to tell you this story in French!

SHIP FASHION AND BRISTOL SHAPED
Number Four – Running Away from Sea

Some of us sailor boys has a saying. We say that the land is like a boarding-house mistress. And we aren't wrong, neither. They're both big. They're both hard. And, if you run into either of them in the dark, I wouldn't give much for your chances. So shiver your timbers, haul in all sail, and let me tell you about the time I ran away to land.

It was after I'd given up doing long trips. They're all very well for a young man, but after a mariner has been marinated for a number of years he's seen it all. He's heard it all, too. And he's made love to a fair amount of it. And then perhaps he meets, shall we say, a buxom barmaid. And suddenly being far from home, with just a gang of hairy hands for company, doesn't have the same attraction. I know, because it happened to me.

I took up herring fishing, as being a way to mix business with pleasure, if you get my drift – which is north to south, generally. But on one trip I found that fishing, me buckos, is a chancy trade. Now herring were known, in them days, as 'silver-darlings'. That was due to their colouration and affectionate nature. But they weren't being especially friendly on that trip.

Some of us sailor boys has a saying. We says that a herring is like a woman, but without the bicycle. If they don't wish to be caught then there's nothing a poor fisherman can do. You can lower your nets. You can nail your colours to the mast. You can do what you like, but they won't be caught if they don't want to. And the same goes for herring, too.

Many's a time I've been tossed on the briny, the wind in me hair and the spray up me nose, casting and heaving, casting and heaving, and nothing to show for it. And then the wind goes round, and, before you know it, you've got them wriggling and gasping over the top of your sea-boots. And the same goes for herring, too.

Well, on this particular trip we'd caught bugger all, if you'll excuse my rough sailor talk. Or even if you won't. We hadn't caught enough fish to satisfy a trollop. So our skipper thought as we should try our luck closer to shore. He took her in as close as he dare, and then called on us to cast the nets.

Some of us sailor boys has a saying. We says that a net is like a woman. They're both heavier than they look. They take a lot of looking after. And, when you finally haul either of them in, you're usually in for a big disappointment.

Well, just as we were casting the nets, up came a squall, out of nowhere. And the next thing I know I'm thrown overboard, in the breakers, with me sea-boots filling up fast. Now there's two things a sailor can do in a circumstance like that. Or three, if you counts drowning. The other two are to swim for the boat, or head for the shore. And all of a sudden I knew something. I knew that my love-affair with the sea was over. She didn't seem so attractive no more, despite her heaving billows and her skin like silk, now that I was actually in her. That's often the case, I've found. So I struck out for land.

Some of us sailor boys has a saying. We say you should never give a breaker an equal suck. What we mean by that I have no notion. But I sucked a few breakers that day, I can tell you, before I finally hauled myself ashore. And when I did I resolved, there and then, never to go to sea again.

I'm not one to go back on my word. Which means I've reached the end of my maritime memories, you lubbers, whether you like them or not. And now my life has flashed before my eyes, I can say I'd have done it all over again, and devil take the hindsight.

Some of us sailor boys has a saying. We say that memory is like a woman. At least, I think we do. I really can't quite remember. Except to say that I've lost both of them in my time. But now the tide's out, and the wind's dropped, and I reckon I'll just go for a walk on the shore. So let go, me proud beauties, and damn your eyes!

The Shoals of Whiting

Oh it was a dark and a dismal day,
Out of Holkham harbour we were lighting,
In the sleet and hail of a force-eight gale,
We went looking for the shoals of whiting.
　　Though the wind did blow, we searched high and low,
　　We were looking for the shoals of whiting.

Oh me mother said I should go to sea,
And the very thought of that was frightening;
But me mother, Jill, she's more frightening still,
So I went looking for the shoals of whiting.

With the pitch and roll soon you're feeling ill;
You are turning green, and your stomach's tightening.
Then you learn a thing; you should face downwind,
When you're looking for the shoals of whiting.

Oh the hours were hard, and the work was long,
And you're wondering why the fish aren't biting;
That's 'cos you forget, you should use a net
When you go looking for the shoals of whiting.

Oh from Warham Hole, down to Scroby Sands,
Through the wind and spray our boat was fighting;
Cast a million trawl, we caught bugger all,
Oh we couldn't find the shoals of whiting.

Then the storm got worse, and the sea did swell,
And our captain he got struck by lightning;
Oh the ship went down, just off Yarmouth town,
And it was there we found the shoals of whiting.
Now there's just our bones, down in Davy Jones;
We got eaten by the shoals of whiting.

THE FOLK-SINGING OLYMPICS
as told by Sid Kipper

As well as a master storyteller, Sid Kipper is also a renowned singer, especially of folk song. His albums, such as Like A Rhinestone Ploughboy, *and* East Side Story, *have been widely acclaimed and sold in their thousands. He has custody of a vast range of material, all the way from simple old songs such as* The Mild Rover, *to the exciting, modern, Cajun beat of* Way Down In The Bayeux Tapestry.

This singing is a family tradition, and Sid's pride in that legacy is evident in this fascinating story from his one-man show, Vaughan Williams Stole My Folk Song.

The Folk Singing Olympics were held in my little village of St Just-near-Trunch in 1919. Now, as you can imagine, it was a huge event for the village. But just in case you can't, I'll tell you, anyway.

Of course, a village didn't get awarded the Olympics, just like that. There was a lot of work to be done first. You had to form a committee to give out the bribes, and then you made your bid, and told them all about your facilities, and so on. With regard to the

173

facilities, St Just said they could use the New Goat Inn, the village hall, and the public conveniences (between 3.30 and 4.00 p.m. on a Wednesday). Plus they could have the Olympic Village at Trunch Bored School, as long as they brought their own tents.

Well, to cut a long story to the quick, St Just got awarded the games, despite some limp competition from South Walsham, and a stiff proposal from Dickleburgh. And for weeks before the event the village was buzzing. Then someone mucked out the public conveniences and the buzzing eventually died down. They swept the streets, cut the grass at the school, put some bunting up outside the Post Office, and then all was ready for the visitors.

People came from near and far (although the attendance from in the middle was frankly disappointing). To start the whole thing off, all the teams paraded round the village green in alphabetical order. Except for Wreningham, who couldn't spell, and insisted on going after Reepham. And except for St Just, of course, because, being the home team, they brought up the rear. What a sight they were, in their team uniform of Arran sweaters and scarlet neckerchiefs, every one of them giving the team salute by putting their fingers in their ears. Of course, being last to go they'd spent the longest in the New Goat, so they didn't parade all that straight. But what they lacked in precision, they made up for in enthusiasm.

Once the teams were all assembled Lord Silver-Darling came down and set the bawl rolling by cutting the tape, declaring it all open, and singing his family song:

'This land is my land, so you keep off it,
I grow my crops here, and reap the profit.
From that big oak tree, to the parish boundary,
This land belongs to me alone!'

Now, the Olympics weren't just important for the village. They were also very important for my family, as well. Because my Grandfather Billy, and Great Uncle Albert, they both won medals in different events.

Of course, there were all sorts of events. For instance, the Marathon Singing was won by a bloke from Bawburgh. He set a new World Record with a song called *The Hard Times Of Old Buckenham*. It starts:

'There's people whose home is a dried up old ditch;
I tell you with them I would happily switch,
For what do they know of the trials of the rich?

And it's oh, the hard times of Old Buck'nham,
In Old Buckenham awfully hard times.'
And it carries on and on. The bloke from Bawburgh would have gone on longer than he did, as a matter of fact, but they had to stop him in the end, so they could lock up the village hall and revive the judges. So nobody ever discovered how the song came out.

Then there was the Speed Singing. That was won by a little woman from Knapton, who got through the test song, *Do You Know Ken Peel*, much faster than anybody else. Then she declared that she couldn't hang about to collect her medal because she'd got things to do, and her husband would expect his dinner on the table, and anyhow she'd only popped in to see what all the fuss was about. They had to use a stand-in for the medal ceremony. So if Cyril Cockle ever shows you the medal they presented to his grandmother, just you bear that in mind.

A bloke from Ditchingham sang the highest, at 7 feet 3 inches, and Bernard Wrigley, from Booton, sang the lowest, at 2 feet 6. There was also Synchronised Singing, various Relays, and how far you could throw your voice.

(Ernie Spratt wanted to go in for the Triple Jump, but his wife was having none of that. Which, according to Ernie, was just 'lack of business, as usual'.)

My Uncle Albert won his gold in the Loud Singing event, which I've explained elsewhere. And Grandfather Billy competed in the blue-ribbon event, which was the Pentathlon.

Now the Pentathlon was made up of five different elements. They were singing-when-drunk, singing-with-your-hands-tied-behind-your-back, singing-while-standing-on-your-head, singing-while-drinking-a-glass-of-water, and, finally, singing-when-sober. That last one was the hardest discipline of all. And up against Billy in the final was his arch rival, Claude Brown, from Caister. Now Claude had quite a reputation as a singer. In fact, he was sometimes known as 'the Caister Nightingale'. Come to think of it, Grandfather Billy was often referred to as 'the Trunch Cock', but that's another matter. Anyhow, the two of them had been at woodcutter-heads for years over who was the top singer (I say woodcutter-heads because we don't call them loggers in Norfolk).

Well, the competition started off smoothly enough. Billy was excellent when drunk, and very good while standing on his head. Just to show off he gave an exhibition song, standing on his head when drunk, which was *Gorleston Town*:

'Now a sailor boy came home from the sea,
He thought he'd have a jubilee.
'Would you like a nice time?' Belinda said.
'No, I'll make do with you instead.'
Now won't you come down, won't you come down,
Won't you come down to Gorleston Town?'

Claude lost points on the singing-when-drunk because he didn't slur his words enough, and got to the climax too quickly, but he made up ground in the standing-on-the-head, because all the change fell out of his pockets and the judges accepted that as a bribe. On the hands-behind-the-back they were pretty even, and on the while-drinking-a-glass-of-water they were both fairly odd. All of which meant they were pegging level when they went into the final event, which was the singing-when-sober.

Now, this event was a bit of an unknown quality, because nobody had seen Billy sober for years. He'd been practising for it by singing while thinking sobering thoughts, such as the price of beer, or imagining Lady Silver-Darling in the altogether. But Claude was a lifelong member of the Caister Temperance Society (except for competition purposes, of course) and this was his best event.

It was the last contest of the whole Olympics. Well, it had to be, really, because every time they got Billy sobered up a bit, somebody won something, and then he got drunk again, helping them to celebrate. But in the end everything else was won, Billy was sobered up, and the singing began. Claude went first, and he sang a Scottish ballad about a dyster lassie:

'Bonny Anne Clyde, dressed in the altogether,
And in the altogether, she dyed.'

Well, it was brilliant. You could have heard a cough drop. And Claude got maximum points, despite the Suffolk judge giving him minus three (he always did that, and they always ignored him, because he wasn't supposed to be there, anyhow).

So now Billy got up. His song was a humorous sort of a song, all about this woman with a huge appetite:

'I know a young lady who opened a fly,
I think I know why she opened that fly,
Oh me, oh my.'

It goes on like that for a while, with lots of stuff about what she swallowed, and things wriggling, and wriggling, and tickling inside her.

Well, once Billy got into the song he just got better and better, till by the time he reached the end everyone was stunned into silence. Then they all leapt to their feet and cheered (except for the Suffolk judge who threw himself on the ground and booed), and Billy got maximum points as well.

So it was a tie, and now it had to go to a penalty sing-out. Well, first they explained the rules about scoring, hesitation, repetition, and so on, and then it began. The chosen song was *The Rollesby Ram*. I expect you know it. It starts:

'As I was leaving Rollesby, all on my billy goat,
I met the littlest ram, sir, that ever got its oats.'

So they set off, and they went at it hammer and sickle, turn after turn, verse after verse. Billy sang:

'The legs all on this ram, sir, they barely reached the ground,
And when it came to a mole hill it had to walk right round.'

And Claude came right back with:

'The fleece upon this ram, miss, was sheared off with nail scissors,
I took it home all to my wife, and she said "What d'you think this is?"'

So then Billy sang:

'The stones upon this ram, ma'am, had been cut off at birth,
They were given away for nothing, which is more than they was worth.'

And Claude responded with:

'The horns upon this ram, your highness, they reached up to his ear,
A little boy went up in January and come down the previous year.'

Each verse was better than the last. Although they didn't know that at the time, of course, because they hadn't reached the last verse yet. And then, all of a sudden, and very dramatically, they did. You see, Claude was singing the verse which goes:

'I brought this ram along tonight, but now I fear I've lost it,
It fell through a hole in my pocket and some great clodhopper squashed it.'

And he suddenly realised that Billy had already sung that verse, and he juddered to a halt. Well, the penalty for that was four pints for a refusal. So Claude got drunk, and then he was disqualified, of course.

Now, to be declared the winner, Billy only had to sing:

'And now my song is over, it all has come to nought,
And if you want any more, then you're dafter than I thought.'

Which he did, and he was, and the Olympics were over.

They carried Billy Kipper through the streets of St Just, and he got the gold medal hung on him by the celebrity guest, who was the Singing Postman's Grandfather. Claude had to try and look pleased with the silver, as Billy was awarded the freedom of the public conveniences (except for 3.30 to 4.00 on a Wednesday).

The celebrations went on long and loud, until they actually ran into the closing ceremony, which was probably just as well since the closing ceremony was not very exciting. It was exactly like the opening ceremony, actually, except that instead of Lord Silver-Darling cutting the tape and declaring it all open, Lady Silver-Darling sewed the tape up again, and declared it all closed.

And that was that. They never had the Folk-Singing Olympics again after that, because alcohol was made a banned substance, so nobody but Claude wanted to enter. And as a consequence of that Grandfather Billy never lost his title. And he never had to sober up again either. He lived to the ripe middle age of 57, dying in 1948, when I was only two years old. So I don't really remember him. But apparently he just got better and better at the drinking, so that if he kissed you goodnight, you'd wake up with a hangover the next morning.

But all that was yet to come. Back in 1919 the Olympics were over, the celebrations had ground to a stupor, and there was nothing for it but to sweep up the village, take down the bunting, rake the Olympic Village, and argue about the results.

And they do say that, after a while, it was almost as if the Olympics had never happened. Except for one thing. It took quite a long time for the buzzing to get back to full volume.

178

BUNFIGHT AT THE OK CHORALE
by Augustus Swineherd

In the 1950s, under pressure to pay off his slate at the Old Goat Inn, Swineherd wrote a number of pot-boilers to raise funds. Most of them, frankly, failed to reach the required temperature, turning out more like plate-warmers.

Bunfight At The OK Chorale, however, does have a certain charm, not least in the novelty of its location. Because, while there have been no end of stories of the American Wild West, tales of the Docile East have been much rarer. The East was the part of the USA that attracted most East Anglians, as a quick look at the place names they took with them reveals. And no doubt Cambridge, Massachusetts and Haverhill, New Hampshire have their own stories to tell. But ours begins further south, some miles inland from the seaport of Norfolk, Virginia.

Of course, Swineherd had never been there. But that need never be a barrier to an author with imagination. And debts.

Well I'll be hog-tied if this here ain't a true story. And I knows that because I was there when it all happened. I was the piano player in the Penultimate Chance Saloon, that day when the Stranger rode into town.

Now East Clintwood was just another quiet, backwoods, Eastern town, only without no woods. We just had the one church, the one store, and the one saloon, but that didn't bother us no never mind. They sure took care of all the praying, spending and drinking we could do. They was strung out down the main street, and that was the way the Stranger came.

He was riding a bald palomino, kind of drifting down the street like tumbleweed, with his spurs a-jangling in the quiet of a long, hot afternoon. Where he came from nobody knowed. Where he was heading for everybody found out soon enough. But in between them times, a whole mess of stuff was about to happen.

Word was that the Stranger had been poking cows and punching horses, back West. He sure looked capable of it. He was lean, mean and clean, and I dare say he liked beans. But as he stood at the bar of the saloon, with one fancy leather boot on the brass rail round the bar, and the other one in the boot rack by the door, you could tell there was only the one thing on his mind. But it weren't

179

drink. And it weren't women. We found out soon enough what it was, because he downed his redeye, and turned slowly round to face the room. It all went quiet. 'Howdy, all,' he said. 'I done heared I might get some action here. Done I heared right?'

Well, nobody didn't answer him, so he picked me out with his eye and said it again. I replied, kinda nervous. 'Well now, Stranger,' I said, 'that all depends on what sort of action you was a-looking for.'

The Stranger spat out a single word. 'Singing,' came the word, from the spittoon. Well, the room went even silenter, and I dived for cover. I'd been a piano-player long enough to know trouble when I smelled it.

'Singing?' I asked from under a table. 'And what sort of singing might it be?'

'Well it ain't no tinhorn folk-singing,' sneered the Stranger. 'It ain't no folk-singing, and it ain't no glee club, neither. It's man's singing I'm looking for. What you might call chor-ee-ale singing. And, in regard of that, I heared you had a buckaroo hereabouts by the name of Orson King. Well, I've got a score to settle with that particular son of a mother.'

It was true. In them days Orson King was a big player in town. He had his own outfit, named after him, and knowed and feared for many's a mile as the OK Chorale. They ran things in town, sing-ing wise.

Now their singing weren't exactly what you'd call perty, but it was sure as darntootin' final. When they sung something it sure as tarnation stayed sung. When they done *The Crucifixion* they really crucified it. And when they sung *Messiah* they didn't bother much with the 'iah' bit. Folks reckoned there weren't another choir any-thing like them, and I reckon they reckoned right. Of course, that may have been on account of the way they all took their teeth out before singing. That came about after an incident when one galloot in the tenors felt lucky, went for a top C, and took a woman in the fifth row clean out with his bottom set.

And, while I was a-telling you all that in flashback, dang me if Orson King himself didn't walk right into the saloon. He just strode up to the bar and ordered the whisky. Then, when he had all the bottles sorted just how he wanted them, he came out from behind the bar and faced the Stranger. Only he weren't no stranger to Orson King.

180

'I knew you'd track me down one day, Chuck Wagon,' he said. 'You're just plum loco enough to think I might be glad to see you. But this town ain't big enough for the both of us. As a matter of fact, it ain't really big enough for me on my own, but I've kind of grown attached to it, so I don't mind. But I reckon you oughta turn around and head back out of town, before I have to do something I'd regret.'

But Chuck Wagon didn't move. 'I ain't about to go nowhere, Orson,' he said. 'Not until you and me have had a show-down. You may have bested me back then, but I reckon you just got lucky. And I'll be hornswoggled if you ain't about to give me a second chance.'

Orson wiped his brow with a spotted banana. 'Now, Chuck, you know I don't give nobody no second chance. Why, a lot of men I don't even give no first chance. Sure, you used to be my sidekick, in the old days. But I gave you your chance, and you paid me back in fool's gold. I trusted you with my wife, and you done cheated on me.'

'But, Orson, we was only singing duets.'

'Only singing duets, you say! What sort of a best friend sings duets in cahoots with another man's wife behind his back? Why, if that varmint of an Apache dancer hadn't winged me, I wouldn't never have cancelled that show, and come home unexpected, and caught you both at it, out there on the hacienda. Do you think it would have stopped at duets? You're darn tooting it wouldn't. It would have been trios and quartets next, and before you knew it there'd have been a full-blown goddam choir. And we all know who'd have been singing the solos.'

Chuck fingered his Stetson, looking kinda stubborn. 'You've got it figured all wrong, Orson. Me and Lisabel was only practising so she could sing with you. She wanted to take you by surprise.'

'Well, she sure as damnation done that!'

'You was madder'n a bull, and I couldn't fight you because you was my pardner, so I vamoosed. Then you left town without leaving no forwarding address. Sure there's bad blood between us, but it ain't me that spilled it.'

Orson chewed his cheroot for a whiles, saying nothing. He took a silver dollar from his pocket and tossed it high in the air. Then, without seeming to take no aim, he spat, and hit the dollar, dead centre, right at the top of it's flight. It seemed to sort of help him in the making up of his mind.

'Me and Lisabel come here to leave it all behind, and start out clean,' Orson said. 'But seeing as you've found me, we'll settle it now, once and for all. We'll do the dog-gone show right here. It's time to sing up, or shut up, Chuck.'

Well, Chuck Wagon's eyes narrowed, and his nostrils flared. He cleared a space around him by kicking away a chair; it went skittering clear across the bar. You could tell he wished he'd used the foot with the boot on. 'Guess a man's gotta croon what a man's gotta croon,' he muttered, and then, before anyone could stop him, he gave us *Auld Lang Syne*, full belt. Well, it sure weren't no sound for the squeamish, I can tell you. By the time he'd finished we was all cowering behind the tables, and the mirror over the bar had smashed itself into a thousand pieces.

'Mighty fine,' said Orson, cool enough, but looking kinda ornery. 'I see you ain't lost none of your edge.' But that weren't the end of it, of course. Like I told you, this here was man's singing. So now Orson had to best him, or lose face in the eyes of his own men.

Without looking round he called out to me: 'Hank,' he said, being as that's my name; 'Hank, give me a D.' Well, I was trepidated. 'Don't do it, Orson,' I pleaded. 'Don't go for the Handel. You ain't no young whippersnapper no more. It could be the finishing of you!'

But Orson weren't one to take no notice of what nobody said. 'Just shut up, Hank, and give me the note,' he said, his eyes never leaving his face. Some men dove clean out of the saloon, clean through the windows. One went to get the Sheriff. But Orson, he just stood there, waiting for me to make a move.

It was like I'd gotten taken over. Like I couldn't stop myself. I opened up that piano lid. My trigger finger hovered over the key. Then that darned finger fell downward, and everyone jumped as a clear note rung out through the room. Well, Orson, he just took a deep breath, threw back his shoulders, and then all hell broke loose. It was cold-blooded carnage. Nobody hadn't never heard no one do that to the *Hallelujah Chorus* before. There was notes in there that a man shouldn't have to hear this side of the grave. There was semi-tones, quarter-tones, accidentals, and even a few deliberates. And all of it come out louder than the scream of a two-bit whore who's just been bitten, twice.

When it was all over no one moved. Every window was blowed out, and tiles had been throwed off the roof. My piano was smashed into pieces, and all the saloon girls were still wobbling.

Well, Orson had won alright, but he never sung no more after

182

that. He was all sung out and plum tuckered. He was took straight to his bed, and died within the week.

We buried him in Boot Hill, and then we all buried our teeth into the finest mess of chow we could muster, it being our way to honour a brave singer, who'd gone in the way he'd have wanted to go. It was the biggest blow-out ever seed in these parts, which is why it become known in Eastern legend as the 'Bunfight At The OK Chorale'.

Of course, what made it so special was it being by way of a triple celebration. Because, being practical folk, we done held the wedding of Lisabel and Chuck right alongside of Orson's burying. Seems she'd been hankering after him all these years and couldn't wait to get back to the duetting.

And the third celebration? You recall as how I said about them saloon girls wobbling, right after Chuck sung? Well, I got one of them kind of steadied down with my hands, and one thing led to another, and now I've got a pardner of my own. We makes beautiful music together, every Sunday night, whether we needs it or not.

Of course, the OK Chorale never sung no more after that. They didn't have no heart for it. And I never played the piano no more, neither, due to there not being no piano to play. And Chuck Wagon? Well, he left town with Lisabel. Got himself fixed up as head wrangler with the New Costessey Minstrels, who soon become so thoroughly wrangled they was every bit as feared as Orson King's outfit had ever been.

And since then things have gone back to being sort of quiet in East Clintwood. Truth to tell, I guess we kinda like it that way. Why, there's even talk of planting some woods out front.

AWFULLY GOOD
(a Musical by Rev. Derek Bream)
as reviewed by Sid Kipper

In 1999 St Just's musical Vicar, Rev. Derek Bream, unveiled an ambitious project designed to make the Old Testament more relevant. He dramatised the entire thing, adding music throughout.

Although he won't admit it, I think Derek had high hopes for this production. I know for a fact that he sent a copy to a well-known composer of musicals, in the hope that it might even make the West End stage. And if only he'd known the difference between Lloyd-Webber and Lloyd Grossman, who's to say that his ambition might not have been achieved?

The show was a huge undertaking, and the full script is far too long for the current volume. So what follows is Sid's description of the very first performance of Derek's epic.

This is the story of Rev. Bream's big show in the village hall. People are still talking about it in the Old Goat Inn, but I reckon the overall verdict is that it wasn't bad, if you like that sort of thing. But I suppose you'll want a bit more detail than that.

The show is a sort of musical extra-gavanza, based on the Old Testament. So it's basically all about God, and awe. Now I happen to know that Derek was originally going to call it *God Awful*, but his wife Bridget reckoned that wouldn't really be a very good advert. So then he had another think, and he came up with *Awfully Good*. That was a cunning ruse, you see. Because he reckoned that if it got reviewed, then, no matter what anyone said about it, he'd still be able to quote them as saying it was 'awfully good'.

Of course, being Derek, and being trendy, he brought the whole thing up to date while he was about it.

Now Derek is best known as a song writer, with hits like *I'm A Happy Clappy Chappy*, and *Leader Of The Flock*. But he thought that for such a big thing he ought to do it with someone else. The only problem was that he couldn't find anyone else who wanted to do it with him. So in the end he did it with everybody, in a way, without any of them knowing about it. That is, he just nicked any songs he fancied, and changed them to suit himself. He built a few local speciality acts into the show and, then, after a few rehearsals (which most of the cast couldn't attend), it was all ready to go. So I went along to the first night to cast my ear over it. I got a seat between Darren Dabb and Penny Pollack. As a matter of fact I think they wanted to sit together, but I knew Darren would have his hip flask on him, so I arranged things to suit myself. While everyone settled down I nosed in on their conversation, and then the show began. First, all the lights went out, leaving the hall in complete darkness. Then the whole place was filled with a terrible sound. That turned out to be Mrs Dace, who'd arrived late and was trying to find her seat in the blackout. So after they'd put the lights back on, and she'd got to her seat, and someone had found Mr Pike's teeth which had been knocked off his lap in the incident, they put the lights out again, and did the show right there.

Act 1

Out of the darkness boomed a voice. It was the Vicar, who was playing God. And He boomed the first words of the show, which were: 'In the beginning was the word-processor' (Like I said, it was all brought up to date).

Then, still in the dark, God started creating. He rattled on for a bit about how if He wanted anything doing around here He always had to do it Himself. Then He went into the first musical number, which was *Bring Me Sunshine,* and a spotlight came out of the dark and picked Him out. Well, it did eventually. At first my nephew, Kevin, who was working the spotlight, didn't know where to point it, what with it being pitch black in the hall. So he held the light the wrong way round by accident, and pointed it straight into his own eyes and completely blinded himself. But after a bit, with God helping by calling out 'Left a bit' and 'Up a bit', and so on, they got it right. Then God proceeded to make the birds and the beasts, and Great Yarmouth. (I should have said that Derek made the whole thing local, as well as up to date.)

Of course, God didn't actually create the real things, live on stage. It's only a small stage, after all. So Derek had cardboard cut-outs instead, that sprang up from the stage. Well, they were meant to spring up, but they kept on getting stuck. So, strictly speaking, on that particular night, the world and all things in it were created jointly, by God, and Cyril Cockle with a crowbar.

After the world had been created God went off, and the setting changed to the nude scene, in the Garden of Reedham. Adam was played by some friend of the Vicar's who nobody had seen before, and Eve was Mrs Barbel from the mobile library. Adam sang *If You Were The Only Girl In The World'*, and Eve gave him the Apple Mac, which was how they got all the knowledge. And that was the really dramatic moment, when they realised they were both totally naked. Mind you, you have to understand we don't have top-line actors available in St Just (except for me, of course, and they couldn't afford me). So Adam didn't play that bit especially well. I mean, it had been obvious to everyone, for some time, that he'd already realised that Eve was totally naked. It stuck out a mile. Anyhow, that led to them being cast out of the garden, but only after Cyril Cockle had to come back on with a bucket of cold water and his crowbar, to prize them apart!

When they'd dried the stage (and thrown out Widow Hake who doesn't understand drama, and was protesting they should have let Adam and Eve finish what they'd started) the whole cast came on and did a big routine of begatting and smiting. Only it's just called sex and violence in the show. And that finished off with everyone joining in a big world-music number called *On Ilkley Moor Begat*.

Then the stage was cleared again and we had the story of Noah, played by Darren's dad, Daniel. Only Noah didn't have an ark: he had a roll-on roll-off ferry instead. Well, they didn't have an actual full-size ferry on stage, for reasons I've already gone into. So they had it on a low-loader in the car park, instead, with just the ramp coming down on to the stage. And they drove all the animals up the ramp, singing *The Animals Went In 4x4s*.

I thought, at that point, Darren might have wanted some help with the hip-flask, celebrating his Dad's success, but he didn't. Anyway, when the animals were all gone, Cyril came on with a shovel and cleaned up the stage for his roses, and we went into the next scene, which was the Tower of Babel. Now Derek spent a long time thinking up all sorts of clever ways to bring the story up to date. He wanted to get across the effect of all those people shouting at each other, with no one making any effort to understand what anyone else was saying. In the end he came up with a very simple idea. He just held a Parish Council meeting on stage. That got the effect across alright!

But Derek hadn't really thought out how the scene was going to end, so of course it didn't. It just went on and on, with points of order, and amendments to the addendum, and so on, and the audience started to get a bit restless. Eventually Cyril came back on and announced that the Old Goat Inn was selling cheap beer, and the Parish Council got off pretty quick then, I can tell you. And Brenda Bream came on and sang *Come On Babel, Light My Fire*, to finish the scene.

Things got moving again with Lot and his family, who were played by the Wilcoxes. Unlike Adam, they didn't have very big parts. I mean, they hadn't been on stage a moment before they had to flee. They were warned not to look back, or else. But of course the audience kept shouting out 'Behind you!' and in the end Mrs Wilcox looked round and was turned into a pillar of salt, which was so realistic it was immediately snapped up by the bloke from the chip shop in Mundesley.

Now the scene changed again, and all the people were exiled to Wroxham, which is a bit like Egypt, but without the pyramids. And with a lot more water. And on came Simon Sturgeon as Joseph, in his Amazing Technicolor Waistcoat, which was actually one of mine which I'd lent them. In my opinion it was the highlight of the show. And Simon met Pharaoh, and did his mind-reading act. That was easy enough, actually, because Pharaoh was played by Farmer Trout, and all he ever thinks about is cows. He's got over 300 cows, and he knows them all by number. So Simon just had to guess if he was thinking of thin cows, or fat ones. And it finished with Pharaoh singing *After The Bull Is Over*, very badly.

Then the pace picked up again. First a woman had a baby in the bulrushes, and then there were lots of plagues. I can't remember them all, but I do know there was a plague of tourists, and a plague of green fly. So all the people got rich, but the roses wilted. Then the baby, who was called Mo, grew up, and was played by my Uncle Len, wearing a false beard.

(Now I may have been rude about the acting, but to give them their due they did give it a proper try. I mean, Len even shaved off his real beard to play the part!)

After a lot of to-ing and fro-ing, Mo parted Decoy Broad, and led the people out of Wroxham. And they all began worshipping a golden calf, which was modelled on one of Briony Bream's. She's got cracking legs, I must say.

Anyhow, Mo went up a small hillock, the thing being set in Norfolk, and came down with the Ten Suggestions. (Derek doesn't like to be too bossy about these things.) And that was when Len got his big solo, which was *Ten Steps To Heaven*. And that was the end of the first half, and still no sign of the hip-flask.

Act Innocent

The interval passed without much incident. Well, it did until the bloke who was playing Adam came round to get a couple of cups of milky coffee for him and Mrs Barbel. He'd completely forgotten to change out of his costume, which was his birthday suit, so that caused quite a stir, I can tell you. Especially when my aunt Ruby pointed at him pointedly, if you see what I mean, and asked him if that was the raffle prize. He forgot all about the coffee and shrank away pretty quick after that.

Then they had the raffle, which was won by someone from Knapton. So he was instantly disqualified, and it was drawn again, and this time the hand-knitted toilet roll cover was won by Lady Silver-Darling by force of habit, even though she wasn't there and she hadn't bought a raffle ticket.

Then we all settled down again, and I persuaded Darren and Penny to stop snogging behind my back, and things went quiet and dark for the second half. And that was when we all heard Mr Pike shouting from the gents' lavatory. At first we thought it was part of the show. But, when he didn't go into a song, Mrs Pike remembered that he wasn't even in the show, and eventually God come down amongst us, along with Cyril Cockle and his crowbar, and they released the jammed lock on the toilet door, and then the second half proper began.

Act 2

It wasn't nearly as exciting as the start of the first half. For quite a while the cast just wandered round in the wilderness, which in this version was Suffolk, and rather boring if you ask me. Then there was a lot of lame stuff about Mo asking God if he'd see the promised land (which was Norfolk, of course), and God answering of course he would, and so on. Only that turned out to be a trick answer, because, just as Norfolk came into sight, Mo dropped dead in the outskirts of Bungay. But not before Len had milked the death scene for a lot more than it was worth. The chorus had to keep singing *Go Down, Moses* over and over again, until eventually one of them tripped him up, and he finally did go down.

Then, after a brief interruption, caused by Mrs Pike going home to feed her cats, there was a loud fanfare of trumpet, played by Kevin. And on came Joshua to fight the battle of Haddiscoe, and the walls came tumbling down. It was all very dramatic. Of course, the walls weren't actually meant to come tumbling down, but they did anyway. It seems somebody tripped over one of the ropes backstage, and the scenery all collapsed. I bet Widow Hake wished she hadn't been thrown out then, because that revealed Adam and Eve catching up with unfinished business. I don't think that's strictly correct to how it is in the bible, but it went down very well on the night. Eventually they managed to get the scenery back up, and the noise from Adam and Eve subsided, and the show went on.

It went on to the story of Samson and Delilah, played by Carl and Karen Cod. First Carl did some weight-lifting, and then he gave a brief display of martial arts, while Karen struck poses in her spangled bikini. Then, while Carl had a rest, Karen gave him a Number Two haircut, and he instantly lost all his strength. As he crawled about the stage he gave a moving rendition of *The Green, Green Grass Of Home*. (I believe the Vicar actually wanted him to sing *My, My, My, Delilah* at that point, but he couldn't find the music, so they had to settle for the next best thing.) Then Samson got his strength back, and brought down the temple. Well, he was meant to bring down the temple, but, given what had happened to the scenery earlier, the backstage crew had lashed everything together double strength. So now the temple wouldn't budge, and it was all down to Cyril and his crowbar again.

Mrs Pike came back in then, smelling of cat food, wanting to know what she'd missed, and then it was time for the Harley quins to do the story of David and Goliath. Larry Harley stood on Harry Harley's shoulders to play Goliath, while Garry Harley got down on his knees to do David, and Barry Harley just stood standing like normal to be Saul, along with his sister, Clarrie. Her part isn't actually in the bible, but the others said they wouldn't appear without her, so that was that. They built the excitement up with lots of 'I'm going to flatten you!' and 'Oh yeah?' and 'Come on then if you think you're hard enough!' and so on. It was all very realistic, even down to Garry going red in the face and trembling slightly. (It turned out later that Larry had said something to him in the dressing-room before they came on.) So then Garry whipped out his catapult, took aim and hit Larry smack between the eyes with a half-inch ball-bearing. Well, Larry went out like a light, and fell right off Harry's shoulders. Garry jumped forward and grabbed Larry's sword as he fell, and it took Harry, Barry and Clarrie to stop him from finishing Larry off for real, there and then, live on stage. It was all very theatrical, and I finally managed to get my hands on Darren's hip-flask during the excitement.

Things calmed down when the ambulance had gone, and we moved on to the story of Solomon. He had 700 wives and 300 concubines, although not all of them were on stage, obviously. A lot of them were in the ferry, as a matter of fact, looking after all the animals. Derek was doubling up as Solomon, and he sang *Help Me Make It Through The Night*, until two women came to see him with a baby. (They used a real baby – you could smell it.) And Solomon saw the baby, and said it was no good looking at him, because he had a thousand alibis. But the women said the argument wasn't about who was the father. They said the argument was about who was the mother. You see, they both reckoned the baby was theirs (but of course it couldn't have been, because they didn't have lesbians in those days). And they said that Solomon was known far and wide for his wisdom, so go on then, smarty pants, what should they do? So then he had to decide which one of them should have the baby. He called for someone to bring him a sword, but they couldn't do that. The only sword they had was down at the police station as evidence, with Garry Harley, who was helping them with their enquiries into the assault on his brother. So they improvised, and Cyril brought him his crowbar instead. And Solomon decreed that the baby should be cut in two with the crowbar, so that the women could have half each. Well, of course, that put them on the spot. That called their bluff. Because they both wanted the top half and neither of them wanted the bottom half. So Solomon said the wise thing would be to toss for it, and that's what they did. But the one who got the bottom half said she'd like to go double or quits, and she lost again, and that meant the other woman got the whole baby. So, that was that sorted out.

Now we came to the bit that I had a hand in: the Proverbs. Derek had asked me to supply him with some, so as to give the whole thing a local flavour (although if you ever tasted what passes for cooking round our way, you'd avoid local flavours like one of those plagues in Wroxham). Anyhow, I let him have a few proverbs on the cheap, and he arranged them into a sort of a song. I remember one bit. It went:

'Beauty's in the eye of the beast, a king may look at a cat.
Charity belongs in a home, and Amman's Amman for all that.'

It sounds better when it's sung. On the night it sounded absolutely awful, because it was sung by Farmer Trout (who only sings in the key of B flat), accompanied by Ms Marsden from the village school (who can only play in F sharp, due to the missing keys on the piano). The result was worth double the entrance money to miss!

So, by the time they'd both finished, in their own times, we were all glad that the end was nigh. Which it was. They quickly whipped through Daniel in the lion's den (partly because they'd been sent the wrong costume, so it was actually the pantomime horse's den). Then Jonah went for a ride in a submarine and sang an Irish song called *Sod 'em And Begorrah*. And then, before we knew it, the lights came up, and the whole thing was over.

Act Of God

Not that they'd got to the end of the show, because they hadn't. There was quite a bit more to go, I think. But the caretaker had had enough, and wanted to lock up and go home. So he announced that he didn't mind which way he did it. He said he could lock up the hall with us in it, or with us out of it, but he thought we might prefer to be given the choice. Which we did, to be fair. I mean, I'm all for a lock-in normally, but not when there isn't a bar. And I'd emptied Darren's hip-flask by then.

So that was that, and now we'll never know how the story comes out. Because the first performance of *Awfully Good* was also the last. Well, it had to be, given the circumstances. Come the next night Larry Harley was still in hospital, and Garry was remanded in custody. Adam and Eve had eloped straight after the show and have never been seen again (although rumour has it they're loving happily ever after, running an ethnic Norfolk Dumpling restaurant in Surrey). Uncle Len had accidentally set fire to his false beard while trying to sneak a quick fag backstage; Farmer Trout caught a chill due to having to get changed in the outside toilet; and Ms Marsden said there was a brand-new scratch on her piano and she was taking it home. So that was that.

But all in all it wasn't a complete failure. After all, they raised some money for the New Organ Fund, and Cyril Cockle's roses came on a treat. But I don't think they'll be putting the show on again in our village. So if you know anyone who'd like to stage the second performance, I'm sure Derek would be delighted to hear from you, care of the Vicarage.

TRANSMATTER™
by Chris Sugden

Sid Kipper here. Chris Sugden reckoned that if he was going to have his name on the cover, then he ought to get at least one story in the book. So here it is. Mind you, I said he could take his name off the cover instead if he liked, but he said no thank you. He said it had to be there, because otherwise this book wouldn't match our previous ones. So I told him that if he was trying to be clever with me he was wasting his time.

'I'll tell you what I think,' said young Cosmo Cockle. 'I reckon I can't be doing with all these here new-fangled contraptions.' That was his considered opinion, delivered gravely to the equally youthful Bing Kipper, over a half-litre of Watneys Traditional Olde Lager. They were sitting in Spratts!, known to the more senior residents of St Just-near-Trunch as the old Old Goat Inn.

Bing mutely agreed with Cosmo. He'd found that to be the best policy. To join in would only encourage his companion to elaborate further. But Cosmo needed no such encouragement, anyway, as he went on to demonstrate.

'I mean, you take this Transmatter™. People being beamed all over the place in an instant. That's not natural. You wouldn't catch me doing it, not for love nor credit. I'll stick to my anti-grav bike, thank you very much, like nature intended. Well, I would if it was working. It's a bugger to push.'

Bing nodded again, the look in his eye suggesting that he was deep in thought about these important matters, whereas, in fact, he was thinking about something else entirely.

It was the new people in the village, the Nimbys, that had set off this unnatural wave of thinking. Their house had appeared about a month ago, in what, before that, had been Farmer Trout's top field. Of course, nowadays, these things were all done remotely. So, one minute there'd been nothing there but a crumbling old barn, and the next there was a five-bedroom Exec. Res. complete with virtual cowshed, containing half a dozen virtual cows.

The Nimbys were commuters. They worked somewhere or other, a long way away. They had said where – Nassau, or Natal, or something like that. Nowhere anybody had heard of, anyway. Every morning they Transmatted™ off to work, and every evening they beamed back again. Or at least they would, if the system operated properly. But, like most new, talked-up innovations, it hardly ever did. The thing was forever crashing. And that had some bizarre consequences.

You see, the Transmatter™ manual was very insistent that you should back yourself up on a regular basis, as a precaution. But most people never even opened the manual. And those who did would do one back-up, then not quite get round to it again. So, when something went wrong, as it often did, they had to go back to a version of themselves from when they first bought it. Which could be very awkward. For instance, what if they'd got married in the meantime? Or had children? The High Court were still considering the matter.

And Cosmo was considering it, too.

What Bing was thinking about was the Nimby's eighteen-year-old daughter, Maxine. He reckoned she was far more worthy of the mental effort. She was what his Great Great Uncle Sid would have called 'a right little crackler'. And what made her especially worth thinking of, for Bing, was that he was fairly certain she'd been giving him the eye.

'And another thing,' said Cosmo, charging on like an out-of-control hover-plough. 'Now that house is there I'm going to have to reprogram the robofox. Otherwise she's liable to go running straight in their front door, with the hounds in full cry behind her. I mean, they're bound to be the sort that would sue over a little thing like wrecking a house.'

'She's certainly different to the local females,' said Bing, dreamily.

'Well, of course she is. She's electronic. You can programme her to do whatever you want.'

'No, that's no good. I tried that once, in that place in North Walsham. No matter how clever they get, it's still not the same as the real thing. For instance, they never ask you to hold on a minute, and stop doing that, while they answer the phone to their friend Trixie.'

From this you can see that each of them was barely listening to what the other was saying. Just to confuse things further the landpeer, Ernie Spratt, decided to join in the conversation.

'Well, I can remember the good old days,' he said. 'All the incomers came from London, then. But at least they only used to bother us at the weekend. And another thing. When they did come they used to spend a bit of money. Kept the Olde Craft and Trinkette Shoppe going for years, they did.'

Ernie was worried about Transmatter™. It might mean that his customers would beam off to the larger, plusher establishments in Aylsham and Cromer. He'd thought of getting one installed in Spratts!, but that might lead to a load of strangers coming into the pub, and he definitely didn't want that. He could express his considered reaction in just two words. He used them now. 'Bugger that.'

Well, it's good to know that the standard of conversation in the old watering-hole remains as high as ever.

The next day: They'd set the weather control to fine and Bing was keeping an eye on the Nimby's place, just in case Maxine happened to appear. Preferably sunbathing again, in her virtual kini®. Now if that were to go on the blink there'd be a real sight for sore eyes, he thought. As he walked up and down the lane behind the house, in what he considered a suitably casual manner, hoping to accidentally-on-purpose catch a glimpse of her, he noted that while the virtual cows didn't add to the international milk lake, they didn't eat real grass either. That field was going to have to be cut soon, otherwise Maxine would be able to sunbathe quite unseen from the lane, and that would never do.

At least he wouldn't have to worry about Cosmo Cockle getting in the way. Because he'd seen him, half an hour before, heading off to Demons Wood with his lazer shotgun. Now, some people said that such guns weren't sporting. But that didn't bother Cosmo and Bing, because they didn't shoot for sport, anyway. They shot for the pot. You could get 25 newgrams of the stuff for a rabbit, and 50 for a pheasant, and it was good quality, too.

Bing heard a door open and saw Maxine coming out into the garden. Today she'd tuned her kini® to black, which showed off her curvaceous figure really well, even if it didn't make much use of the gadget's possibilities. He wondered if it had the Own-Skin setting, in which the kini® read the colour of the wearer's skin and tinted itself to match it exactly. Well, if it did, she never used it.

As it happened, Maxine was thinking about Bing at that very moment. Oh, she hadn't spotted him. He was far too good a poacher for that. But she'd seen him around the village, and noticed the effect she had on him, and she was wondering why he hadn't tried to do anything about it. She had thought about ringing him up, pretending it was a wrong number, but she'd been rather shocked to discover that he'd still got last year's model of vidphone, which didn't have the pretend-wrong-number feature! It didn't have the lost-sock alarm either, but that wasn't so bad, because nobody had been able to find any use for that anyway.

Well, she was thinking, if he wouldn't do anything about it, then she would have to. She knew he attended the village folk club at Spratts!, so she'd just have to go along and accidentally run into him there. But just now, she thought, I'm going to lie in the sun and try out the Own-Skin setting on my kini®. Which is exactly what she did. As she let her concentration begin to drift she thought she heard a noise, but thankfully never realised that it was the sound of a very excited young man tripping over his own feet, due to not looking where he was going.

Tuesday, the night of the folk club, arrived, as Tuesdays will if you're patient enough. Which, to be frank, Maxine wasn't. At Spratts! Ernie programmed the EnviroMeant to the Happy Folkie setting. In no time at all the standard titanium and plastic fittings had converted themselves into old-looking, unmatched wooden chairs, rustic tables with candles in bottles, and so on. There were even ashtrays. Obviously nobody was going to break the law by actually smoking tobacco, but they did add an authentic, old-world touch. And so the place was made exactly and precisely like every other franchise in the chain. Of course, a few modern features had to remain. Authenticity was one thing, but discomfort was quite another. So the drinks-dispenser stayed, and the air-conditioning countered the atmospheric, but totally unnecessary, Perma-logg fire.

Folk music had become popular again when the New Age Party came into power. Now various chains had opened up. As well as the Happy Folkie there were The Ballad Bar and Song U Like. All had much the same format, with local singers going first, singing from the menu provided, followed by a live holographic transmission of whoever the guest performer was that week.

Usually there was a charity raffle, raising funds for deprived areas such as London which, since the advent of regional government, was largely ignored by the rest of the country.

At Spratts! Bing was one of the first to arrive. He chatted briefly to Ernie, while the latter adjusted the precise position of one of the tables. There had been a bit of an embarrassment the previous week, when the hologram of the guest artist had appeared right in the middle of Tansy Trout. No harm done, of course, but it's hard to get the full effect of a really powerful old folk song, like Puff The Magic Dragon©, when the singer and their stylophone are intimately entangled with one of the locals.

Other people gradually turned up, and eventually the singing began. Bing was in the middle of his Great Great Grandfather George's amazingly prophetic song, 'Barley, Barley and Barley-Oh', when Maxine opened the door and looked around a little nervously. When he'd finished the song a game of cat and mouse began, as both she and Bing tried to arrange to bump into each other accidentally. It was finally resolved when she got fed up with all that, walked straight up to him and said, 'Hello, Bing, I'm Maxine.'

For a moment he was tongue-tied. 'Yes, I know I'm Bing,' he said. 'No, I mean, I know your kini®. That is, hello Maxine.'

It wasn't a great start, but she laughed with him rather than at him. He bought her a bottle of JohnBarleycorn.com, and after that they sat down and chatted together the whole night, much to the annoyance of everybody else, who wanted to listen to the singing. But by then Maxine and Bing were quite oblivious to such things.

Later he walked her home, and, well, Mother Nature took care of the rest. If you want to know the details you must supply them yourselves. But nothing too kinky, if you don't mind. It wasn't like that.

And now that boy has successfully met girl, and vice versa, by tradition that's the end of the story. Apart from the tidying up bits. She now makes sure that he has an up-to-date vidphone, and he encourages her to use the Own-Skin setting when she sunbathes. They honeymooned in Croydon. They didn't intend to honeymoon in Croydon, but that's Transmatter™ for you. They say that it will work properly, any day now. Anyhow, Bing and Maxine were so much in love that they didn't really care where they were.

And now that they've settled down, and signed up to ImmortaliT treatment, I can genuinely declare that they are going to live ever after. Although the advertisements make one thing absolutely clear. Happiness is by no means guaranteed.

Barley, Barley and Barley-Oh

In Spring look out upon the land,
A thousand acres at your command,
See all the hedgerows blooming, and
Have them all grubbed out.
If April showers should come your way,
They bring the flowers that bloom in May;
So give out orders now to spray,
Before such weeds can sprout.
The seasons round fight every foe
Of barley, barley and barley-oh.

In Summer have your barley grow
In neat and tidy perfect rows;
Where the bee sucks I don't know,
But not round here, that's clear.
When blackbirds sing on every bough
Of trees grown high, and standing proud,
Send out your men to cut them down;
They serve no purpose here.
The seasons round fight every foe
Of barley, barley and barley-oh.

In Autumn, when the weather's fair,
Let sounds of singing fill the air
Inside the tractor cab, for there
Be tuned to Radio 2.
And now there's real work to be done,
For you must sit and do your sums,
To make sure that your bounty comes
On time from the EU.
The seasons round fight every foe
Of barley, barley and barley-oh.

When Winter winds are whistling, and
Drifts of snow hide all the land,
Fly to Barbados, to get tanned,
And rest there, at your ease.
And soon the year will come round when
Your barley will be all GM,
Which sews and reaps itself, and then
Farewell to drudgery.
The seasons round fight every foe
Of barley, barley and barley-oh.

CLEVERCLOGS AND THE THREE BEARS
as told by Sid Kipper

*This is one of the many stories first published by the Grim brothers – Ghastly
and Grotty – who were based in the tiny Norfolk village of Bradfield. Most
of their tales were deeply depressing, as their stock in trade was doom,
death and disaster. This is partly explained in the introduction to one of
their collections of stories,* Miserable Ever After:
*'If people, as they almost universally profess, really wanted happy
endings then they would not make the sort of choices in life that
they do. They would not marry unsuitably, court ill health, or live
in a small community with their sibling. Yet observation suggests
that these are exactly the things that they do choose to do. We
therefore draw the conclusion that it must be unhappy endings
they seek, and herein set out to provide them in multiplicity.'*
*This version, however, has been changed, as it has passed through the hands
of generations of tellers, such that it is almost unrecognisable as the same
story at all.*

Once upon a time, if not more, there were three bears. Actually,
there were thousands of bears, but there were three in particular
who were involved in this story. Well, four really, but I don't want
to give away the surprise ending. And these three particular bears
lived in a cottage in the very middle of Demons' Wood, in between
the Three Big Pigs and the Little Good Wolf.

The three bears were Baby Bear, Mummy Bear, and Mummy

Bear's friend, Uncle Teddy. And the story begins one morning when Mummy Bear got up dark and late to make the porridge. She did that to remind them all exactly what Daddy Bear was doing at the moment. But the porridge was too hot to eat. So, being too stupid to think of blowing on it, they all went for a walk in the bear garden while they waited for it to cool down.

But they didn't lock the door behind them. They did try locking the door in front of them, but that way they couldn't get out, so they gave it up as a bad job and threw away the key – which was a trick they'd learned at Daddy Bear's trial.

And while they were out a-walking, along came a big girl who had long golden locks, large blue eyes, and a couple of other size-able attributes as well. She was known as Cleverclogs, because she was clever, and she did clog-dancing, although quite how those two things go together I don't know.

Normally Cleverclogs lived in the village of Bradfield with her two grim brothers. But today she was lost in the woods, so she went into the three bears' cottage, because she was tired and cold, and hungry.

Well, when she saw three chairs she sighed. 'I'm so tired, I could do with a sit down,' she said. So first she tried Uncle Teddy's chair – although properly speaking it was really Daddy Bear's chair. Except that it wasn't, which was part of the reason why he was away for a while.

Whoever's chair it was really doesn't matter, anyway, because when she tried it she couldn't get comfortable, what with the very high arms and the built in pipe-rack, so she moved on. Then she tried Baby Bear's chair, but that one was too small for her, and she broke it into smithereens (which are very small smithers). So when she'd got herself out of the wreckage, and got the splinters out of her tender bits, she tried Mummy Bear's chair. And, lo and behold, it was just right for her, so there she sat.

And as she sat there she saw the porridge. 'I'm so hungry,' she said – which was stupid really, because there was no one listening to her. On the other hand it's very handy for us, because otherwise we wouldn't have any idea what she was doing, hopping from chair to chair and trying all the different porridges. Because that's what she did. And she preferred Mummy Bear's porridge, and she ate it all up. Or down. I can't be certain because I don't know if she was standing on her head or not at the time.

Well, by now she was full up – or down – and very tired, which come to think of it was no surprise if she'd been standing on her head. That can be very tiring. So she went upstairs, and came to all the bedrooms. First she went into Mummy Bear's room and tried her bed, but it was all chintzy, with frilly bits on the pillows and such, and she didn't like it at all.

So then she tried Baby Bear's bed, but it was rather small and not very comfortable, what with the rubber sheet on it because of his little problem, and she didn't like that one either.

Well, the fact is she ended up in Uncle Teddy Bear's bed, and she fell straight away into a deep, deep sleep.

And while she slept deep upstairs, the three bears came home to see if their porridge was cool. When they saw what had happened Baby Bear said, 'Somebody's been sitting in my chair, and it's all broken.' And Mummy Bear said, 'Somebody's been eating my porridge, and it's all gone.' So Uncle Teddy Bear went upstairs to check and he saw Cleverclogs asleep in his bed, with her long golden locks spread across his pillow, and her breath making the coverlet slowly rise and fall, and her silk underthings strewn all over the floor. And he came straight back downstairs and said to the others, 'Well, there's nothing up there.'

So, that night, when they all went to bed early at Uncle Teddy Bear's insistence, Mummy Bear and Baby Bear wondered who it was that had been in the house and broken the chair and eaten the porridge. And Baby Bear went to sleep in his little bed with the rubber sheet. And Mummy Bear went to sleep in her chintzy bed with the frills on the pillows. And Uncle Teddy – well, Uncle Teddy Bear had a nasty surprise.

At first when he hopped in beside her Cleverclogs was fast asleep, and seemed only too pleased to cuddle up to him. But when he got even more cuddly she suddenly woke up, and that was when he discovered that she'd been clever enough to go to bed with her clogs on. And he walked with a limp for some considerable time afterwards.

And Cleverclogs ran all the way home, leaving her silk underthings behind, and told the story to her two grim brothers, who immediately sold it to a newspaper. And next to her story was a big engraving of Cleverclogs in a tasteful pose without her silk underthings just to prove it.

Things between Mummy Bear and Uncle Teddy were never quite the same after that. Well, you see, she found the silk underthings in his room and demanded to know whose they were. The only excuse he could think of was to say that they were his, otherwise she might have reported him and he'd have been arrested for attempted humanality.

In fact, Mummy Bear was very understanding about it. She insisted that he wore them all the time from then on.

And another thing – whenever she suggested that they go for a walk in the bear garden while the porridge cooled he always acted like a bear with a sore head. Only it wasn't his head that was sore, of course.

And Cleverclogs's picture in the paper caused a great stir. Lots of men wrote in and said it was a shame about her underwear, and they'd be happy to buy her some more, and when should they come round to measure her up? And lots more men wrote in to say that they'd search for her underwear until it was recovered. But despite a great deal of effort it was never found – which was probably just as well for Uncle Teddy.

But to this very day, big girls still like cuddling teddy bears.

And to this very day men are still going around, looking at big girls, and trying to see if any of them are wearing those long lost silk underthings.

THE BEAR FACTS

Cuddly, curvaceous Cleverclogs, the Bradford Bombshell, went down to the woods last week, and we couldn't believe our eyes. The blonde HONEY went for a little sun-bathing to get BROWN, when she had a GRIZZLY experience. She had BEARLY stripped off when all her clothes were stolen by a passing family of bears. Without PAWS for thought, she set off home without a stitch, so she certainly wasn't in disguise. Luckily our CUB reporter was there, so Cleverclogs wasn't the only one who got everything down! You'll be GROWLING with delight as she BEARS all on page 3. That's how we PANDA to our readers' wishes!

(from the *Daily Squit*)

DEREK'S *EIGHTH* LETTER
TO THE TRUNCHEONS

This is the last of Rev. Derek Bream's collection of letters. After its broadcast was brought to the attention of the church authorities, Derek's mission was abruptly terminated, and he was returned to his parish duties. An incident in Gissing seems to have been at the heart of the matter, but Derek pointedly refuses to comment.

Life's like that, isn't it? Only the other day I was going through Gissing, when a man strode up and addressed me in a rather blunt manner. 'Who the Heck are you?' he demanded. Well, he didn't actually say 'Heck'. But then, he certainly didn't say 'Heaven', either.

'Call me Derek', I was about to say, when he suddenly struck me. But I wasn't really aware of that at the time, because it had struck me first, just the moment before. For we all want to know who the Heck we are, don't we? I mean, we most of us know our names, most of the time, but do we really know exactly *who* we are? And is the who that we are the same person as the who that other people think we are? For example, many of my parishioners think that I'm an idiot, but then, that's not who I really am, is it? No, that's *what* I really am. So who, then, am I?

You see what I'm saying, don't you? Somewhere inside us is the real who. It is the part of us which will eventually go to Heaven or, just possibly, Heck. And I think we may never know, in this world, just who we really are.

However, in the meantime, I have made some enquiries about the blunt man in Gissing, and he can rest assured that I know exactly who *he* is. And where he lives.

So let him just remember this. If The Good Lord had wanted blunt men from Gissing to go around assaulting passing Vicars willy nilly, He would never have made said Vicar good mates with some of the larger lads at the Senior Youth Club.

VAUGHAN WILLIAMS STOLE
MY FOLK SONG
from the show by Sid Kipper

Folk-song collectors were never popular with the Kipper family. And they encountered quite a few. From Cecil Sharp to the present day, all the great folk-song collectors have tried to get their material from them. Various efforts are chronicled elsewhere, but only one was ever successful. Here Sid tells that story, followed by some thoughts on Lucinda Wormwood (the one collector who found some favour with the family), and some revelations that even Sid himself is not aware of.

As a member of the Kipper family, I can tell you that we never wanted to have any of our old songs collected. So we used to keep them well away from those folk-song correctors (we called them that because they were always mucking the songs about). But there was one that got away, and it was one of the very oldest ones. A song called *Polly On The Floor*.

Of course, years ago, collecting folk songs was all the rage. Posh people from London used to go round the country, getting poor people's songs off them. Take the bloke who nicked my song. Now he didn't come from London direct. He started off in Australia, actually. He was called Rolph Vaughan Williams, only he was so posh that he didn't have the sense he was born with, and he pronounced his first name Rofe. Rofe first got interested in our family when he was collecting songs back in Australia. You see, someone told him about my ancestor, Bruce Kipper. Now Bruce was famous, because he was the only person ever to get transported to Australia, and then transported back again by the Australians. I don't know what he did out there, but there are a lot of people in Australia called Bruce!

Anyhow, Rofe reckoned Bruce might have made off with some Australian songs, so he followed his trail to our village. And, of course, Bruce did bring some songs back. *Walsingham Matilda* was one. *All Around My Head* was another.

Well, once old Rofe got on our trail he wouldn't let it go. He was after our songs for years. He'd tried getting us drunk, which we didn't mind, because we just made sure we got too drunk to sing – that's what they call 'ceilidhed'. He'd tried tricking us, but we were too stupid for that. He'd tried hiding in all sorts of places, like behind the wainscoting, and under the beds, but the dogs always sniffed him out.

In fact, it was only by accident that he got the one he did. You see, one day he was hanging about the Old Goat Inn, hoping to get someone to sing for him, when he decided to go to the Gents. Which just goes to show that he was no coward! But he left his collecting notebook on the table. Well, just then my Uncle Albert came into the pub. He'd been trying for some time to remember the words of this particular song, and it had just come to him. So when he saw the notebook and pencil, he opened the book and jotted the song down there and then. Because writing a song down is the very best way to fix it in your mind.

Old Rofe was gone some time. He was probably looking for paper, and wishing he'd taken his book with him. So when he came back Albert had finished, and shut the book again. So Rofe didn't know the song was there, and Albert didn't know who's book it was. It wasn't till Rofe got back to London that he saw it, and realised what he'd got. But, of course, he'd only got the words. Now he had to think about how he might get the tune. Because those collectors were mad for tunes.

Well, the next time Rofe came to Trunch he tried the sideways approach. He went into the Old Goat and he said to Albert, 'I say, my good man, do you happen to know a song called *Polly On The Floor*?' And Albert said, 'Yes, I do, thank you, my good man.'

So then Rofe said, 'I wonder if you'd be good enough to hum me the tune? I just want to see if it's the same as the one I've already got.'

But Albert was too sharp for that. He said, 'I tell you what, you be good enough to hum your tune and then I'll tell you if it's the same.' Of course, old Rofe couldn't do that, so he made his excuses and walked away.

But he'd set Albert thinking about that tune. And you know how it is. Once you get thinking about a tune it just goes round and round in your head, until somehow it finds a way to get out. Eventually you find yourself humming it, or whistling it, or whatever. Well, Albert didn't even realise that he'd started tapping the tune out on his teeth with a pencil (which was pretty clever, anyway, seeing as he didn't have his teeth in his mouth at the time). But Rofe realised, and he stood behind Albert, with his notebook, and wrote it down first time. When Albert turned round he saw him. He looked at the notebook, and remembered where he'd seen it before, and then he realised he'd been outmanoeuvred. So, with the mutual respect of one kidder for another, Albert punched Rofe straight on the nose.

But old Rofe got out of there like a flash, and now he'd got the song, and from that day on our family had lost it.

Until the other year, that is. You see, I got a phone call one day from someone who said she was his granddaughter, Eff Vaughan Williams (I thought that was her initial at first, but I found out later that she'd been christened Elf). She said she'd inherited the song, and since I was now more famous than her grandfather would I like to have it back? And, to cut a long story short, I got it. Mind you, they hadn't looked after it very well. For a start the tune had been removed and used for a piece called *The Mole Descending*. And the words were in a pretty bad way, all bent and twisted. But I've spent some time on it, straightening it out and putting the éds back, and now I can sing it again, which I do in my show.

But before I get off the subject, there was one collector we didn't mind as much as the others. That was Miss Wormwood. She wasn't sneaky like them. She just asked for the songs straight out. Mind you, we still didn't give her any of them, but we did appreciate the way she went about it. She even used to muck in and help about the house sometimes. And my Uncle Albert, he took a real shine to her. I reckon he fancied her something rotten, as a matter of fact. He always said that if things had been different, then they would never have been the same.

The only thing I'll say against Miss Wormwood is that she did give up rather easily. I mean, she only came round three or four times, and then we never saw her again. And we never did find out why. I think it would have broken Albert's heart, if he'd had one.

The following, found recently in a cobwebbed corner of the Vaughan Williams library, at Cecil Sharp's House in London, seems to shed some light on the matter.

Report by Lucinda Wormwood (Miss)
to the English Folk-Song And Dance Society, 1934
As requested by the Society, I recently visited my half-cousin Doyley Silver-Darling in St Just-near-Trunch, in order to collect the

songs of the Kipper family. We have known for some time that this family are the custodians of a number of old songs, a part of our English heritage which has been handed down to them. They have, to date, stubbornly refused to hand them back.

I decided that I must gain their confidence in some way, so I called at their cottage in my best country clothes and asked if there was any way in which I could assist them. My offer was taken literally, I fear, and I was forced to perform a number of household and farmyard chores of a rather unpleasant nature.

On my second visit I met one Albert Kipper. Having made it plain that I was not there to engage in manual labour, I took the opportunity to hint that he might have something that I wanted. At first this approach seemed quite promising, but Mr Kipper clearly misunderstood my hint. I left with an old copper kettle and four lucky horseshoes, the latter still attached to a lucky horse. I had, apparently, purchased these items. I do hope the Society will be able to find some use for them.

By my third visit I felt I had gained Mr Kipper's confidence, and so I asked him directly if he knew any songs. He said that he did, and actually offered to sing them for me. Eagerly I prepared my notebook and pencil, and soon, having settled himself, legs akimbo, before the fire, he cleared his throat and began to sing. Imagine my shock as I found myself transcribing an appalling thing called *The Black Bottom*, a modern song of the sort known as 'popular'. I knew better than to stop him, however, and wrote the whole thing down. When he had finished I asked if he didn't know any other, older songs. He said that he did, and stood stiffly in the corner of the room to sing *My Grandfather's Clock*. Again I dutifully noted it down, and then asked for something older still. He declared that he knew just what I wanted, wiped his nose on his arm, and sang me *Greensleeves*.

I thanked him, of course. Then I asked if he didn't have any of the old traditional songs for which his family was famed. 'Well now, Mrs Woodworm,' he said, 'if that's what you want you've come too late.' I asked what he meant, and he said that they had given them all to someone who had called the week before, in exchange for a goldfish. 'We had a good clear out of all them old songs,' he declared, 'In order to make room for some nice new songs in better condition.' I cannot believe that he was telling me the truth, but I was forced to leave empty-handed.

My fourth visit proved to be the final one. Albert Kipper, it seemed, had somehow gained the impression that I might be interested in him in a 'personal' way. Why he thought a lady such as myself should have any interest in a creature of his ilk I have no idea. It is only to rescue these lovely songs from the unsavoury clutches of the likes of him that I am induced to have anything to do with him at all. I should have thought that was obvious. However, it was only when we were alone in the sordid slum he calls 'the parlour' that I sensed there was something wrong.

Reaching behind him he declared that he had something to show me. Could it be, I asked, that he had followed the example of Mr Copper of Sussex, and written down his songs into a book? No, he declared, he was going to show me his third leg. Instantly I recalled the disgusting song I had collected from the Cockle family, in which the self-same term is used to describe something which appears rather prominently in the story. I was forced to leave immediately, pursued by the shameless wretch, who was calling out that I could try it on if I liked.

And so I regret to report that the songs of the Kipper family remain uncollected.

Polly On The Floor

Lord Weasenham-St-Peter has gone to a far count-er-ee,
Leaving behind his gay Lady.
But he's left her under the watchful eye
Of his faithful parrot:
His faithful parrot in the window high.

And while Lord Weasenham-St-Peter sailéd the sea,
This gay Lady longéd for company.
Till a handsome chambermaid she engagéd,
Who served her mistress;
She served her mistress, in and out of bed.

Said the Lady to the parrot, 'If your tongue you will hold,
You shall have the usual cage of gold;
Keep your beak shut about the maid and me,
Or you'll very, very soon;
You'll very, very soon an ex-parrot be!'

When His Lordship caméd home from that far count-er-ee,
With wondrous goods, all of duty free,
Thus to his Lady did he speak;
'Tell me why are you holding;
Why are you holding the parrot's beak?'

'Now tell me Polly, while I cross-eyéd the sea,
Was my gay Lady true to me?'
'Oh yes, yes I was,' said Lady Polly,
'Just you ask the parrot;
Ask the parrot if you don't believe me.'

'Then speak now bird, be not taciturn,
And an emerald mirror you shall earn.'
So it told him of the maid and the gay Lady,
Adding 'That's not natural;
That's not natural, if you ask me.'

'Oh did you have her in my Hall,
Where first we kisséd and playéd with the ball?
Oh did you have her in our bed,
Where first I took;
Where first I took your maidenhead?'

'Oh yes I had her in your hall,
On your floor and against your wall,
Dangling from your chandelier, and in our bed.
But tell me what makes you think;
What makes you think you took my maidenhead?'

Now Lord Weasenham-St-Peter pulléd out his sword so quick,
And through his own broken heart drove it.
And with his dying words he did bequeath,
To his faithful parrot;
To his faithful parrot, all his lands and money.

Lady Polly cried, 'Fetch me a club, a gun, a sword,
That I may slay this meddling bird.'
And as from its perch the parrot keeled,
Stunnéd, shot and stabbéd;
Stunnéd, shot and stabbéd, these last words it squeeled;

'Oh come all you parrots, and mina birds,
Think before you choose your words;
For gold and jewels I never did wish,
All I wanted was a bell and a cuttle fish.
So if long life you would enjoy,
If I were you;
If I were you I'd stick to 'Who's a pretty boy?'

DOT KIPPER'S HANDY
HOUSEHOLD HINTS

This final recipe from Dot Kipper seems to be more ceremonial than nutritious. However, it is still prepared occasionally, the last time being just before the death of Sid's supposed father, Henry, on 29th July, 1999.

PECK OF DIRT – They reckon you have to eat a peck of dirt before you die, so here's my favourite way of doing it.

METHOD – Take a peck of dirt (or, if you must use new-fangled measurements, take 2 gallons of dirt, although I don't reckon it's anything like as good in gallons, and you can't tell me different). Wash it, eat it, and die.

TIP – Some people want to eat it with chop-sticks, but everyone knows that chop-sticks should only be used for eating chops.

Also available from Mousehold Press, by the same authors:
Prewd and Prejudice (1994)
The Ballad of Sid Kipper (1996)
Crab Wars (1999)

Earlier (and shorter) versions of the following stories appear on the album *Spineless*, recorded by Sid Kipper (with Rev Derek Bream and Chris Sugden), available on Leader Records, LER2117:
'Cleverclogs and the Three Bears', 'Crackers For Fanny', 'Derek's First Letter To The Truncheons' (as 'The Lesson of Len's Lorry'), 'The Digression of the Three Gruff Billy Goats', 'The Headless Horse Man of Happisburgh', 'Piering Out To Sea', 'The Sirens of Scroby Sands' and 'Sir Wayne, The Green Knight'.

Sid Kipper has recorded 'Breasting The Waves', and 'The Shoals of Whiting' (with Dave Burland) on *Boiled In The Bag*, Leader Records LER2118, and 'Haul The Deck', 'Polly On The Floor', and 'The Sailor In Diss Dress' on *East Side Story*, Leader Records LER2120.
All songs are copyright Chris Sugden.

For further information about Sid Kipper, his writings, recordings and appearances, join his mailing list by writing to:
10 Perseverance Road, Queensbury, Bradford, England, BD13 1LY.